'**Whether you accept it or not you are a woman, not a man, and I wish to paint you as one. Something else you are hiding under those terrible dresses you favour,**' he said, tracing the line of her throat with his fingers, brushing lightly over her breasts.

She caught her breath as he touched her. Without being conscious of it she stepped towards him, wanting his hand to cup her, yearning in the purest, most thoughtless of ways for him to satisfy the craving she had been feeling for days. It was nothing to do with aesthetics. She knew that. It was elemental—purely carnal.

'You have the most delightful curves. Did you know that this is what your English painter Hogarth called "the line of beauty"?' His fingers slid down, brushing the underside of her breast, to the indent of her waist and round, to rest on the curve of her bottom and pull her suddenly hard up against him. 'You, Cressie, have the most beautiful line.'

His e   in
absol   ld
kiss   at
she w

AUTHOR NOTE

When I wrote my *Princes of the Desert* historical mini-series a couple of years ago, it was published with the strapline 'Where English Roses meet Desert Sheikhs.' The English Roses referred to were sisters, Lady Celia and Lady Cassandra, the eldest daughters of Lord Armstrong, a distinguished British diplomat. There were five Armstrong sisters in all, and it was always my intention to tell each of their stories eventually.

I had always envisaged Cressie as the bookish, intense sister (being the eldest of four sisters myself, I know how readily labels such as this are applied!). In an age where such bluestocking traits were not only discouraged but frowned upon, especially in young women of marriageable age, Cressie is an intellectual with a serious hang-up about her looks. Giovanni is a brooding and fatally attractive Italian artist, touched by genius, with a sordid and shameful past. Hardly the most obvious of matches, but definitely one which will generate a lot of sparks.

Cressie and Giovanni's story touches on a number of seemingly conflicting concepts—truth versus beauty, science versus art, logic versus instinct, duty versus freedom—but it's not *about* any of that. It's about two people from different worlds who have an irresistible connection and who, in attempting to find themselves, find each other. What could be more romantic than that?

I fully intend to complete the Armstrong sisters cycle by writing Caro and Cordelia's stories some time in the near future. But for the time being I hope you enjoy Cressie's tale.

THE BEAUTY WITHIN

Marguerite Kaye

First published in Great Britain 2013
by Mills & Boon, an imprint of Harlequin (UK) Limited.
Harlequin (UK) Limited, Eton House, 18-24 Paradise Road,
Richmond, Surrey TW9 1SR

© Marguerite Kaye 2013

ISBN: 978 0 263 89825 5

Harlequin (UK) policy is to use papers that are natural, renewable
and recyclable products and made from wood grown in sustainable
forests. The logging and manufacturing process conform to the
legal environmental regulations of the country of origin.

Printed and bound in Spain
by Blackprint CPI, Barcelona

Born and educated in Scotland, **Marguerite Kaye** originally qualified as a lawyer but chose not to practise. Instead, she carved out a career in IT and studied history part-time, gaining a first-class honours and a master's degree. A few decades after winning a children's national poetry competition she decided to pursue her lifelong ambition to write, and submitted her first historical romance to Mills & Boon®. They accepted it, and she's been writing ever since.

You can contact Marguerite through her website at: www.margueritekaye.com

Previous novels by the same author:

THE WICKED LORD RASENBY
THE RAKE AND THE HEIRESS
INNOCENT IN THE SHEIKH'S HAREM†
  (part of *Summer Sheikhs* anthology)
THE GOVERNESS AND THE SHEIKH†
THE HIGHLANDER'S REDEMPTION*
THE HIGHLANDER'S RETURN*
RAKE WITH A FROZEN HEART
OUTRAGEOUS CONFESSIONS OF LADY DEBORAH
DUCHESS BY CHRISTMAS
  (part of *Gift-Wrapped Governesses* anthology)

Highland Brides

and in Mills & Boon® Historical *Undone!* eBooks:

THE CAPTAIN'S WICKED WAGER
THE HIGHLANDER AND THE SEA SIREN
BITTEN BY DESIRE
TEMPTATION IS THE NIGHT
CLAIMED BY THE WOLF PRINCE**
BOUND TO THE WOLF PRINCE**
THE HIGHLANDER AND THE WOLF PRINCESS**
THE SHEIKH'S IMPETUOUS LOVE-SLAVE†
SPELLBOUND & SEDUCED
BEHIND THE COURTESAN'S MASK
FLIRTING WITH RUIN
AN INVITATION TO PLEASURE

**Legend of the Faol*
†linked by character

and in M&B *Castonbury Park* Regency mini-series

THE LADY WHO BROKE THE RULES

and in M&B eBooks:

TITANIC: A DATE WITH DESTINY

For Arianna,
who helped me enormously with all things Italian,
though any mistakes are all mine.
Grazie mille!

Prologue

'Absolutely marvellous. A triumph.' Sir Romney Kirn rubbed his meaty hands together enthusiastically, his fingers like plump sausages, as he gazed at the canvas which had just been unveiled to him. 'Quite, quite splendid. I'd say he's done me justice, would not you, my love?'

'Indeed, my dear,' his good lady agreed. 'One would even go so far as to say he has made you more handsome and distinguished than you are in the flesh, if that were possible.'

Sir Romney Kirn was not a man short of flesh, nor much given to modesty. The glow which suffused his already ruddy and bloated face was therefore most likely attributable to a surfeit of port the previous evening. Lady Kirn turned, her corsets creaking disconcertingly, towards the artist responsible for her husband's portrait. 'Your reputation as a genius is well deserved, *signor*,' she said with a simpering little laugh, her eyelashes fluttering alarmingly.

She was clearly smitten, and in front of her husband to boot. Had she no shame? Giovanni di Matteo sighed. Why did women of a certain age insist on flirting with him? In fact, why did women of all ages feel it necessary to throw themselves at him? He gave the merest hint of a bow, anxious to be gone. 'I am only as good as my subject, my lady.'

It worried him that the lies flowed with such practised ease. The baronet, a bluff man whose interests began and ended with hop farming had, over the course of several sittings, imparted his encyclopaedic knowledge of the crop while he posed, a copy of Adam Smith's *Wealth of Nations* in his hands—a volume which he admitted bluffly had not previously been opened, let alone read. The library which formed the backdrop to the portrait had been purchased as a job lot and had, Giovanni would have been willing to wager, remained entirely unvisited since its installation in the stately home—also recently acquired, following Sir Romney's elevation to the peerage.

Giovanni eyed the glossy canvas with the

critical eye his clients sorely lacked. Technically, it was a highly accomplished portrait: the light; the angles; the precise placing of the subject within the composition, Sir Romney being posed in such a way as to minimise his substantial girth and make the most of his weak profile; all were perfect. An excellent likeness, his clients said. They always did, and indeed it was, in as much as it portrayed the baronet exactly as he wished to be seen.

It was Giovanni's business to create the illusion of authority or wealth, sensuality or innocence, charm or intelligence, whichever combination his sitter desired. Beauty—of a kind. This polished, idealistic portrayal was what his clients sought in a di Matteo. It was what he was famed for, why he was sought after, and yet, at the peak of his success, ten years since arriving in England, the country he had made his home, Giovanni stared with distaste at the canvas and felt like a failure.

It had not always been like this. There had been a time when a blank canvas filled him with excitement. A time when a finished work made him elated, not desolate and drained. Art and sex. He had celebrated one with the other back in those days. Illusions both, like the ones he now painted for a living. Art and sex. For him, they used to be inextricably linked. He had given up the latter. Nowadays, the former left him feeling cold and empty.

'Now then, *signor*, here is the—er—necessary.' Sir Romney handed Giovanni a leather pouch rather in the manner of a criminal bribing a witness.

'*Grazie.*' He put the fee into the pocket of his coat. It amused him, the way so many of his clients found the act of paying for their portrait distasteful, unwilling to make the connection between the painting and commerce, for beauty ought surely to be priceless.

Refusing the dainty glass of Madeira which Lady Kirn eagerly offered, Giovanni shook hands with Sir Romney and bade the couple farewell. He had an appointment in London tomorrow. Another portrait to paint. Another blank canvas waiting to be filled. Another ego waiting to be massaged. And another pile of gold to add to his coffers, he reminded himself, which was the whole point, after all.

Never again, no matter if he lived to a hundred, would Giovanni have cause to rely on anyone other than himself. Never again would he have to bow to the wishes of another, to shape himself into the form another expected. He would not be his father's heir. He would not be any woman's plaything. Or man's for that matter—for there were many men of a certain type, wealthy and debauched, who liked to call themselves patrons but who were more interested in an artist's body than his body of work. His answer to those proposals had always been succinct—a dagger held threateningly to the throat—and always had the desired effect.

Never again. If he had to prostitute something to maintain his precious independence, then let it be his art and nothing else.

The room rented for the evening by the London Astronomical Society in Lincoln's Inn Fields was already crowded when the young man slipped unnoticed into his seat, anxious to remain inconspicuous. The meetings of this learned body of astronomers and mathematicians were not open to the public, but the way had been paved for his attendance by one of the members, Charles Babbage. The connection had initially been a family one, Mr Babbage's wife, Georgiana, being a remote cousin of Mr Brown, the name by which the young gentleman went by upon occasions such as this, but a shared passion for mathematics had cemented the acquaintance into a somewhat unconventional, some might even say subversive, friendship.

Tonight, the Society's president, John Herschel, was presenting his paper on double stars which had recently won him a gold medal. Though it was not an area in which the young man held a particular interest, primarily due to the fact that he had no access to a telescope of his own, Mr Brown took notes assiduously. He had not yet given up hope of persuading his father to purchase such an instrument by stressing the educational benefits which young minds, namely the younger siblings so indulged by his parent, could derive from star-gazing. Besides, Mr Herschel's process of deduction based on reason and repeated observation was a technique common to all of the natural philosophies, including Mr Brown's own particular area of interest.

Candles fluttered on the walls of the panelled room, which was dimly lit and stuffy. As the lecture progressed, coats were loosened and the levels of the decanters fell. The erstwhile Mr Brown, however, partook not a drop of wine nor removed his hat, never mind unbuttoned the bone buttons of his over-large frock coat. He was considerably more tender in years than the other members, if appearances were to be believed, with a soft cheek which looked to be untouched by a razor. His hair, what could be seen of it, was dark brown and corkscrew-curled giving him, frankly, a rather effete appearance. His eyes were an unexpected blue, the colour of a summer sea. Wide-spaced and dark-fringed, a close observer would perceive in them a hint of a sparkle, as if he were laughing at his own private joke. Whether from reticence or some other motive, Mr Brown took care not to allow any such close observation, hunching over his notebook, meeting no glances, chewing on his lower lip, shading his face with his hand.

The fingers in which he held his pencil were delicate, though the nails were sadly bitten, the skin around them picked raw and peeling. His slenderness was emphasised by the heavy folds of his dark wool coat. Under-developed, he looked to be, or simply under-nourished as studious youths often were, for they neglected to eat. At the Astronomical Society they were accustomed to such types.

As soon as the lecture was over, the applause given and the myriad of questions addressed, Mr Brown got to his feet, huddling into a voluminous black cloak which made him seem even slighter. To a kind enquiry as to whether he had enjoyed the President's lecture he nodded gravely but did not speak, hurrying out of the room ahead of the other attendees, down the shallow steps of the building and into Lincoln's Inn Fields. The gardens across the way loomed, silent and slightly foreboding, the trees dark shapes which logic told him were simply trees but which felt menacing all the same. 'Be a man,' he muttered to himself. The words seemed to amuse him, and his amusement served to banish his trepidation.

The other buildings, once grand town houses, were these days almost all given over to offices of the law. Though it was after ten at night, lights burned in several windows. The shadow of a clerk huddled over his desk could be made out in the nearest basement. Conscious of the lateness of the hour, determinedly ignoring the lurking danger which any sensible person must be aware accompanied the location, the gentleman skirted Covent Garden and made his way towards Drury Lane. It would have been an easy thing to procure a hackney here, but his destination was relatively close, and besides he had no wish to speed his arrival. Head down, keeping the brim of his hat over his face, he passed the brothels and gaming houses. Eschewing the quickest route along Oxford Street, he headed for the genteel streets of Bloomsbury where he allowed his pace to slacken.

A distinct change came over Mr Brown as he neared Lord Henry Armstrong's substantial town house in Cavendish Square. The sparkle left his eyes. His shoulders hunched as if he were retreating into himself. His steps slowed further. A combination of illicit thrill and intellectual stimulation had charged his blood and his brain during the meeting he had attended. Looking up at the tall, shuttered windows of the first-floor drawing room which stared blankly down at him, he felt as if those sensations were literally draining away. Though he fought it, he could not conquer the feeling, not quite of dread but of dejection, which enveloped him. He did not belong here, but there was no escaping the fact that it was his home.

Through the closed drapes of the window on the ground floor to the left-hand side of the door, light glimmered. Lord Armstrong, a distinguished senior diplomat of many years standing who had contrived to retain his post and increased his influence in the newly elected Duke of Wellington's government, was working in his book room. Heart sinking, the young gentleman turned his key in the lock and made his way as silently as he could across the reception hall.

'Cressida, is that you?' the voice boomed.

The Honourable Lady Cressida Armstrong halted in her tracks, one foot on the bottom step of the staircase. She cursed in a most unladylike manner under her breath. 'Yes, Father, it is I. Goodnight, Father,' she called, foolishly crossing her fingers behind her back and making for the staircase, diving as fast as she could for the sanctity of her bedchamber before she was discovered.

Chapter One

London—March 1828

The clock in the reception hall downstairs chimed noon. Having spent much of the morning working and re-working a piece which transcribed the basics of her theory on the mathematics of beauty into a form which could be easily understood by the readers of *The Kaleidoscope* journal, Cressie now stared unhappily at her reflection in the tall looking-glass. Had she allowed sufficient time to summon her maid, perhaps her unruly curls would bear less resemblance to a bird's nest, but it was too late now. The morning gown of brown-printed cotton patterned with cream and burnt-orange flashes and trimmed with navy satin ribbon was one of her favourites. The sleeves, contrary to the current fashion, were only slightly puffed, and came down almost to her knuckles, hiding her ink-stained fingers from sight. The skirts were, also contrary to fashion, not quite bell-shaped, and the hem was trimmed with only one flounce. Sombre and serious was the effect she was aiming for. Cressie pulled a face. Washed-out, plain and rather ragged around the edges was what she had achieved. 'As usual,' she muttered, turning away from her reflection with a shrug.

Making her way downstairs, she braced herself for the encounter ahead. Whatever the reason behind her father's request to speak with her, she could be certain it was not going to be a pleasant experience. 'Be a man,' Cressie said to herself with a defiant swish of her skirts as she tapped on the door of the book room. Curtsying briefly, she took a seat in front of the imposing walnut desk. 'Father.'

Lord Henry Armstrong, still handsome at fifty-five years of age, nodded curtly. 'Ah, Cressida, there you are. I had a letter from your stepmother this morning. You may congratulate me. Sir Gilbert Mountjoy has confirmed that she is increasing.'

'Again!' Bella had already produced four

boys in eight years, there was surely no need
for yet more—and in any event, Cressie had
supposed her father to be well past that sort
of thing. She screwed up her nose. Not that
she wanted to contemplate her father and Bella
and *that sort of thing.* She caught his eye and
attempted to rearrange her expression into
something more congratulatory. '*Another* half-
sibling. How very—agreeable. A sister would
make a most pleasant change, would it not?'

Lord Armstrong drummed his fingers on
his blotter and glared at his daughter. 'I would
hope Bella would have the good sense to produce me another son. Daughters have their uses
but it is sons who provide the wherewithal to
secure the family's position in society.'

He made his children sound like chess pieces
in some arrogant game, Cressie thought bitterly, though she chose not to voice it. She knew
her father well enough, and this was a mere
preamble. If he wanted to speak to her it invariably meant he wanted her to do something for
him. Daughters have their uses right enough!

'To the matter in hand,' Lord Armstrong
said, bestowing on Cressie the sort of benev-
olent smile that had averted a hundred diplomatic incidents and placated a myriad of
courtiers and officials across Europe. The ef-

fect on his daughter was rather the opposite. Whatever he was about to say, she would not like. 'Your stepmother has not been in her customary rude health. The good Sir Gilbert has confined her to bed. It is most inconvenient, for with Bella indisposed, it means Cordelia's coming-out will have to be postponed.'

Cressie's rather stiff smile faded. 'Oh no! Cordelia will be most upset, she has been counting the days. Cannot my Aunt Sophia take Bella's place for the Season?'

'Your aunt is a fine woman and has been an enormous support to me over the years, but she is not as young as she was. If only it were just a question of Cordelia. I have no doubt that your sister will go off quickly, for she's a little beauty. I have Barchester in mind for her, you must know, he has excellent connections. However, it is *not* simply a question of Cordelia, is it? There is your own unmarried state to consider. I had intended that Bella would act as escort for you both this Season. You cannot prevaricate indefinitely, Cressida.'

The veteran diplomat looked meaningfully at his daughter, who wondered rebelliously if her father had any idea of what he'd be up against, trying to coerce Cordelia into wedding a man whose full, gleaming set of teeth owed their existence in his mouth to their removal from the gums of one of his tenants, if rumour was to be believed. 'If Lord Barchester is your ambition for Cordelia,' Cressie said, keeping her eyes fixed on her clasped hands, 'then it is to be hoped that he is more enamoured with her than he was with myself.'

'Hmm.' Lord Armstrong drummed his fingers again. 'That, Cressida, is an excellent point.'

'It is?' Cressie said warily. She was not used to praise of any sort from her father.

'Indeed. You are twenty-eight now.'

'Twenty-six, actually.'

'No matter. The point is you have scared the devil out of every eligible man I've put your way, and the fact is that I intend to put some of them your sister's way. They'll not want you standing beside her like a spectre when I do. As I mentioned earlier, your Aunt Sophia is too advanced in years to adequately present two gals in one Season, so it seems I must choose. Cordelia will likely fly off the shelf. I think my ambitions for you will have to be temporarily put into abeyance. No, do not, I pray, feign disappointment, daughter,' Lord Armstrong added caustically. 'No crocodile tears, I beg you.'

Cressie's clasped hands curled into fists. Over the years, it had become her determined

policy never to let her father see how easily he
could bruise her feelings. That he still managed
to do so was one of the things which vexed her
most. She understood him very well yet still,
no matter how predictable were his barbs, they
invariably hurt. She had long ceased thinking
that he would ever understand her, far less
value her, but somehow she felt compelled to
keep trying. Why was it so difficult to fit her
emotions to her understanding! She sighed. Because he was her father and she loved him,
she supposed. Though she found it very hard
to like him.

Lord Armstrong frowned down at the letter
from his spouse. 'Do not, either, delude yourself that you are entirely off the hook. I have
another pressing problem that you can assist
me with. Apparently that damned governess
of the boys has fled her post. James put a pig's
bladder filled with water in her bed, and the
woman left without giving any notice.' The diplomat gave a bark of laughter. 'Chip off the old
block, young James. We used to get up to the
same jape at Harrow when I was a stripling.'

'James,' Cressie said feelingly, 'is not *high-
spirited* but utterly spoilt. What's more, where
James leads Harry follows.' She might have
known that this would turn out to be about

her father's precious sons. She loved her half-brothers well enough, even if they were thoroughly spoilt, but her father's preoccupation with them to the exclusion of everything, and everyone, else, grated.

'The nub of the matter is that my wife is clearly in no position to secure a suitable new governess post-haste, and I myself, it goes without saying, have many weighty matters of state to attend to. Wellington relies on me completely, you know.' It was an illusion, Cressie knew, but she could swear that her father visibly puffed up as he made this pronouncement. 'However, my boys' education must not be interrupted,' he continued, 'I have great plans for all of them. I have pondered on this, and it seems to me that the solution is obvious.'

'It is?' Cressie said doubtfully.

'It certainly is to me. You, Cressida, will be governess to my sons. That way, Cordelia will be able to come out this Season as planned. Placing you in the position of governess removes you most expediently from Cordelia's arena, and spares you from being a burden by making use of that brain you are so proud of. My sons' education will not be jeopardised. With a bit of luck we may even have Cordelia married by the autumn. And there is the added bonus of having you on hand at Killellan Manor while Bella is indisposed, thus providing you with the opportunity to forge a more amenable relationship with your stepmother than hitherto.' Lord Armstrong beamed at his daughter. 'If I say so myself, I have devised a most elegant and satisfactory solution to a potentially difficult situation. Which, one supposes, is why Wellington values my diplomatic skills so highly.'

Cressie's thoughts were, however, far from diplomatic. Presented with what she had no doubt was a *fait accompli*, her instinct was to find some way of sabotaging her father's carefully laid plans. But even as she opened her mouth to protest, it came to her that perhaps she could turn the situation to her advantage.

'You wish me to act as governess?' Her brain worked feverishly. Her brothers were taxing, but if she could manage to teach James and Harry the principles of geometry using the primer she had written, it might provide her publishers with the evidence they needed to commit to a print date. Freyworth and Son had initially been most enthusiastic when she first visited their offices, and most reassuring on the subject of discretion. The firm had, Mr Frey-worth told her, several lady writers on their books who wished, for various reasons, to remain anonymous. Surely such practical proof as she would obtain from successfully instructing her brothers would persuade him that her book really was a viable commercial proposition? Selling her primer would be the first step to financial independence, which was the first step towards freedom. And who knew, if she managed his precious boys better than any of the other governesses, she might finally gain her father's approbation. Although that, Cressie conceded, was unlikely.

Even more importantly, accepting his proposal meant that she would not have to spend a seventh Season mouldering away on the shelf while her father schemed and plotted an alliance. So far, he had stopped short of taking out an advertisement on the front page of the *Morning Post* along with the intimations of patents pending, but who knew what he might do if he became desperate enough. *One daughter, without looks but of excellent lineage and diplomatic connections, offered to ambitious man with acceptable pedigree and political aspirations. Tory preferred, but Whig considered. No tradesmen or time wasters.*

Now she thought of it, it was a distinct possibility for, as Lord Armstrong never tired of pointing out, she possessed neither the poise nor beauty of any of her other sisters. That she was the clever one was no consolation whatsoever to Cressie, when she thought of how incredibly foolishly she had behaved during that fiasco of her third Season, by surrendering her one marketable asset to Giles Peyton. That she could have been so desperate—Cressie shuddered. Even now, the memory was mortifying. It had been a disaster in every possible way save one—her reputation, if not her hymen, was intact, for her erstwhile lover and intended husband had hastily taken up a commission shortly afterwards, leaving her in sole possession of the unpalatable facts.

In more recent Seasons, her father's attempts to marry her off had smacked of desperation, but he had never once flagged in his manipulations. He thought he was manipulating her now, but if she kept her cards close to her chest, she might just manage to turn the tables. Cressie felt a small glow inside her. Whether it was self-satisfaction or a feeling of empowerment she wasn't sure, but it was a feeling she liked. 'Very well, Father, I will do as you ask and act as governess to the boys.'

She kept her voice carefully restrained, for to hint that she wished to do as he said would be a major tactical error. It seemed she had hit just the right note of reluctant compliance, for Lord Armstrong nodded brusquely. 'Of course they will require a proper male tutor before they go to Harrow, but in the meantime the rudiments of mathematics, Latin and Greek—I believe I can rely on you for those.'

'Rudiments!'

Lord Armstrong, seeing that his remark had hit home, smiled. 'I am aware, Cressida, that you consider your erudition rather above the requirements of my sons. It is my fault. I have been an over-indulgent parent,' he said in all sincerity. 'I should have put an end to these studies of yours long ago. I see they have given you a most inflated view of your own intellect. It is no wonder that you have failed to bring any man up to scratch.'

Was it true? Was she conceited?

'Next year,' Lord Armstrong continued inexorably, 'when Cordelia is off my hands, I shall expect you to accept the first offer of marriage I arrange for you. It is your duty, and I expect you to honour it. Do I make myself clear?'

It had always been made abundantly clear to her that, as a daughter, as a mere female, her purpose was to serve, but her father had never before laid it out so clearly and unequivocally.

'Cressida, I asked you a question. Do I make myself clear?'

She hesitated, torn between bitter hurt and impotent fury. Silently, she pledged that she would use this year to find a way, any way save telling him the awful, shameful truth of her dalliance with Giles, of placing herself firmly on the shelf and just as importantly, of establishing herself as an independent and wholly *un*-dependent female. Cressie glared at her father. 'You make yourself abundantly clear.'

'Excellent,' Lord Armstrong replied with infuriating calm. 'Now, to other matters. Ah—' he broke off as a tap on the study door heralded the arrival of his butler '—that will be him now.'

'Signor di Matteo awaits his lordship's pleasure,' the butler intoned.

'The portrait-painter fellow,' Lord Armstrong casually informed his daughter, as if this should be the most obvious thing in the world. 'You shall relieve your stepmother of that burden also, Cressida.'

He had obviously walked in on some sort of altercation, for the atmosphere in the study fairly crackled with tension as Giovanni entered the room in the portly wake of Lord

Armstrong's butler. The manservant, either oblivious to the strained mood or, more likely in the way of English servants, trained to give that impression, announced him and departed, leaving Giovanni alone with the two warring factions. One of them was obviously Lord Armstrong, his client. The other, a female, whose face was lost under a mass of unruly curls, stood with her arms crossed defiantly over her bosom. He could almost taste the pent-up frustration simmering away beneath the surface, could guess too, from the way she veiled her eyes, the vulnerability she was trying to hide. Such a mastery of her emotions was intriguing, for it required, as Giovanni could attest, a lifetime's practice. Whoever she was, she was not your typical simpering English rose.

Giovanni made his perfunctory bow, just low enough and no more, for it was one of the advantages of his success that he no longer had to feign deference. As was his custom, his dress was austere, even severe. His frock coat with its high shawl collar and wide skirts would be the height of fashion were it any colour other than black. Similarly his high-buttoned waistcoat, his stirrupped trousers and highly polished square-toe shoes, all unrelieved black, making the neat ruffles of his pristine shirt and carefully tied cravat gleam an impossible white. It amused him to create an appearance in such stark contrast to the flamboyant and colourful persona his high-born sitters expected of a prestigious artist—and an Italian one at that. He looked as if he were in mourning. There were times, of late, when he felt that he was.

'Signor de Matteo.' Lord Armstrong sketched an even more shallow bow. 'May I present my daughter, Lady Cressida.'

The glance she shot her father was a bitter dart. It was received with a small smile. Whatever had transpired between them was the latest in what Giovanni surmised had been a lifetime of such skirmishes. He made another bow, a little more sincerely this time. Looking into a pair of eyes the azure blue of the Mediterranean Sea in summer, he saw they were overly bright. 'My lady.'

She did not curtsy, but offered her hand to shake, like a gentleman. 'How do you do, *signor.*' A firm clasp she had, though her nails were in an atrocious state, chewed to the quick, the skin bleeding around the edges. She had a pleasant voice, to his ear, the vowels clipped and precise. He had the impression of a fierce intelligence blazing from her eyes under that intense frown, though not beauty. Indeed, her dreadful gown, the way she rounded her posture, curling into herself as she sat down, made it clear that she cultivated plainness. But for all that—or perhaps because of that—he thought she had an interesting face.

Was she to be his subject? A pique of interest flared momentarily but no, the commission was for a portrait of children, and Lady Cressida was most definitely well past her girlhood. A pity, for he would have liked to try to capture the vitality behind the shimmering resentment. She was no empty-headed society beauty, nor appeared to have any aspirations to be depicted as such. He cursed the paradox which made the most interesting of subjects the least inclined to be painted, and the most beautiful subjects the ones he was least inclined to depict. Then he reminded himself that beauty was his business. A fact he was having to remind himself of rather too often.

'Sit, sit.' Lord Armstrong ushered him to a chair and resumed his own seat, surveying him shrewdly from behind the desk. 'I wish you to paint a portrait of my boys. James is eight. Harry six. And the twins, George and Frederick, are five.'

'Four, actually,' the daughter intervened.

Her father waved away her comment. 'Still

in short coats, is the important thing. You'll paint them together, as a group.'

It was, Giovanni noted, an instruction rather than a question. 'And the mother too?' he asked. 'That is the usual...'

'Lord, no. Bella's not—no, no, I do not wish my wife depicted.'

'What, then, of their sister?' Giovanni asked, turning towards Lady Cressida.

'Just the boys. I want you to capture their charms,' his lordship said, looking pointedly at his daughter, whom he obviously considered to possess none.

Giovanni repressed a sigh. Another tedious depiction of cherubic children. Sons, but no daughter. The English aristocracy were no different from the Italian in their views in that regard. It was to be a pretty and idealistic portrait totally lacking in any truth, the licit products of Lord Armstrong's loins displayed in the family gallery for posterity. His heart sank. 'You wish me to show your sons as charming,' he repeated fatalistically.

'They *are* charming.' Lord Armstrong frowned. 'Proper manly boys, mind. I want you to show that too, nothing namby-pamby. Now, as to the composition...'

'You may leave that decision with me.'

Forced to paint a vision far removed from reality he might be, but his fame had at least allowed him some element of control. As Giovanni had expected, his lordship looked put out. It was all so predictable. 'You may have every confidence in my choice. I presume you have seen my work, my lord?'

'Not seen as such, but I've heard excellent reports of it. I wouldn't have summoned you here if I hadn't.'

This was new. Across from him, he could see that it was news also to Lady Cressida, who looked appalled.

'I fail to see how my being unfamiliar with your work is at all relevant.' Lord Armstrong frowned heavily at his daughter. 'As a diplomat, I have to trust the word of others constantly. If there's a problem in Egypt, or Lisbon, or Madrid, I can't be expected to hotfoot it over there in person. I ask myself, who is the best man for the job, and then I get him to deal with it. It's the same with this portrait. I have taken soundings, sought expert advice. Signor di Matteo was consistently highly recommended—in point of fact,' he said, turning to Giovanni, 'I was told you were the best. Was I misinformed?'

'Certainly, demand for my portraits far outstrips the rate at which I can produce them,' Giovanni replied. Which was true, and ought to cause him a great deal more satisfaction than it did, even if it did not actually answer Lord Armstrong's question. His success was such that he could command an extremely high premium for his portraits, even if that very success felt not like freedom but a prison of his own making. Another thing Giovanni was discovering recently, that success was a double-edged sword. Fame and fortune, while on the one hand securing his independence, had severely compromised his creativity. It was a price worth paying, he told himself every day. No matter that he felt his muse recede ever faster with every passing commission.

His newest patron, however, seemed quite satisfied with his response. To possess what others desired was sufficient for Lord Armstrong, as it was for most of his class.

His lordship got to his feet. 'Then we are agreed.' He held out his hand, and Giovanni stood too, taking it in a firm grip. 'My secretary will handle the—er, commercial details. I look forward to seeing the finished product. I must make my excuses now, for I am expected at Apsley House. There is a chance I may have to accompany Wellington on his trip to St Petersburg. Inconvenient, but when one's country calls, what can one do! I shall leave you in my daughter's charge, *signor*. She will supervise her brothers during the sittings. Anything you need Cressida can provide, since Lady Armstrong, my wife, is currently indisposed.'

With only a curt nod in his daughter's direction, Lord Armstrong hurried from the room, content that he had in one fell swoop neatly resolved all his domestic problems and could now concentrate his mind fully on the much more important and devilishly tricky matter of how best to address the issue of Greek independence without standing on either Turkish or Russian toes.

Left alone with the artist, Cressida surveyed him properly for the first time. She had been so absorbed in trying to maintain control of her temper that until now she had noted merely that Signor di Matteo's dress was not at all like the peacock she expected, that he was younger than she had surmised from his reputation, and that his English was excellent. What struck her now with some force was that he was starkly and strikingly beautiful. Not merely handsome, but possessing such an ethereal magnetism and sense of physical perfection that she could almost question whether or not he was real.

Aware that she was staring, she took a mental inventory in an attempt to unscramble her reeling senses. High cheekbones and a high brow, the sleek line of his head outlined by the close-cropped cap of raven-black hair. His eyes were dark brown under heavy dark lids. It was a classically proportioned face, albeit vaguely saturnine. The planes of his cheeks were sharp, accentuated by the hollows below. He had a good nose. A near enough perfect nose, in fact. And his mouth—it was wasted on a man, that mouth. Full lips, top and bottom, deeply sensual, sculpted, and at the same time it curved up just enough to make him look as if he was on the verge of a smile, just enough to take the edge off his forbidding expression. Even without measuring the precise angles, Cressie could tell she was looking at the physical embodiment of perfect mathematical beauty. A face which would launch a thousand ships—or flutter a thousand female hearts more likely, she thought cynically. But it was also the epitome of her theory. And at that thought, her heart gave a little unaccustomed flutter.

She was being rude, though, judging from the way Signor di Matteo was returning her gaze. Haughty and at the same time wearily resigned, he was clearly accustomed to being stared at. No wonder, and even less of a surprise was his indifference to her, for he had painted some famous beauties. Unlike her father, Cressie had studied several examples of Signor di Matteo's work in the course of her research for her treatise. Like the man himself, his paintings were perfectly proportioned and classically beautiful. Too perfect, almost. His subjects were portrayed flawlessly and flatteringly. There was, in the small number of portraits she had managed to view, a similarity in the way their faces conformed to an ideal, the result of which was undoubtedly a very accomplished likeness, but also moulded the individual features from a kind of template of beauty. Which was exactly the premise of the theory that Cressie had developed. Beauty could be reduced to a series of mathematical rules. It would be fascinating to see first-hand how Signor di Matteo, the famous artist, set about creating his works.

A famous artist who, Cressie now noted with deep embarrassment, was tapping his fingers impatiently on her father's desk. She flushed. How rude he must think her. 'I trust you have in mind a suitably flattering composition, *si-*

gnor. As you will no doubt have noticed, my father dotes on his sons.'

'His *charming* boys.'

Was there just the lightest hint of irony in his voice? Could this artist actually be mocking his patron? 'They *are* very good-looking,' Cressie conceded, 'but they are most certainly *not* charming. In fact, you should know that they have a particular liking for practical jokes. Their governess has recently left without notice as a result of one such, which is why I shall be taking her place, their reputation being—'

'*You!*'

Cressie stiffened. 'As I have already informed my father, I am perfectly capable of teaching the *rudiments* of mathematics.'

'That is not what I meant. It is merely that the Season is almost upon us. I would have thought you would have had parties to attend—but forgive me, it is none of my business.'

'I have already experienced several Seasons, *signor*, and have no wish to endure another. I am six-and-twenty, and quite beyond dances and parties. Not that I ever—but that is of no account.'

'You have no wish to find a husband, then?'

The question was extremely impertinent, but the tone of his voice was not, and Cressie was, in any case, eager to vent her spleen now that the real object of her wrath had departed. 'There are some women whom marriage does not suit. I have concluded I am one of them.' Which was not quite a lie, but more like putting the truth through a prism. 'Until I am at least thirty and saying my prayers, however, my father will not accept that. His gracious permission to excuse me this year is more to do with ensuring I do not intrude on my youngest sister's chances of making an excellent match. Once she is safely betrothed, I am to be wheeled back on to the market. My role as governess is merely a temporary expedient.'

Her frankness had obviously perplexed him. It had taken her aback too. A small frown marred that perfect brow of his, and confusingly there was also a hint of upward tilt of that far too perfect mouth. Was he laughing at her? Cressie bristled. 'It was not my intention to provide you with a source of amusement, *signor.*'

'I am not amused, merely—interested. I have not before met a lady so determined to boast of her unmarried state and the fact that she understands more than the—er—the *rudiments* of mathematics.'

He *was* mocking her. 'Well, now you have.' Indignation and anger made Cressie indiscreet.

'And I do understand *considerably* more than the rudiments, if you must know. In fact, I have published a number of articles on the subject, and even reviewed Mr Lardner's book, *Analytical Treatise on Plane and Spherical Trigonometry*. I have also written a children's geometry primer which a most respected publisher has shown an interest in printing, and I am currently writing a thesis on the mathematics of art.'

So there! Cressie folded her arms over her chest. She had not meant to blurt out quite so much. Having done so, she waited for Signor di Matteo to laugh, but instead he raised his brows and smiled, not a condescending smile, but rather as if he was surprised. His smile made her catch her breath, for it transformed his beauty from that of a haughty statue to something much more human.

'So you are a published author.'

'Under the pseudonym Penthiselea.' Cressie had just betrayed yet another jealously guarded secret without meaning to. What was it about this man? He had her spilling her innermost thoughts like some babbling child.

'Penthiselea. An Amazonian warrior famed for her wisdom. It is most—apt.'

'Yes, yes, but I must urge you to discretion.

If my father knew...' Cressie took yet another deep breath. '*Signor*, you must understand that in my position—that is to say— my father thinks that my facility for mathematics is detrimental to his ambition to marry me off, and I must confess that it is my own experience too, by and large. Men do not value intelligence in their wives.'

Signor di Matteo's smile had a cynical twist to it now, his dark eyes seemed distant, turned in on some unpleasant memory. 'Blood and beauty rule supreme, *signorina*,' he said. 'It is the way of the world.'

It was a stark little expression, which said more precisely than she ever could exactly what Cressie herself believed. Beauty was this man's business, but she wondered what he knew of the burden of pedigree. She could not find a way of framing such a personal question without inviting offence.

He put an end to her attempts, with a question of his own. 'If you are studying the relationship of mathematics to art, you must have read the definitive work by my fellow Italian. I refer to Pacioli, his *De Divina Proportione*?'

Pleased to discover that he was not the type of man to assume her sex prevented her from understanding such an erudite work, Cressie

The Beauty Within
the title of the book sounded when spoken by
a native Italian. 'You have read it?' she asked
foolishly, for he obviously had.

'It is a standard text. You agree with what he
says, that beauty can be described in the rules
of symmetry?'

'And proportion. These are surely the basic
rules of any art?'

Signor di Matteo began to prowl restlessly
about the room, frowning. 'If painting was simply about getting angles and proportions right,
then anyone could be an artist.'

'How did you learn to paint so well?' Cressie
countered.

'Study. Of the Old Masters. In the studios as
apprentice to other painters. Practice.'

'So it is a skill. A craft, with rules which can
be learned. That is exactly my point.'

'And my point is that art is not simply a
craft.' There was anger in his tone now.

'I don't understand what I've said to upset
you, *signor*. I was paying you a compliment.
The primary purpose of art is to adorn, is it
not? And if it is to adorn, it must be beautiful.
And if it is beautiful, then it must conform to
what we know is beautiful—to the mathematical rules of symmetry and proportion which

we see in nature, as your countryman Signor Fibonacci has shown us. To be reckoned the best, not only must you have mastered the technical skills of the draughtsman, but you must obviously have the firmest grasp of these underlying rules.'

'So I paint by rote, that is what you are saying?'

'I am saying that you are a master of the rules of nature.'

'Yet nature has created you, my lady, and you hardly conform to those rules. By your process of deduction, you cannot then consider yourself beautiful.'

The cruelty of his words was like a slap in the face. She had been so caught up in propounding her theory that she had unwittingly insulted him, and his response, to turn her own plainness against her, was much more painful than it ought to be. The light of intellectual conviction died from her eyes, and Cressie tumbled back down into harsh reality. Signor di Matteo possessed the kind of looks which made women cast caution to the winds, though most likely the caution they cast was physical rather than intellectual. 'I am perfectly well aware, *signor*, that I am not beautiful.'

'There is beauty in everything if you know how, and where, to look.'

He was standing too close to her. She was acutely aware of his brooding physical presence. Cressie got to her feet, intending to push him out of the way, but he caught hold of her arm. His fingers were long, tanned and quite free of paint, she noted absently. Her head barely reached the broad sweep of his shoulders. This close, there was no mistaking the strength which lurked underneath that lithe exterior. Being so near to him made her breathing erratic. It was embarrassment which was making her hot. Every propriety must be offended. 'What do you think you're doing? Unhand me at once.'

He ignored her, instead tilting her chin up and forcing her to meet his piercing gaze. She could escape quite easily, and yet it did not occur to her. 'It is true,' he said softly, 'that your nose is not perfectly straight and so spoils the symmetry of your profile.'

Cressie glowered. 'I am perfectly aware of that.'

'And your eyes. They are too wide-spaced, and so not in the proportion to your mouth which Pacioli requires.'

One long finger traced the line he mentioned. His own eyes had a rim of gold at the edges. The lashes were black and thick. His touch was doing strange things to her insides. It made her jittery. Nervous. Was he flirting with her? Definitely not. He was merely punishing her for her unintended insult. 'And my ears are out of alignment with my nose, the ratio between my chin and my forehead is wrong,' Cressie said, with an insouciance she most certainly did not feel. 'As for my mouth…'

'As for your mouth…'

Signor di Matteo trailed his finger along the length of her bottom lip. She felt the most absurd urge to taste him. He growled something in Italian. His fingers splayed out over her jaw. He bent his head towards her. He was going to kiss her.

Cressie's heart thudded. He really was going to kiss her. The muscles in her calves tensed in preparation for flight, but she didn't move. His fingers slid along her jaw to tangle in her hair. She watched, urging herself to escape, but at the same time another part of her brain was enthralled, mesmerised, by that perfectly symmetrical face. Let him, she thought. Let him kiss me, if he dares!

His lips hovered a fraction over hers, just long enough for her to have a premonition of

melting, a premonition of what it would be like
to cede, to unleash whatever it was he kept restrained. Just long enough for Cressie to come
to her senses.

She yanked herself free. 'How dare you!' It
sounded very unconvincing, even to herself.
She was struggling to breathe, praying that
the heat which flooded her cheeks, which was
surely mortification, was not too apparent. The
nerve of him! He was outrageously attractive
and he obviously knew it. Also, he was Italian.
Everyone knew that Italian men were quite unable to control their passions. Obviously, it was
not such a cliché as she had thought.

'To return to your point, *signor*, I concede
that my mouth is too wide to be considered
beautiful,' Cressie said, relieved to hear that
her voice sounded almost composed.

'Beauty, Lady Cressida, is not exclusively
about symmetry. Your mouth is very beautiful, in my humble opinion.'

Giovanni di Matteo did not look the least
abashed. 'You ought not to have kissed me,'
Cressie said.

'I did not kiss you. And *you* ought not to
have spoken so scathingly of my work, especially since you have never seen it.'

'Do not assume that I am so ignorant as my

father. I have studied it, and I did not speak scathingly! I merely pointed out that you—that painting—that any art—'

'Can be reduced to a set of principles and rules. I *was* listening.' But even as he curled his lip, Giovanni had a horrible suspicion that this wholly unorthodox female had somehow managed to get to the root of his dissatisfaction. In the early days, when he painted for the simple pleasure of creating something unique, he had channelled that tangible connection between canvas and brush and palette and blood and skin and bone, painting from the heart and not the head. It had earned him nothing but mockery from the so-called experts. *Naïve. Emotional. Lacking discipline and finesse.* The words were branded on his heart. He learned to hone his craft, eradicate all emotion from his work. To his eye it rendered it soulless, but it proved immensely popular. The experts acclaimed it, the titled and influential commissioned it. He chose not to disillusion any of them. Giovanni made his bow. 'Much as I have enjoyed our discussion, Lady Cressida, I must go and continue with the more prosaic task of capturing the likeness of my current client. I bid you good day.'

He took her hand, raising it to his lips. As he

kissed her fingertips, the spark of awareness took him by surprise. Judging by her shocked expression, he was not the only one affected by it.

Chapter Two

Giovanni leapt down from the gig as it drew to a halt in front of Killellan Manor, the country estate of the Armstrong family, airily dismissing the waiting footman's offer to escort him to the door. He had travelled to Sussex on the mail, which had been met at the nearest posting inn by Lord Armstrong's coachman. It was a cold but clear day, the clouds scudding across the pale blue sky of early spring, encouraged by the brisk March breeze. Pulling his greatcoat more tightly around himself, he stamped his feet in an effort to stimulate the circulation. There were many things about England he admired, but the weather was not one of them.

Lord Armstrong's impressive residence was constructed of grey sandstone. Palladian in style, with the main four-storey building flanked by two wings, the façade which fronted on to the carriage way was marred, in Giovanni's view, by the unnecessary addition of a much later semi-circular portico. Enclosed by the high hedges into which the gates were set, the house looked gloomy and rather forbidding.

Wishing to stretch his legs after the long journey before announcing his presence, Giovanni followed the main path past a high-walled garden and the stable buildings to discover a prospect at the front of the house altogether different and much more pleasing to the eye. Here, manicured lawns edged with bright clumps of daffodils and narcissi stretched down, via a set of wide and shallow stone steps, to a stream which burbled along a pebbled river bed towards a watermill. On the far side of the river, the vista was of gently rolling meadows neatly divided by hedgerows. Despite the fact that the rustic bridge looked rather suspiciously too rustic, he couldn't help but be entranced by this quintessentially English landscape.

'It is a perfect example of what the poet, Mr Blake, calls *England's green and pleasant land*, is it not?'

Giovanni started, for the words came from someone standing immediately behind him.

The rush of the water over the pebbles had disguised her approach. 'Lady Cressida. I was thinking almost exactly that, though I am not familiar with the poet, I'm afraid. Unless— could it be William Blake, the artist?'

'He is more known for his verse than his art.'

'That will change. I have seen some of his paintings. They are…' Giovanni struggled to find an appropriate English word to describe the fantastical drawings and watercolours which seemed to explode out of the paper. 'Extraordinary,' he settled on finally and most unsatisfactorily. 'I find them beautiful, but most certainly they would fail your mathematical criteria.'

'And this?' She waved at the landscape. 'Would you consider this beautiful?'

'I suspect your father has invested rather a lot of money to ensure that it is. That bridge, it cannot possibly be as old as it appears.'

'There is also a little artfully ruined folly in the grounds, and you are quite correct, neither are older than I am.'

It had been more than two weeks since their first meeting in London. In the interval, Giovanni had replayed their conversation several times in his head, and that almost-but-not-quite kiss too. It had been a foolish act to take such a liberty with the daughter of the man who was paying his commission, and a man of such palpable influence too. He couldn't understand why he had been so cavalier. Attempting to recreate Lady Cressida feature by feature using charcoal on paper had proved entirely unsatisfactory. He had been unable to capture the elusive quality that had piqued his interest. Now, as she stood before him, the sun shining directly behind her, making a halo of her wild curls, the dark shadows under her startlingly blue eyes, the faintest trace of a frown drawing her brows together giving her a delicate, bruised look, he could see that it was nothing to do with her features but something more complex which drew him to her. It puzzled him, until he realised that her allure was quite basic. He wanted to capture that ambiguity of hers in oils.

'You look tired,' Giovanni said, speaking his thoughts aloud.

'My brothers are—energetic,' Cressie replied. *Exhausting* would be more accurate, but that would sound defeatist. Two weeks of shepherding four small boys intent on making mischief had taken their toll—for the twins, though not formally included in her lessons, insisted on being with their brothers at all times. Until they had become her responsibility, she had been dismissive of Bella's complaints that the boys wore her down to the bone. They were mere children—all they required was sufficient mental stimulation and exercise, Cressie had thought. She realised now that her contempt had been founded on blissful ignorance.

Her evenings had therefore been spent making a guilty effort to become better acquainted with a stepmother who made it plain that her company was welcome only in the absence of any other, for Cordelia had hastened to London the day after Cressie's arrival at Killellan, fearful that either Lord Armstrong or Aunt Sophia might change their minds about her impending coming-out season. Cressie was alone for the first time in the house without any of her sisters for company. She was becoming short-tempered and grumpy with the boys, which in turn made her annoyed with herself, for she wanted to like her brothers as well as love them. She tried not to blame them for the lack of discipline which made them unruly to a fault. Every morning she told herself it was just a matter of trying harder. 'I fear I rather underestimated the effort it takes to keep such active minds and bodies occupied,' she said, smiling wanly at the portrait painter.

'Still, I believe teaching will bring its own reward. At least—I hope it will.'

Giovanni looked sceptical. 'You should demand fair payment from your father. I think you would be amply rewarded if you did so, if only by his reaction.'

'Goodness, he would be appalled,' Cressie exclaimed. 'The fact is I'm doing this for my own reasons, not merely to accommodate my father.'

'And those reasons are?'

'No concern of yours, Signor de Matteo. You do not like my father much, do you?'

'He reminds me of someone I dislike very much.'

'Who?'

'That is no concern of yours, Lady Cressida.'

'Touché, signor.'

'You do not much like your father either, do you?'

'You ought not to have to ask such a question. And I ought to be able to answer positively.' Cressie grimaced. 'He enjoys making things difficult for me. And I him, if I am honest.'

The mixture of guilt and amusement on her face was endearing. The wind whipped a long lock of hair across her face, and without thinking, Giovanni made to brush it away at the same time as she did. His gloved hand covered her fingers. The contact jolted him into awareness, just as when he had kissed her hand, and the arrested look in her eyes made him aware that she felt it too. Her eyes widened. She shivered. The sun dazzled her eyes, and the moment was gone.

Cressie wrapped her arms around herself as the wind caught her again. She had come out without even a wrap. 'We should go inside,' she said, turning away, thrown off balance not just by the tangle of her gown, which the breeze had blown around her legs, but by her own reaction to Giovanni de Matteo's touch. She was not usually a tactile person, but he made her acutely conscious of her body, and his. She did not want him to see the effect he had on her, though no doubt he had the same effect on every female he encountered. 'I should take you to meet my brothers now. My stepmother does not like me to leave them with the nursery maid for too long.'

'Let them wait a little longer. I would like to see something of the house in order to find a suitable place to set up my easel. Lady Armstrong cannot object to you assisting me, can she? And you, Lady Cressida, you cannot ob-

ject to my company over your brothers', even if
we seem to disagree on almost every subject.'

She couldn't help laughing, and her laughter
dispelled her awkwardness. 'After the morning I have had in the schoolroom I assure you I
would take almost any company over my brothers', even yours. I most certainly do not object.
Come, follow me.'

The portrait gallery ran the full length of
the second floor. Light streamed in through
windows which looked out over the formal
gardens. The paintings were hung in strict an-
cestral sequence on the long wall opposite. 'I
thought you might wish to set up your studio
here,' Cressie said.

Giovanni nodded approvingly. 'The light is
good.'

'The yellow drawing room and music room
are through these doors, but neither are much
used for Bella, my stepmother, prefers the
smaller salon downstairs, and since Cassie—
Cassandra, my second sister—left home some
years ago, I doubt anyone has touched the pi-
anoforte, so you will not be disturbed.'

'Except by my subjects.'

'True. I do not know how you prefer to work,

whether they must sit still for hours on end, but...'

'That would be to expect the impossible, and in any event not necessary.'

'That is a relief. I was wondering whether I would have to resort to tying them to their chairs. Actually, I confess that I have been wondering whether I must resort to doing just that in order to keep them at their lessons. I had hoped that my primer—' Cressie broke off, tugging at the knot of hair which she had managed to tangle around her index finger, and forced herself to smile brightly. 'My travails as a teacher cannot possibly be of interest to you, *signor*. Let us look at the paintings.'

Though her determination to shoulder the blame for her brothers' failings intrigued him, there was a note in her voice that warned Giovanni off from pursuing the subject. He allowed her to lead him from portrait to portrait, listening while she unravelled for him the complex and many-branched Armstrong family tree, enjoying the cadence of her voice, taking the opportunity to study, not the canvases, but her face as she talked animatedly about the various family members. There was something deep within her that he longed to draw out, to capture. He was certain that beneath the veneer of scientific detachment and tightly held emotions, there was passion. In short, she would make a fascinating subject.

He must find a way of painting her portrait. Not one of his idealised studies, but something with some veracity. He had thought the desire to paint from the heart had died in him, but it seemed it had merely been lying dormant. Lady Cressida Armstrong, of all unlikely people, had awakened his muse.

But tantalising glimpses, mere impressions of her hidden self would not suffice. A certain level of intimacy would be required. In order to paint her he needed to know her—her heart and her mind, though most definitely not her body. Those days were past.

And yet, he could not take his eyes from her body. As she moved to the next painting he noticed how the sunlight, dancing in through the leaded panes in the long windows, framed her dress, which was white cotton, simply made, with a high round neck. The sleeves were wide at the shoulder as was the fashion, tapering down to the wrists, the hem tucked and trimmed with cotton lace. With a draughtsman's eye he noted approvingly how the cut of the gown enhanced her figure—the neat waist, the fullness of her breasts, the curve of her hips.

In this light, he could clearly see the shape of her legs outlined against her petticoats. One of her stockings was wrinkled at the ankle. The sash at her waist was tied in a lopsided knot rather than a bow, and the top-most button at her neck was undone. She employed no maid, Giovanni surmised, and she had certainly not taken the time to inspect herself in the mirror. Haste or indifference? Both, he reckoned, though rather more of the latter.

He followed her to the next painting, but the pleasing roundedness of her *fondoschiena*, the tantalising shape of her legs, distracted him. He wanted to smooth out the wrinkle in her stocking. There was something about the fragile bones in a woman's ankle that he had always found erotic. And the swell of a calf. The softness of the flesh at the top of a woman's thighs. He had tasted just enough of her lips to be able to imagine how yielding the rest of her would be.

Giovanni cursed softly under his breath. Sex and art. The desire for both had been latent until he met her. Painting her was a possibility, but as for the other—he was perfectly content in his celibate state, free of bodily needs and the needs of other bodies.

'This is Lady Sophia, my father's sister,'

Lady Cressida was saying. 'My Aunt Sophia is—you know, I don't think you've been listening to a word I've said.'

They were standing in front of the portrait of an austere woman who bore a remarkable resemblance to a camel suffering from a severe case of wind. 'Gainsborough,' Giovanni said, recognising the style immediately. 'Your aunt, you were saying.'

'What were you really thinking about?'

'Is there a painting of you among the collection?'

'Only one, in a group portrait with my sisters.'

'Show me.'

The painting had been hung between two doors, in the worst of the light. Lawrence, though not one of his best. There were five girls, the eldest two seated at a sewing table, the younger three at their feet, playing with reels of cotton. 'That is Celia,' Lady Cressida said, pointing to the eldest, a slim young woman with a serious expression and a protective hand on the head of the youngest child. 'Beside her is Cassie. As you can see, she is the beauty of the family. Cordelia, my youngest sister who makes her come out this Season, is very like her. Caroline is beside her, and that is me, the odd one out.'

Giovanni nodded. 'You certainly have very different colouring. What age were you when this was painted?'

'I don't know, eleven or twelve, I think. It was before Celia married and left home.'

'I am surprised that your mother is not in this painting. Lawrence would usually have included the mother in such a composition.'

'She died not long after Cordelia was born. Celia was more of a mother to us than anyone.' Lady Cressida's voice was wistful as she reached out to touch her sister's image. 'I haven't seen her for almost ten years. Nor Cassie, for eight.'

'Surely they must visit, or you them?'

'It is a long way to Arabia, *signor.*' Obviously sensing his confusion, Lady Cressida hastened to explain. 'Celia married one of my father's diplomatic protégés. They were in Arabia, sent on a mission by the British Ambassador to Egypt, when Celia's husband was murdered by rebel tribesmen. I remember it so well, the news being broken to us here at Killellan. We were told that Celia was being held captive in a harem. My father and Cassie and Aunt Sophia went to Arabia to rescue her only to discover that she didn't want to be rescued. Fortunately for Celia, it turned out that her desert prince was hugely influential and fantastically rich, so my father was happy to hand her over.'

'And your other sister—Cassie, did you say?'

'When she narrowly escaped a most unfortunate connection with a poet, our father packed her off in disgrace to stay with Celia. He should have known that Cassie, a born romantic, would tumble head over heels in love with the exotic East. When he found out that he had lost a second daughter to a desert prince he was furious. But this prince too turned out to have excellent diplomatic connections and was also suitably generous with his riches, so my father magnanimously decided to be reconciled to the idea.'

'Such a colourful history for such a very English family,' Giovanni said drily.

She laughed. 'Indeed! My father decided two sheikhs, no matter how influential, was more than sufficient for any family. I think he fears if any of us visit them, the same fate would befall us, so we must content ourselves with exchanging letters.'

'And are they happy, your sisters?'

'Oh yes, blissfully. They have families of their own now too.' Lady Cressida gazed lovingly at the portrait. 'It is the only thing which makes it bearable, knowing how happy they are. I miss them terribly.'

'But you are not quite alone. You have your stepmother.'

'It is clear you have not been introduced to Bella. My father married her not long after Celia's wedding. I think he assumed Bella would take on Celia's role in looking after us three younger girls as well as providing him with an heir but Bella—well, Bella saw things differently. And once James was born, so too did Papa. His only interest is his male heirs.'

'Sadly, that is the way of the world, Lady Cressida.'

'Cressie. Please call me Cressie, for no one else here does, now Caro has married and Cordelia has gone to London. I am the last of the Armstrong sisters,' she said with a sad little smile. 'I think you have heard more than enough of my family history for one day.'

'It seems to me a shame that there are no other portraits of you. May I ask—would you—I would like to paint you, Lady—Cressie.'

'Paint *me*! Why on earth would you want to do that?'

Her expression almost made him laugh, but the evidence it gave him of her lack of self-worth made him angry. 'An exercise in mathematics,' Giovanni replied, hitting upon an inspired idea. 'I will paint one portrait to your rules, and I will paint another to mine.'

'Two portraits!'

'*Si*. Two.' An idealised Lady Cressida and the real one. For the first time in years, Giovanni felt the unmistakable tingle of certainty. Ambition long subdued began to stir. Though he had no idea as yet what this second portrait would be, he knew at least it would be his. Painted from the heart. 'Two,' Giovanni repeated firmly. 'Thesis and antithesis. What better way for me to provide you with the proof you need for your theory—or the evidence which contradicts it?' he added provocatively, and quite deliberately.

'Thesis and antithesis.' She nodded solemnly. 'An interesting concept, but I don't have the wherewithal to be able to pay you a fee.'

'This is not a commission. It is an experiment.'

'An experiment.'

Her smile informed him that he had chosen exactly the right form of words. 'You understand, it will require us to spend considerable time alone together. I cannot work with any distractions or interruptions,' he added hastily, realising how ambiguous this sounded. 'You will need to find a way of ridding yourself of your charges for a time.'

'Would that I could do so altogether.' Cressie put her hand over her mouth. 'I did not mean that, of course. I will find a way, but I think it would be prudent if we keep our experiment between ourselves, *signor*.' She grinned. 'You and I know that we are conducting research in the name of science, but I do not think Bella would view our being locked away alone together with only an easel for company in quite the same light.'

As Bella Frobisher, Lady Armstrong had been a curvaceous young woman when she first met her future husband, with what his sister, Lady Sophia, called 'fine child-bearing hips'. Those hips had now borne four children, all of them lusty boys, and were, like the rest of Bella's body, looking rather the worse for wear. A naturally indolent temperament, combined with a spouse who made little attempt to hide his indifference to every aspect of her save her ability to breed, led Bella to indulge her sweet tooth to the full. Her curves were now ample enough to undulate, rippling under her gowns in a most disconcerting manner, her condition having forced her to abandon her corsets. At just five-and-thirty, she looked at least ten years older, dressed as she was in a voluminous cherry-red afternoon dress trimmed with quantities of frothy lace which did nothing for her pale complexion. A pretty face with a pair of sparkling brown eyes was just about visible sunk amid an expanse of fat.

Though she had never aspired to being a wit, Bella had been happy to be labelled vivacious, and had always been extremely sociable until her husband made it clear that her lack of political nous made her something of a liability. He summarily replaced her at the head of his political table with his sister and, having made sure that she was impregnated, consigned his wife to the country. Here, Bella had remained, popping out healthy Armstrong boys at regular intervals, taking pleasure in her sons but in very little else. Though she knew it would displease her husband, she longed for this next child to be a daughter, the consolation prize she surely deserved, who would provide her mama with the affection she craved.

Disappointed from a very early stage in her marriage, unable to express her disappointment to the man responsible, Bella had turned her ire instead on his daughters, who made it very easy for her to do so since they made it all too obvious that they thought her a usurper. Her malice had become a habit she did not even contemplate breaking. Pregnant, bloated, lonely and bored, it was hardly surprising, then, that Giovanni, his breathtaking masculine beauty enhanced by the austerity of his black attire, would appear to her like a gift from the gods she thought had abandoned her.

'Lady Armstrong, it is an honour,' he said, bowing over her dimpled and be-ringed hand as she lay on the *chaise-longue*, 'and a pleasure.'

Bella simpered breathlessly. She had never in all her days seen such a divine specimen of manhood. 'I can tell from your delightful accent that you are Italian.'

'Tuscan,' Cressie said tersely, unaccountably annoyed by the extraordinary effect Giovanni was having on her stepmother. She sat down in a chair opposite and gazed pointedly at Lady Armstrong's prostrate form. 'Are you feeling poorly again? Perhaps we should leave you to take tea alone?'

Flushing, Bella pushed aside the soft cashmere scarf which covered her knees, and struggled upright. 'Thank you, Cressida. I am quite well enough to pour Signor di Matteo a cup of tea. Milk or lemon, *signor*? Neither? Oh well, of course I suppose you Italians do not drink much tea. An English habit I confess I myself am very fond of. Cake? Well then, if you do not, I shall have to eat your slice else cook will be mortally offended, for Cressida, you know, has not a sweet tooth. Perhaps if she did, her temperament might improve somewhat. My stepdaughter is very *serious*, as you will no doubt have gathered by now, *signor*. *Cake* is far too frivolous a thing for Cressida to enjoy. You know, of course, that she is presently acting governess to two of my sons? James and Harry. You will be wishing to know more about them, I dare say, if you are to do justice to my angels.' Finally stopping for breath, Bella beamed and ingested the greater part of a wedge of jam sponge.

'Lord Armstrong informs me that his sons are charming,' Giovanni said into the silence which was broken only by his hostess's munching. She nodded and inhaled another inch or so of cake. Fascinated by the way she managed to consume so much into such a comparatively small mouth, he was momentarily at a loss.

Brushing the crumbs from her fingers, Bella launched once more into speech, this time a eulogy on the many and manifold charms of her dear boys. 'They are so very fond of their little jokes too,' she trilled. 'Cressida claims they lack discipline, but I tell her that it is a question of respect.' Bella cast a malicious smile at her stepdaughter. 'One cannot force-feed such intelligent children a lot of boring facts. Such a method of teaching is all very well for little girls, most likely, but with boys as lively as mine—well, I am not one to criticise, but I do think it was a mistake, not hiring a *qualified* governess to replace dear Miss Meacham.'

'Dear Miss Meacham left because she could no longer tolerate my brothers' so-called liveliness,' Cressie interjected.

'Oh, nonsense. Why must you always put such a negative slant on everything your brothers do? Miss Meacham left because she felt she was not up to the job of tutoring such clever children. "I wish fervently they get what they deserve" is what she said to me when she left, and I heartily agree. I don't know what your father was thinking of, to be perfectly honest, entrusting you with such a role, Cressida. Though perhaps it is more of a question of not knowing *what* role to assign you, since you are plainly unsuited to play the wife. After—how many years is it now, since I launched you?'

'Six.'

Bella shook her head at Giovanni. 'Six years, and despite the best efforts of myself and her father, she has not been able to bring a single man up to scratch,' she said sweetly. 'I am not one to boast, but I had Caroline off my hands with very little fuss, and I have no doubt that Cordelia will go off even more quickly. You have not met Cressida's sisters, but sadly she has none of their looks. Even Celia, the eldest, you know, who lives in Arabia, has her charms, though it was always Cassandra who was the acknowledged beauty. I suppose one plain sister out of five is to be expected. If only she were not such a blue-stocking, I really do believe I could have done *something* with her.' Bella shrugged and smiled sweetly again at Giovanni. 'But she scared them all off.'

Realising that she was in danger of looking like a petulant child, Cressie tried not to glower. The words so closely echoed her father's that she was for a moment convinced he and Bella were conspiring to belittle her. Though Bella had said nothing new, nor indeed anything which Cressie had not already blurted out to Giovanni upon their first meeting, it was embarrassing to have to listen to her character being dissected in such a way. So much for all her attempts to think more kindly of her stepmother. As to what Giovanni must be making of Bella's shocking manners, it didn't bear thinking about.

She put down her tea cup with a crack, determined to turn the conversation to the matter of the portrait, but Bella, having refreshed herself with a cream horn, was not finished. 'I remember now, there was a man your father and I thought might actually make a match of it with you. What was his name, Cressida? Fair hair, very reserved, a *clever* young man? You seemed quite taken with him. I remember saying to your father, she'll surely reel this one in. In fact, as I recall, you actually told us he was going to call, but he never did. He took up a commission shortly after, now I come to think of it. Come now, you must remember him, for it is not as if you were *crushed* by suitors. Oh, what *was* his name?'

She could feel the flush creeping up her neck. Think cold, Cressie told herself. Ice. Snow. But it made no difference. Perspiration prickled in the small of her back. Having taught herself never to think of him, she had persuaded herself that Bella would have forgotten all about...

'Giles!' Bella exclaimed. 'Giles Peyton.'

'Bella, I'm sure that Signor di Matteo...'

'He was actually quite presentable, once one got over his shyness. My lord thought it was a good match. He is not often wrong, but in this instance—the fact is, men do not like clever women. My husband's first wife, Catherine, was reputed to be a bit of a blue-stocking, and look where it got her—five daughters, and dead before the last was out of swaddling. When he asked for my hand, Lord Armstrong told me that it was my being so very *different* from his first wife that appealed to him, which I thought was a lovely compliment. No, men do not like a clever woman. I am sure you agree, *signor*?'

Blithely helping herself to another pastry, Bella looked enquiringly at Giovanni, but before he could speak, Cressie got to her feet. 'Signor di Matteo came here to paint my brothers' portrait, Bella, not to discuss what he finds attractive in a woman.' She swallowed hard. 'I beg your pardon. And yours, Signor di Matteo. If you will excuse me, I have a headache, which is making me forget my manners.'

'I hope you are not thinking of retiring to your room, Cressida. James and Harry...'

'I am perfectly aware of my duties, thank you.'

'If you wish to be excused from dinner, however, I am sure that Signor di Matteo and I can manage quite well without your company.'

'I am sure that you can,' Cressie muttered, wanting only to be gone before she lost her temper completely, or burst into tears. One or other, or more likely both, seemed imminent, and she was determined not to allow Bella the satisfaction of seeing just how upset she was.

But as she turned to go, Giovanni got to his feet. 'I must inform you that you are mistaken on several counts, Lady Armstrong,' he said curtly. 'Firstly, there are many enlightened men, and I include myself among them, who enjoy the company of a clever woman very much. Secondly, I am afraid that I prefer to dine alone when I am working. If I may be excused, I would like the governess to introduce me to her charges.'

With a very Italian click of the heels and a very shallow bow, Giovanni took his leave, took Cressie's arm in an extremely firm grip and marched them both out of the drawing room.

'Lady Cressida. Cressie. Stop. The boys can wait a few moments longer. You are shaking.' Opening a door at random, Giovanni led her into a small room, obviously no longer used for it was musty, the shutters drawn. 'Here, sit down. I am not surprised that you are so upset. Your stepmother's bitterness is exceeded only by her ability to devour cake.'

To his relief, Cressie laughed. 'My sisters and I used to think her the wicked stepmother straight out of a fairytale. I don't know why she hates us so—though my father is right, we have given her little cause to love us.'

'Five daughters, all cleverer than she, and all far more attractive...'

'*Four* of them more attractive.'

'To continue the fairytale metaphor, why are you so determined to be the ugly sister?'

Cressie shrugged. 'Because it's true. Because it's how it has always been. Do you have any brothers or sisters?'

'No.' At least, none who acknowledged him, which amounted to the same thing. 'Why do you ask?'

'I wondered if all families are the same. In mine, we were labelled by my father, pretty much from birth. Celia is the diplomat, Cassie the pretty one, Caroline the dutiful one who can always be depended upon, Cordelia the charming one and I—I am the plain one. Upon occasion I am classed the clever one, but believe me, my father uses that only as an insult. He doesn't see beyond his labels, not even with Celia, whom he was most proud of because of her being so useful to him.'

Giovanni frowned. 'But he does precisely the same to your stepmother. She is the brood mare—it is her only purpose. It is no wonder she feels inferior, and no wonder that she must disguise it by trying always to put you in your place. She is vulgar and brash and lonely, so she takes it out on you and your sisters. It is not excusable, but it is understandable.'

'I hadn't thought—oh, I don't know, perhaps you are right, but I am not feeling particularly charitable towards her at the moment.'

Cressie had been worrying at a loose thread of skin on her pinkie, and now it had started to bleed. Without thinking, Giovanni lifted her hand and dabbed the blood with his fingertip before it could drip on to her gown. He put his finger to his lips and licked off the blood. She made no sound, made no move, only stared at him with those amazingly blue eyes. They reminded him of early morning fishing trips back home in his boyhood, the sea sparkling as his father's boat rocked on the waves. The man he'd thought was his father.

With his hand around her slender wrist, his lips closed around her finger and he sucked gently. Sliding her finger slowly out of his mouth, he allowed his tongue to trail along her palm, let his lips caress the soft pad of her thumb. Desire, a bolt of blood thundered straight to his groin, taking him utterly by surprise. What was he doing?

He jumped to his feet, pulling the skirts of his coat around him to hide his all too obviously inflamed state. 'I was just trying to prevent—I'm sorry, I should not have behaved so—inappropriately,' he said tersely. She should have stopped him! Why had she not stopped him? Because for her, it meant nothing more than he had intended, an instinctive act of kindness to prevent her ruining her gown. And that was all it was. His arousal was merely instinct. He did not really desire her. Not at all.

'It has been a long day,' Giovanni said, forcing a cold little smile. 'With your permission, I think I would like to meet my subjects now, and then I will set up my studio. I will dine there too, if you would be so good as to have some food sent up.'

'You won't change your mind and sup with us?'

She looked so forlorn that he almost surrendered. Giovanni shook his head decisively. 'I told you, when I am working, distractions are unwelcome. I need to concentrate.'

'Yes. Of course. I understand completely,' Cressie said, getting to her feet. 'Painting me would be a distraction too. We should abandon our little experiment.'

'No!' He caught her arm as she turned towards the door. 'I want to paint you, Cressie. I *need* to paint you. To prove you wrong, I mean,' he added. 'To prove that painting is not merely a set of rules, that beauty is in the eye of the artist.' He traced the shape of her face with his finger, from her furrowed brow, down the softness of her cheek to her chin. 'You will help me do that, yes?'

She stared up at him, her eyes unreadable, and then surprised him with a twisted little smile. 'Oh, I doubt very much that you'll be able to make me beautiful. In fact, I shall do my very best to make sure you cannot, for you must know that my theory depends upon it.'

Chapter Three

Cressie stood at the window of the schoolroom at the top of the house, and looked on distractedly as James and Harry laboured at their sums. The twins, George and Frederick, sat at the next desk, busy with their coloured chalks. An unusual silence prevailed. For once, all four boys were behaving themselves, having been promised the treat of afternoon tea with their mama if they did. In the corner of the room, a large pad of paper balanced on his knee, Giovanni worked on the preliminary sketches for their portrait, unheeded by his subjects but not by their sister.

He seemed utterly engrossed in his work, Cressie thought. He would not let her look at the drawings, so she looked instead at him, which was no hardship—he really was quite beautiful, all the more so with the perfection of his profile marred by the frown which emphasised the satyr in his features. That, and the sharpness of his cheekbones, the firm line of his jaw, which contrasted so severely with the fullness of his lips, the thick silkiness of his lashes, made what could have been feminine most decidedly male.

His fingers were long and elegant, almost unmarked by the charcoal he held. Her own hands were dry with chalk dust, her dress rumpled and grubby where Harry had grabbed hold of it. No doubt her hair was in its usual state of disarray. Giovanni's clothes, on the other hand, were immaculate. He had put off his coat and rolled up the sleeves of his shirt most precisely. She could not imagine him dishevelled. His forearms were tanned, covered in silky black hair. Sinewy rather than muscular. He was lithe rather than brawny. Feline? No, that was not the word. He had not the look of a predator, and though there was something innately sensual in his looks, there was also a glistening hardness, like a polished diamond. If it had not been such a cliché, she would have been tempted to call him devilish.

She watched him studying the boys. His

gaze was cool, analytical, almost distant. He looked at them as if they were objects rather than people. Her brothers had, when first introduced to Giovanni, been obstreperous, showing off, vying for his attention. His utter indifference to their antics had quite thrown them, so used were they to being petted and spoilt, so sure were they of their place at the centre of the universe. Cressie had had to bite her lip to stop herself laughing. To be ignored was beyond her brothers' ken. She ought to remember how effective a tactic it was.

She turned her gaze to the view from the window. This afternoon, it had been agreed, Giovanni would begin her portrait. Thesis first, he said, an idealised Lady Cressida. How had he put it? A picture-perfect version of the person she presented to the world. She wasn't quite sure what he meant, but it made her uncomfortable, the implication that he could see what others could or would not. Did he sense her frustration with her lot? Or, heaven forefend, her private shame regarding Giles? Did he think her unhappy? *Was* she unhappy? For goodness' sake, it was just a picture, no need to tie herself in knots over it!

Giovanni had earmarked one of the attics for their studio, where the light flooded through the dormer windows until early evening and they could be alone, undisturbed by the household. In order to free her time, Cressie had volunteered to take all four boys every morning, leaving Janey, the nursery maid, in charge in the afternoons, which Bella usually slept through after taking tea. Later today, Giovanni would begin the process of turning Cressie into her own proof, painting her according to the mathematical rules she had studied, representing her theorem on canvas. Her image in oils would be a glossy version of her real self. And the second painting, depicting her alter ego, the private Cressie, would be the companion piece. How would Giovanni depict that version of her, the Cressie he believed she kept tightly buttoned-up inside herself? And were either versions of her image really anything to do with her? Would it be the paintings which were beautiful or the subject, in the eyes of their creator? So excited had she been by the idea of the portraits she had thought of them only in the abstract. But someone—who was it?—claimed that the artist could see into the soul. Giovanni would know the answer, but she would not ask him. She did not want anyone to see into her soul. Not that she believed it was true.

Turning from the window, she caught his unwavering stare. How long had he been looking at her? His hand flew across the paper, capturing what he saw, capturing her, not her brothers. His hand moved, but his gaze did not. The intensity of it made it seem as if they were alone in the schoolroom. Her own hand went self-consciously to her hair. She didn't like being looked at like this. It made her feel— not naked, but stripped. No one looked at her like that, really looked at her. Intimately.

Cressie cleared her throat, making a show of checking the clock on the wall. 'James, Harry, let me see how you have got on with your sums.' Sliding a glance at Giovanni, she saw he had moved to a fresh sheet of paper and was once again sketching the boys. Had she imagined the connection between them? Only now that it was broken did she notice that her heart was hammering, her mouth was dry.

She was being silly. Giovanni was an artist, she was a subject, that was all. He was simply analysing her, dissecting her features, as a scientist would a specimen. Men as beautiful as Giovanni di Matteo were not interested in women as plain as Cressie Armstrong, and Cressie would do well to remember that.

* * *

It was warm in the attic, the afternoon sun having heated the airless room. Dust motes floated and eddied in the thermals. Giovanni removed his coat and rolled up the sleeves of his shirt. In front of him, a blank canvas was propped on his easel. Across the room, posed awkwardly on a red velvet chair, was Cressie. He had discovered the chair in another of the attic's warren of rooms and had thought it an ideal symbolic device for his composition. It was formal, functional and yet sensual, a little like the woman perched uncomfortably on it. He smiled at her reassuringly. 'You look like the French queen on her way to the guillotine. I am going to take your likeness, not chop off your head.'

She laughed at that, but it was perfunctory. 'If you take my likeness, then you will have lost, *signor*. I am—'

'If you remind me once more of your lack of beauty, *signorina*, I will be tempted to cut off your head after all.' Giovanni sighed in exasperation. Though he knew exactly how he wished to portray her, she was far too tense for him to begin. 'Come over here, let me explain a little of the process.'

He replaced the canvas with his drawing

board, tacking a large sheet of paper to it. Cressie approached cautiously, as if the blank page might attack her. All morning, she had been subdued, almost defensive. 'There is nothing to be afraid of,' he said, drawing her closer.

'I'm not afraid.'

She pouted and crossed her arms. Her buttoned-up look. Or was it buttoned-down? 'I have never come across such a reluctant subject,' Giovanni said. 'You are surely not afraid I will steal your soul?'

'What made you say that?'

She was glaring at him now, which did not at all augur well. 'It is said that a painting reflects the soul in the same way a mirror does. To have your image taken, some say, is to surrender your soul. I meant it as a jest, Cressie. A mathematician such as yourself could not possibly believe such nonsense.'

She stared at the blank sheet of paper, her brow furrowed. 'Was it Holbein? The artist who painted the soul in the eyes, I mean. Was that Holbein? I couldn't remember earlier, in the schoolroom.'

'Hans Holbein the Younger. Is that what you are afraid of, that I will not steal your soul but see into it?'

'Of course not. I don't know why I even

mentioned it.' She gave herself a little shake and forced a smile. 'The process. You said you would explain.'

Most of his subjects, especially the women, were only too ready to bare their soul to him, usually as a prelude to the offer to bare their bodies. Cressie, on the other hand, seemed determined to reveal nothing of herself. Her guard was well and truly up, but he knew her well enough now to know how to evade it. Giovanni picked up a piece of charcoal and turned towards the drawing board.

'First, I divide the canvas up into equal segments like this.' He sketched out a grid. 'I want you to be exactly at the centre of the painting, so your face will be dissected by this line, which will run straight down the middle of your body, aligning your profile and your hands which define the thirds into which the portrait will be divided, like this—you see how the proportions are already forming on the vertical?'

He turned from the shapes he had sketched in charcoal to find that Cressie looked confused. 'There is a symmetry in the body, in the way the body can be posed, that is naturally pleasing. If you clasp your hands so, can you not see it, this line?'

Giovanni ran his finger from the top of her

head, down the line of her nose, to her mouth. He carried on, ignoring the softness of her lips, tracing the line of her chin, her throat, to where her skin disappeared beneath the neck of her gown. The fabric which formed a barrier made it perfectly acceptable for him to complete his demonstration, he told himself, just tracing the valley between her breasts, the soft swell of her stomach, finally resting his finger on her hands. 'This line…' He cleared his throat, trying to distance himself. 'This line…' he turned towards the paper on the easel once more and picked up the charcoal '…it is the axis for the portrait. And your elbows, they will form the widest point, creating a triangle thus.'

To his relief, Cressie was frowning in concentration, focused on the drawing board, seemingly oblivious to the way his body was reacting to hers. It was because he so habitually avoided human contact, that was all. An instinctive reaction he would not repeat because he would not touch her again. Not more than was strictly necessary.

'Are you always so precise when you are structuring a portrait?' she asked. 'This grid, will you draw it out on the canvas?'

'*Si*. And I will also block out the main shapes, just as I have shown you.' Giovanni guided her back towards the chair, encouraging her to question him, relieved to discover that by distracting her with the technical details of his craft, the various pigments he preferred, the precise recipe of oils and binding agents he used to create his paints, he could distract himself too, from his awareness of her as a woman, of himself as a man, which had no place here in his studio.

Cressie's face, which was quite plain in repose, when animated was transformed. He fed her facts, drew her out with questions as to the detail of her theory and sketched quickly, trying to capture her in charcoal and when he had, he replaced the paper with his canvas and repositioned his sitter. This he did quickly lest she remember the purpose of this session and become self-conscious once again.

'Tell me more of this book you are using to teach your brothers,' he said as he began to paint in the grid.

'It is a children's introduction to geometry. I am hoping that if I have evidence of its practical application I will be able to persuade my publisher to print it. At present, he is unwilling to do so at his own expense, and I have not the wherewithal to fund it myself. Unfortunately, to date my brothers have not exactly proved to be the most interested of pupils.'

'It seems to me that your brothers have been raised to find only themselves of interest.'

Cressie grinned. 'That is a dreadful thing to contemplate, but I am afraid it is quite true. Save for my father, they have been raised to care for no one's opinion but their own.'

'And your father cares for none but them, you say?'

'Blood and beauty,' Cressie said with a twisted smile. 'Your words, *signor*, and most apt. Your own father—is he still alive? He must be immensely proud of you and your success.'

'Proud! My father thinks...' Giovanni took a deep breath and unclenched his fists, surprised by the strength of his reaction. He never thought of his father. Not consciously. He had no father worthy of the name. 'What I know from bitter experience is that you might succeed in mollifying your father by doing as he bids, but he will only see it as his right, his due. You cannot make a man such as that proud of you, Cressie. And in the process of trying, you are making yourself thoroughly miserable.'

'I am not miserable. I have no option but to try. I am not like you, free to please myself, I have no independent means, and my one talent is hardly going to support me.'

Her arms were crossed again, she was hugging herself tight across her chest, eyes bright, expression bleak. If her father only knew how unhappy she was—but that was exactly the point, was it not? Lord Armstrong did not care, any more than his own father, Count Fancini, what unhappiness he inflicted on his children in the name of the bloodline. Seeing her like this, knowing she would go on suffering as long as she continued to try to do what she thought she ought, made him furious. 'Why do you pander to them, your father, his wife, his sons! Why do you allow them to trample on you?'

'How dare you! What gives you the right...?'

Cressie jumped up from her seat and tried to push past him, but Giovanni grabbed her by the arms, wishing he could shake some sense into her. Her unruly curls tumbled from the loose knot which held them. 'I am not trying to hurt you, Cressie,' he said, more gently now. 'Quite the reverse. I am actually trying to help. You *are* unhappy, and will only become more so as long as you keep trying to please your father. Trust me on this.'

'Why should I?'

She was right—why should she listen to him when he was not able to explain? Giovanni shook his head. 'I have said too much. I wished merely to discover the person I wish to paint. The person you are, the woman inside here...' he touched her forehead '...and here...' he placed his palm over her heart '...that is who I wish to discover.'

She breathed in sharply. 'You might be disappointed by what you find.'

'I doubt it.' Her eyes were wide open, such a startling colour. Cobalt, ultramarine, Prussian blue, none of those pigments would capture the exact shade. Beneath his hand, he could feel her heart beating. How could he have thought of her face as plain? What was she thinking now, looking at him like that?

Dio! He snatched his hand away from her breast and took a step backwards. '*Mi dispiace.* I am sorry. I should not—but there are such emotions inside you jostling to be heard. I could never be disappointed by what I find in you.'

Cressie flushed, obviously unused to any sort of compliments, never mind such a strange one as he had just paid her. 'Thank you,' she said awkwardly. 'I think we should stop for the day. I must go and see how Bella fares.'

She whisked herself out of the room before he could reply. Giovanni dropped into the chair she had vacated and tugged his neckcloth loose, closing his eyes. It was his own fault, introducing his father to the conversation, but the similarities in their situations were impossible to ignore. Fourteen years since their paths had crossed, his and Count Fancini's. The memory of that last interview at the palazzo in Firenze was still painfully clear. Their voices echoing round the marble chamber as they argued. His footsteps sounding larger than life, walking across the courtyard as he left. The count's cold fury turned to scorn and threats when he realised that his son was not going to bend to his will.

You will come back with your tail between your legs. No one will buy those pretty jottings of yours. Mark my words, you will be back. And I will be waiting.

Giovanni rubbed his eyes with his knuckles. Was the count waiting still? Had word of Giovanni's fame reached him? He cursed and got to his feet. He did not care. Why should he!

Cressie hovered in the doorway at the far end of the gallery, watching Giovanni at work, carefully measuring oil from a glass bottle before mixing it with pigments on his palette. The wooden case which looked like a travelling medicine chest, in which he kept his various

binders and oils, stood open on the table beside
him. As usual when he worked, he had taken
off his coat and rolled up his pristine white
shirtsleeves. His waistcoat was grey today, the
satin back stretched across his shoulders, displaying the lean lines of him to advantage. As
ever, when she saw him, she was struck by
the perfection of his physique, and as ever she
reminded herself that her reaction was purely
aesthetic.

Her gaze drifted down, to the slight curve
of his buttocks outlined by his black trousers. For a man so lithe, he was surprisingly
shapely. He had the body of one of those stat-
ues of Greek athletes. A javelin thrower, perhaps? She would like to see him pose with a
spear, muscles tensed, gracefully poised. She
would like to be able to capture him in such a
pose—simply for the sake of illustrating symmetry. He had the type of body which would
appear very much to advantage when naked
rather than clothed. Unlike hers.

She placed the backs of her hands on her
burning cheeks. Giles, the one man she had
seen naked, had looked a little ridiculous and a
little threatening, holding himself, so strangely
proud of his jutting manhood. He had been
so offended when she had been unable to dis-

guise her—how had she felt? Anxious. Ever so slightly hysterical, unable to reconcile the enormity of what she was about to do with the awkward mechanics of the act itself. And they had *both* been awkward. Giles was not nearly as experienced as he had implied. He had not liked her questions, had taken her nervous request for instruction badly, calling her analytical. And unwomanly. That hurt. Still hurt.

All in all, it had been a most lamentable experience for both of them. In fact, with hindsight, she had the distinct impression that Giles would have been much happier if she'd lain back and said nothing at all while he got on with her deflowering. Which was exactly what she did, in the end. And it had been so unrewarding for him that if his pride would have allowed him he would have decided there and then that once was enough. Which was what she decided for herself, in the end.

Though she did not doubt it was mostly her fault, for she had ample proof that she was not the kind of woman men desired, neither could Cressie imagine that Giovanni would be as inept as Giles in the same situation. Those artistic fingers of his were surely incapable of being anything other than expert. And his mouth, the fullness of his lips, the way the top lip bowed. The other day, during the first of their portrait sessions, she had been sure he was going to kiss her. During the second session, she had been even more certain, but again he had not, and since then, he had been almost brusque with her. She was acting like a silly chit, allowing her imagination to take flight like this, imagining Giovanni naked, imagining him touching her in a way Giles never had, in a way no man ever had.

'Cressie?'

She jumped, opened her eyes and guiltily snatched her hand away from her breast. 'Giovanni.'

He smiled. 'I like the way you say my name.'

She was blushing! Lord, it was as well no one, not even the world's most renowned portrait painter, could actually read her thoughts. All the same, she dared not look at him. 'I came to tell you that the boys—they will be here in a moment if you are ready for them.'

He gestured towards the easel, the palette with its oils already mixed. 'As you see, I am prepared.'

'They have been very difficult today. I am not sure that they will be keen to sit for long.' Cressie fixed her gaze on Giovanni's top waistcoat button. 'I would bribe them with sweet-meats if I had any.'

'There is no need.'

'There is, you have no idea…'

He smiled, and caught a strand of her unruly hair with his finger, pushing it back from her brow. 'Trust me.'

The barest touch, yet she jumped, acutely aware of him, the more so for the shocking nature of her thoughts just moments before. 'I shall go and—if you're ready then, I shall…'

But there was no need. A shout, the stampede of four pairs of feet, followed by the nursery maid's gentle remonstration not to run, wholly ignored, and the four boys were upon them in a tangle of blonde hair, deceptively cherubic faces and chubby limbs. Janey, her mob cap askew, her apron covered in ink, dropped a harassed curtsy. 'I'm sorry, my lady, only the minute you left them alone with me they was like caged animals. Harry broke James's slate, and Freddie got hold of the ink pot and when I tried to take it back from him…'

'There's no need to apologise, Janey, it's not your fault.'

'Them being cooped up because of the rain don't help one little bit, my lady. If only the sun would come out, we could get them to run

some of those flitters out of their legs. If you'll
excuse me now, I will go and change my apron.
It's quite ruined.'

'Now, then,' Giovanni said, when the maid
had bustled out of the room, still tutting and
shaking her head at the mess of her uniform,
'I have devised a game for the boys to play.'

'A game?' Cressie said. 'But I thought you
needed them to sit still for their portrait.'

'The game requires them to be seated. You
must trust me, Cressie.'

'You are forever saying that.'

'And today I shall provide you with proof.'
Giovanni clapped his hands together to gain the
boys' attention, and when this had no effect on
the scrapping twins, pulled them bodily apart,
dangling one from each hand by the seats of
their nankeen breeches. Freddie and George
were so astonished that they were silenced.
Watching him walk towards the table, effort-
lessly carrying the boys aloft, Cressie found it
difficult not to be impressed. What was that
other thing that Greek athletes were so often
depicted throwing? A discus. Yes, she was willing to wager that Giovanni would be skilled
at that too. Dressed only in one of those little
tunics which stopped short at the top of his

thighs. When he lunged to make the throw the fabric would ripple, revealing...

'Cressie?'

For the second time that morning, she jumped and blushed.

'You too,' Giovanni said, holding out one of the chairs which stood at the table for her. The boys were already seated, staring at her expectantly.

'I?'

'You are to join in the game, Cressie. You are to sit beside me because I'm the eldest,' James said, casting Harry a superior look.

'I want Cressie to sit beside me because I'm Mama's favourite,' Harry replied, instantly goaded.

'You are not! I'm the favourite because I'm Papa's heir and I shall one day be Lord Armstrong.' James puffed out his chest in a frighteningly good impression of his father. 'Papa says—'

'Do you wish to play the game or not?'

Giovanni did not raise his voice, but he gained the attention of all four boys immediately. He didn't sound angry or flustered but— bored? Cressie hid her grin behind her hands. Indifference, that was the key. Her brothers were hanging on his every word as he handed them pieces of paper and charcoal and explained the rules of his drawing game. They were looking up at him, all four of them, with their mouths wide open, their eyes expectant. It was only when she realised that Giovanni had stopped speaking and was now looking in her direction that Cressie found she really was required to join in. 'I can't draw,' she said nervously.

Giovanni showed his teeth. 'Anyone can draw. It is simply a question of ratio and proportion—you told me so yourself.'

'That is not fair. There is a difference between theory and execution.'

'Interesting. The first time I suggest you test your own theory you start to make excuses. You do not relish being challenged, do you? No, don't deny it—you have already crossed your arms. Next you will glare at me.'

'I won't. I am not so predictable,' she responded, glaring.

'Cressie does that when she's being scolded,' James piped up. 'And when Mama talks to her. And Papa.'

'I do not! Do I?' Cressie turned to her brothers, appalled. When both James and Harry nodded solemnly, she pulled a face, making a show of unfolding her arms. 'That is very rude of me, boys. I hope that you know better than to follow my example.'

James shrugged. 'Mama and Papa aren't ever angry with us. Are you going to play this game or not?'

'You really expect me to draw a horse?' Cressie looked pleadingly at Giovanni.

'I really expect you to *try* to draw a horse,' he replied. 'Whether you will succeed or not—that I will judge when you have all finished. There will be a prize for the best effort. In the meantime, I am going to get on with my own work.'

He pulled the canvas, upon which the portrait of the boys was beginning to take shape, towards him, picked up his brushes and began to paint. All four boys did the same, concentrating hard on their drawings. Cressie stared down at her blank sheet of paper, completely intimidated by it. She couldn't even remember what a horse, that most familiar of animals, looked like. Glancing up, she caught Giovanni's sardonic look and hurriedly picked up her charcoal. It was just a question of ratio and proportion, for goodness' sake. Cressie furrowed her brow and began to make tentative marks on the paper.

An hour and many false starts later, the animal which looked back at her bore no resemblance whatsoever to anything equine. She had tried to draw it side-on and had produced something which looked rather like a hippopotamus on stilts. Her galloping horse was drawn mid-air in an impossible acrobatic leap which made it look as if each of its legs were being pulled towards a different point of the compass. Her rearing horse looked like a lap dog which had been trained to beg for its food, and, having decided that perhaps the legs were the problem, she attempted a horse lying down with its limbs folded under its body. It looked like a cross between a cat and a sheep.

Her final attempt was a horse's face looking straight out of the paper. This drawing had character, there was no denying it. With its toothy grin and long-lashed eyes, it looked very like Aunt Sophia, who in turn looked very like one of the camels which Cressie had ridden on her single visit to Arabia.

'Camels are a kind of horse,' she said to Giovanni as he examined her masterpiece. His mouth twitched, and she forced herself not to fold her arms across her chest. She would *never* fold her arms across her chest again. 'If I had had the benefit of lessons...' She stopped, suddenly remembering that she had. When Mama was alive, there had been a drawing master who had toiled in vain to improve her artistic skills. 'Oh very well, I admit it, it is not just a question of applying rules. I have no talent whatsoever. Are you happy now?'

'Cressie's horse looks like old Aunt Sophia,' Harry said. 'Look, James.'

She hurriedly retrieved the drawing from her brothers. The last thing she needed was for it to find its way into her father's hands. Or worse, into her aunt's. 'Never mind my drawing, since I am obviously not the winner. Let us judge your attempts.'

Freddie and George had each produced a series of round blobs with lines, the same shape they drew for almost everything. Instead of dismissing them, though, Giovanni took the time to praise each and to find individual merit in each too, eventually declaring that they were all so good that they were equal winners, since each was the best in a different way. Such highly competitive children did not usually take to a decision like this, but once again Cressie was surprised to discover them not only compliant but proud and, most importantly, not bickering. Their prize was an individual portrait, swiftly executed, which managed to be both comic and remarkably accurate. A few strokes of Giovanni's charcoal brought James to life as a king, Harry as a general, Freddie as a lion tamer complete with whip, and George, fists raised, as a boxer.

She had thought Giovanni oblivious to her brothers' chatter and boasting as he took their likenesses in the schoolroom and in this make-shift studio. She had been quite wrong, for he had depicted each of them exactly as they most wished to be seen. Looking over Harry's shoulder at his drawing, Cressie was filled with admiration for Giovanni's skill, though the free-form cartoons were nothing like the carefully executed portrait which was emerging from the canvas. These sketches of her brothers were impish, unrestrained, full of movement and humour. For the first time, she had an inkling of the depths of his ability. In the drawings there were no rules, no careful proportion, only a highly evocative image. Admiration ceded to unease. He saw so much. What would he see in her, that she did not wish to have exposed?

Having sent the boys back up to the nursery for their midday meal, Cressie wandered over to stand beside Giovanni in front of the portrait. Here, there were none of the subtly subversive qualities of the charcoal sketches. This painting would be exactly as her father requested, showing his sons only to best advantage. 'There is more truth in those drawings, the work of moments, than in this meticulously assembled canvas,' she said.

'But much more beauty in this painting, yes?'

'So it is a lie, is that what you are saying?'

Giovanni shrugged. 'It is your father's truth. And your stepmother's. It is the truth of what people want to see, what most people do see, for they do not look beyond the first impression.'

'But you do, Giovanni. Why do you not paint it?'

His smile was bitter. 'Because it is more profitable to sell lies. But I will paint the truth when I paint you for a second time. We will continue with the first portrait this afternoon, yes?'

'The portrait which will provide my proof, which is a lie. What am I to make of that for my thesis, I wonder?' Cressie picked up one of the sable brushes from the box which lay open on the table, and stroked the soft bristle over the back of her hand. 'You were very good with my brothers today. They heed you in a way they never listen to me.'

'You think so? Yet they fought for the privilege of sitting beside you to draw. Stop thinking of them as your father's sons. They are not your rivals—they are just boys.'

'I wish I had been a boy.'

'You think Lord Armstrong will be any less manipulative with his sons than his daughters?'

'He won't force them into marriage.'

'He cannot force you.'

'He can make my life unbearable.'

Giovanni caught the curl which persisted in hanging down over her forehead, and once again brushed it back into place. 'It is you who are doing that, trying to be what you are not, wishing to be who you are not.'

His hand still lay on the nape of her neck. His touch made her skin tingle. She was so conscious of him, her body so aware of his proximity in a way that confused her. 'I wish you would not persist with the notion that I am unhappy, Giovanni.'

He ignored her. 'This afternoon, when you sit for me, I want you to wear something different. Something with a *décolleté*. Whether you accept it or not, you are a woman, not a man, and I wish to paint you as one. Something else you are hiding under those terrible dresses you favour,' he said, tracing the line of her throat with his fingers, brushing lightly over her breasts.

She caught her breath as he touched her, her nipple tightening as he grazed it. Without being conscious of it, she stepped towards him, wanting his hand to cup her, yearning in the purest, most thoughtless of ways, for him to satisfy the craving she had been feeling for days. It was nothing to do with aesthetics, she knew that. It was elemental, purely carnal.

'Curves,' Giovanni said, his hand tightening on her breast just exactly as she hoped. 'You have the most delightful curves. Did you know that this is what your English painter Hogarth called the line of beauty?' His fingers slid down, brushing the underside of her breast, to the indent of her waist and round to rest on the curve of her bottom, and pull her suddenly hard up against him. 'You, Cressie, have the most beautiful line.'

His eyes were dark. She was trembling, and in absolutely no doubt this time that he would kiss her. Nor in any doubt at all about what she wanted. Cressie stood on her tiptoes and lifted her mouth in invitation.

Darkness, a swirling, dangerous darkness, enveloped her as his lips met hers, not gently but passionately, in a hard, hungry kiss that sent her reeling into a hot, heady place, crimson with desire. His fingers tightened, digging into her *derrière* as he pulled her against him, bracing her against the hard muscles of his thighs, his tongue stroking into her mouth, touching hers, sending a pulse of heat through her. She arched against him, angling her mouth against his, the better to taste him, mindlessly opening to him, wantonly kissing him back, every bit as hungry as he. It was as if they had both been wild dogs restrained, now freed to ravage, devour, a bursting open of pent-up passion which she could not believe, now it was released, had ever been contained.

She could feel the hard length of his manhood against her belly. No thought of it being ridiculous, no thought of that other time, when she had stared with analytical interest at Giles, what she wanted from Giovanni was violent, unrestrained and utterly base. She heard herself whimpering as one of his hands left her bottom, then a guttural moan as he covered her breast, stroking her nipple into an aching nub. His kiss deepened as he pushed her against the table, lifting her up on to it. She clutched at him, opening her legs to pull him between them, impatient with the voluminous folds of her gown, desperate to get closer, pulsing with heat and wet with desire, reaching for the thick length of his erection.

Giovanni groaned as her fingers stroked him through the wool of his trousers. She stroked him again. He muttered something in Italian, leaning over her, pressing her down on to the table. She could smell linseed oil from the palette. Something clattered to the floor. His curse was violent this time, as he released her so suddenly that she fell back, her head colliding with the jar which held his paintbrushes.

The sound brought them both to their senses. Cressie scrabbled from the table, shaking out the skirts of her gown, blushing wildly. 'I must go,' she muttered. He tried to stop her, but she shook him off, fleeing from the room in a flutter of muslin.

Giovanni pulled out a chair and sat down heavily. *Inferno!* What was it about her that made it so difficult for him to keep his hands to himself? She was insecure and defensive, and what's more she was abrasive, challenging and she was far too opinionated. Yet she provoked a reaction in him that no woman ever had.

For years he had embraced the cold kiss of chastity with barely any effort. Why did Cressie make him rail against his self-imposed restraint? He should not have kissed her. He should not have touched her at all. Yet when he had—a fire that threatened to be all-consuming, like a blaze ripping through a tinder-dry forest. His instincts had been right. That buttoned-down front she presented to the world masked a smouldering passion. Just thinking about her response, about her mouth on his, the way her lips clung, the way her hands touched him, stroked him— *Dio*, he was hard. Another few minutes and they would have...

'No!' Celibacy was his strength, the cornerstone of his success. He was confusing his desire to paint her with his desire to make love to her. It was an echo, a residue from the past, when art and sex were so inextricably mixed. His desire for her was so strong because his desire to capture her was irresistible. And yet, the Cressie who kissed him was the one he wanted to paint. The one he needed to paint, with a passion equal to the one she had aroused. To show her to herself, and to reflect that back in his art. His true art. To paint from the heart. *That* was what he wanted most passionately of all.

Giovanni jumped to his feet and began to gather together his palette, brushes and knives for cleaning. He must complete the first portrait, without further compromising himself. He must detach himself from the process, and paint Lady Cressida with as much precision as any other professional commission. The terrible drawing she had executed lay before him on the table. Almost persuaded that he had explained the shocking lapse away, Giovanni folded it up and tucked it into his trouser pocket.

Chapter Four

Cressie had decided to take her brothers for a walk through the estate's park since the sun had eventually condescended to show its face. Bella had been taken poorly again and demanded Janey's soothing presence at her bedside. Cressie was glad of the excuse to avoid sitting for Giovanni. She needed time to think.

The grass was damp underfoot, the trees only barely budding, but the sky was a clear, fresh blue above her head. Freddie and George had abandoned their hoops and were perched on the bank of a small stream, peering into the reedy waters in search of tadpoles. Their older brothers had run ahead into the woods, engrossed in some private game of their own. The skirts of Cressie's gown were muddied, her hair a wild tangle, for she had come out without a bonnet in the vain hope that the breeze would clear the jumble of conflicting emotions in her head. Perching on the top of a stone boundary wall, she kept one eye on the twins, trusting that so long as she could hear the elder two shouting to each other they would be perfectly safe.

She must have taken leave of her senses in the gallery this morning. How had it happened? She could not even remember who made the first move towards the other, only that it felt inevitable and irresistible—words that she, a mathematician, a woman who lived by logic, should not even be thinking, let alone acting upon. Never in a thousand years would she have believed that she could have behaved so outrageously. Never before had she lost control in such a way. Making love to Giles had been a very deliberate act. Kissing Giovanni had been elemental.

It was her own fault. Her own fault for having conjured up those shocking images of Giovanni naked, poised with a javelin, clad only in a tunic. It was her own fault for having allowed her thoughts so consistently to dwell on the perfection of his face, on the clean, pure lines of his body. Her own fault for utterly fail-

ing to recognise that what she took for anal-
ysis and aesthetic appreciation had somehow
metamorphosed into lust. Base, animal lust.
She should, in all truth, be ashamed of herself.

The breeze ruffled her hair. She swiped a
rebellious curl out of her eyes. The movement
reminded her that this was what Giovanni had
done, just before he had kissed her. Or before
she threw herself at him and made it impossible
for him not to kiss her. Not that he had resisted.
But then why would he, when he must be quite
accustomed to women doing exactly that! And
now she was behaving just like those females,
even though she knew perfectly well she was
not, nor could ever be, because she had none
of the attractions which went with successful
seduction.

So why, then, had he kissed her, and kissed
her as if he really had desired her every bit
as much as she desired him? Cressie jumped
down from the wall and began to make her
way towards the twins, who had given up on
the search for tadpoles and were now hurrying after their older brothers, intent on join-
ing the game from which they would without
doubt be refused entry. 'Let us go and look at
the baby sheep,' she said, holding out a hand to
each of the boys and leading them towards the

far field, where lambs like little woolly puffs of cloud were cavorting while their mothers chewed complacently at the rich green grass.

She helped Freddie and George up on to the wall, keeping a supporting hand around the back of each. In the far corner of the field one black lamb stood alone, not bleating, but watching the others frolic without showing any inclination to join in. It would be too easy to think of herself as the black sheep of the family, but that was exactly how she felt. Even if Giovanni didn't agree in his determination to get under her skin, to discover this mystical person he claimed was the real Cressie. The Cressie he wanted to paint.

And that, of course, was why he'd kissed her, she thought ruefully. He wanted to disconcert her, make her react. It was simply part of his technique, to rouse her in order to incorporate her reaction into his painting. No doubt it was a technique he had deployed many times, and equally doubtless it was a highly successful one, for who could reject the kisses of a man so perfectly irresistible?

The best thing to do would be to pretend it had not happened. She would not pander to his ego—not that he seemed to wish it. On the contrary, in fact, he was consistently deprecating about his appearance, now she came to think of it.

Lifting the twins down from the wall and calling to Harry and James to join them, Cressie turned back towards the house. She could not resist putting her fingers to her lips. It had been a professional kiss, Giovanni's motives had been purely artistic, but his kiss had been more deliciously decadent than anything she had ever imagined. Professional or no, she could not pretend she had done anything other than relish it. Her reaction had been proof positive. There could be no denying that, since proof was her stock-in-trade.

Cressie entered the attic studio nervously. For over a week she had sat every day while Giovanni worked on her portrait, saying little, barely acknowledging her presence, save to adjust her pose, occasionally to explain a technical point. The atmosphere between them was claustrophobic, tense. He would not allow her to see the painting, *Not until it is finished to my satisfaction*, he had insisted, though he said he was making good progress with it. He had not once made any reference to their kiss. Which was a good thing, she told herself repeatedly, because she had no intention of mentioning it either. He was an artist, she was his sitter. This room, this situation, did not represent real intimacy but rather a form of artistic intensity. Yes, that was it, she decided, satisfied that she had now explained it logically.

She tugged at the neckline of her gown in a vain attempt to make it cover more of her chest. Yesterday Giovanni had reminded her that he wished her to pose in something more revealing. Today she wore an evening dress and felt horribly exposed. Perhaps it was because it was still daylight and the rich crimson velvet gown, with its low *décolleté* and tiny puffed sleeves, showed far more flesh than she was used to displaying. It had belonged to her mother, and was cut in the old-fashioned style made popular by the Emperor Napoleon's wife, Josephine. An overdress of figured black gauze trimmed with gold spangles gave it a decadent appearance. With her corsets much more tightly laced than usual, Cressie's breasts were, to her mind, all too conspicuous, her nipples only just covered. When first she had seen her reflection in the looking-glass she had been shocked by the change in herself, but also by what her reflection said about Mama, whom she had not previously thought of as the kind of woman to wear a gown so obviously designed to seduce.

Cressie's attempt to dress her hair appropriately had not been overly successful. Unwilling to fuel gossip below stairs, she had dismissed her maid once her corsets were laced. What she had intended was a knot in the Grecian style which would complement the dress, but something had gone sadly awry. Very sadly, she thought dejectedly as she put her hand to her coiffure and came away with several hair pins, which she was attempting to replace when Giovanni arrived.

He halted on the threshold, staring at her. She almost crossed her arms over her breasts, but managed to stop herself. 'You said you wanted me to wear something more—but I didn't have anything of my own. Naturally I have evening gowns, but even though I am six and twenty, I am still considered a girl as far as the marriage mart is concerned and so I—so I borrowed this. It was my mother's, but if it's not suitable, I will...' She stuttered to a halt, blushing, as he continued to stare at her. 'I will go and change into something else.'

'No! Cressida, it is *perfecto. Sei bellisima.*'

'Well, it is a very nice gown, I have to agree. I think the fashions of Mama's youth...'

'It is not the gown, it is you.' Giovanni smiled. 'Though the hair—if you will permit me?'

She stood still, hardly daring to breathe as he quickly adjusted her falling tresses. He smelled of fresh soap and turpentine. There was a bluish stubble on his jaw. Why did he have to look so—and why did she have to react so…?

'There! This is inspired.'

He gently pushed her back into the chair and arranged the folds of her gown and then retreated behind his easel, pulling the covering sheet from the canvas. What on earth had she been expecting? That he would fall at her feet, or pull her into his arms, or bury his head in the valley of her really quite impressive bosom? His stubble would be abrasive on her skin. The *décolleté* of Mama's gown was so low that the least movement would expose her nipples to his attentions. Would he use his tongue? 'Oh, dear.'

'Is there something wrong?'

'No, no. It's nothing.'

'The dress is uncomfortable?'

'No. It is just a little—no.'

'You and your mother must share a very similar figure. It fits you perfectly.'

'Does it?' Cressie eyed herself doubtfully.

'You are very similar in looks too, if her portrait in the gallery is a good likeness.'

'You are flattering me today. Am I to be painted blushing with your compliments?'

Giovanni put down his brush. 'You think my compliments are professional artifice?'

Cressie shrugged. 'It doesn't matter, does it, so long as they are effective?'

Anger flashed in his eyes, but it was quickly suppressed. He made a point of focusing on his palette. Cressie fought the urge to pick at her fingers, another habit she was trying to cure herself of since Giovanni had pointed it out to her. 'Is it beautiful?' she asked. 'The picture, I mean. Are you pleased with it?'

He nodded. '*Sì.* I am satisfied. It is what I said it would be. It will be finished sufficiently for me to begin the second portrait very soon.'

'Have you decided how I should be depicted?'

'I thought of you as the Amazonian, Penthiselea, since it is your pen name, but as a warrior queen she would traditionally be portrayed with her breast bared...'

'I feel as if my breast is all but bared in this dress. It is verging on the indecent.' Too late, she realised she had drawn his attention to her bosom, which Giovanni was now staring at, his eyes dark with something that did not look at all painterly. He had looked the same when he had kissed her. It made her feel as before, a sort of hot, unspecified anticipation. A hunger. 'I am not so sure that I really am a warrior queen,' Cressie said hurriedly, embarrassed by the turn her thoughts had taken. 'I am not even brave enough to face up to my father, never mind Achilles.'

'You do yourself an injustice! The first time I met you, you had just been facing up to your father—I remember it most clearly, the defiant look on your face when I walked into the room. And despite what you have told me of his attempts to marry you off, you remain stubbornly unwed.'

'I am unwed because I am unasked.' *Give or take one belated proposal offered under duress, that is.* 'You overestimate my charms, as I have several times pointed out.'

'And you are determined to rate yourself even lower than your father does, as I have also several times pointed out. Had you chosen to, I have no doubt that you could have elicited offers from any number of Lord Armstrong's candidates for your hand. But you did not choose to. In fact, I am willing to wager that you were the very opposite of conciliatory. What is the real truth, Cressie? Why are you not married? Was it that man your stepmother mentioned? Did he break your heart?'

Be careful what you wish for, Cressie Arm-

strong! That would teach her to hope Giovanni would break his silence. 'What about you?' she countered. 'Are you married? Have you ever been in love?'

'No and no. And we were discussing you.'

'*I* was not discussing anyone.'

'Now you sound just like one of your little brothers.' Giovanni laughed. '*Ti ho messo con le spalle al muro.* You don't like having your back against the wall, do you?'

'I do not—I have not—my back against the wall. Why are you suddenly interested in Giles Peyton?'

'I am not, but I am interested in the effect he had on you. I want to understand you better, now that the first portrait is almost complete and my knowledge will not cloud the purity of the image. Do you understand?'

'So this—this interrogation—is just another of your techniques?'

'For the love of God!' Giovanni threw his brush at the easel. It bounced off the wooden strut and landed on the floor. 'There is a woman hidden inside you, a passionate, witty, *interesting* woman. I have seen her, I have touched her, I have kissed her. But you won't admit she exists, never mind set her free.'

He stooped to retrieve his paintbrush. Straightening, he crossed the room to stand before her. 'You think that no one sees you, and yet you want to be seen. You want people to know that there is more to you than mere bloodstock. I can help you, I can show that person, but only if you will let me see her.'

Cressie bit back the automatic denial just in time, forcing herself to consider his words. 'I don't want you to capture my weaknesses, my past mistakes and indiscretions,' she said with difficulty. 'What happened with Giles, it was because I was so young and so naïve and so—I don't know, so desperate to please. But I'm none of those things now, Giovanni.'

'Then show me the real you. Think of this studio as a form of confessional. We are bound by a solemn vow of secrecy. Whatever is said here, remains here. You have my word on it.'

'And if I do confess? Unfortunately you cannot absolve me of my sins.' She hadn't meant to sound so defensive, but she was not at all sure she liked where this conversation was heading. She had never discussed Giles with anyone. She could hardly bring herself to think of it. 'You are offering to play not only the artist but the priest, are you?'

Giovanni stiffened. 'I do not *play* at being an artist.'

'I am not the only one who dislikes having my back against the wall,' Cressie retorted, leaping at the chance to get her own back, for that remark had stung. 'You do play at it, by your own admission. That canvas in front of you, it is not a portrait but an exercise in aesthetics. You have enormous natural talent, I've seen it in those drawings you did of my brothers, but you choose not to use it, and to instead paint what people wish to see. You could be an artist, but you choose to play the painter.'

She wanted only to deflect his questions, but for a moment she thought she had gone too far. Giovanni's mouth tightened, his eyes flashed, darkly threatening, but even as she watched, his anger faded, brought to heel like a disobedient hound. Running his fingers through his short crop of hair, and rubbing his eyes with his knuckles, he smiled wanly. 'You are right. It is what I have built my career on. And it is no longer enough.'

He pulled at his neckcloth, setting the perfect knot awry, and sat down on an ancient chest at right angles to her, throwing up a cloud of dust which clung to his black trousers. It was the first time Cressie had ever seen him dishevelled, the first time she had seen his expression naked, confused. The first time she had seen him look vulnerable. He was resting his chin on his hands, his elbows on his thighs.

Cressie twisted one of the spangles on her overdress round and round, until the thread which held it came loose. 'I'm frightened,' she admitted finally. 'I'm frightened that the person you paint will be a pathetic, unattractive creature.'

The spangle came loose, leaving a tiny hole in the gauze. Cressie stared at it, for she could not bring herself to look at Giovanni. 'You don't understand. How could you, for you cannot possibly have had any problem in attracting women, but—'

His harsh crack of laughter interrupted her, and forced her to look up. 'This,' he said, indicating his face, 'you think this is an asset? You think I like to be fawned over and petted? You think I like it that this perfect profile is the only thing people see?'

'Is that why you won't socialise with us, Bella and I? Why you eat alone, and...'

'Sleep alone. Always. Since—always. There, now you have me confessing to you.' Giovanni got to his feet, catching her hand in his and pulling her with him. 'From the moment I met you, I saw something different in you, Cressie. It's something I can't really explain but I know if I don't capture it I'll regret it for the rest of my life. To capture you, I need to know you. Do you see?'

She was acutely conscious of his body, of his skin, of his mouth, and just as acutely aware that he had confided in her, in *her*, things that he had not told anyone else. It made him vulnerable and even more enticing, it made her want to hold him tightly, and to kiss him and to beg to know more, to know it all. But she owed him a confidence back in return for his candour, and for that she needed to steel herself.

'Very well, here is the truth of it, if you must have it.' Cressie disengaged herself, making for the dormer window, where she gazed out absently at the view. 'I was in my third Season. Despite what you think Giovanni, I had done my best to make myself—amenable—to the men my father brought forwards. But it didn't work. I was so gauche, and when I wasn't completely tongue-tied I was boring my potential suitors to death by talking endlessly about my studies. Bella is right, you know—no man can abide a blue-stocking.'

'No men of your father's acquaintance perhaps,' Giovanni said sardonically. 'Which says much about Lord Armstrong.'

Cressie smiled weakly. 'Thank you. It does

not alter the facts, however. The more I tried, the more I seemed to scare the candidates for my hand away, and the more desperate I became. You have to understand, I have been raised to accept that marriage is not only a duty but my only option. Back then, I did not even consider an alternative. I *had* to make a match. So when Giles came along, and actually showed a modicum of interest in me rather than my family, I managed to persuade myself that he would make a good husband.

'I was not in love with him, but I thought with time—for that is what my Aunt Sophia counselled, you know, that one grew into affection. Only I suppose that my lack of certainty must have shown—and it was hardly flattering—for just when I began to think of Giles as mine, he began to lose interest. I could not have borne it—or so I believed—to lose him when I had already told my father that I expected Giles to call. I had never seen Father so proud of me before. "That's my girl," he said, "always knew you'd come up trumps in the end." So I—I...' She took a deep breath and dug her nails hard into her palms. 'I thought that if I allowed Giles to make love to me, then he would be obliged to marry me,' she confessed painfully.

Moments passed. Cressie pressed her heated

forehead to the cool of the window glass. Running her finger down the pane, she was surprised to discover that it was clean and realised this must be Giovanni's doing, on account of the light. She felt sick, but now that she had started, she had no choice but to finish. 'It was a dreadful thing to do,' she continued, turning back to face him. 'To try to manipulate Giles like that, it was shameful. That my stupidity had quite the opposite effect from the one I intended is my only saving grace. That, and the fact that no one else knows,' she finished with a pathetic attempt at a smile.

'Are you telling me that you gave yourself to this man, and he abandoned you?'

The stark disbelief in his voice made her squirm. 'No, no. Giles was an honourable man. He did offer for me—at least, he said he would marry me, because he ought to—but I knew he didn't mean it. I knew it would be like a death sentence for us both, even worse than having to endure my father's bitter disappointment. I had achieved my goal, and yet I simply couldn't bring myself to accept.'

Cressie dropped her head into her hands. She wouldn't cry, she wouldn't, but the memory of that dreadful scene between her and Giles was a wound that could still inflict much pain. She took another deep breath, muffling her distress by speaking determinedly to her shoes. 'Poor Giles, in a way he was every bit as naïve as I. I tried to make light of it at first you see—during—when—in the bedchamber. I thought to put us both at ease, but I must have sounded like an idiot. And when that did not work, I resorted to asking for instruction, only my questions rather brought Giles's lack of experience to the fore and—I will leave the rest to your imagination, though I doubt very much you can imagine anything so truly awful. Anyway, the net result was that I turned down my only offer of marriage, and Giles left to join the army soon after. I think he was as mortified by the whole episode as I was.'

Cressie forced herself to look up. 'It was a salutary lesson, for I realised I am simply not the kind of woman whom men—who can enjoy that kind of thing. If I could have analysed less and felt more—but that is not in my nature. Logic and facts, supposition and proof, those are the things I am good at. I decided that I would find a way, somehow, to make mathematics rather than matrimony my destiny. You know where you are with formulae.' She straightened her shoulders. 'There you have it, the whole sordid tale. It was some years ago now,' she said firmly. 'I am quite over it.'

'You think so!' Giovanni exclaimed. 'I am not so certain. To think, if the experience had been only a little less unpleasant, you would have married this man, making your father happy and yourself miserable.'

'Why are you so angry?' Cressie's own hackles began to rise. She had never told anyone what had happened between her and Giles. It was shocking and shameful, yet Giovanni seemed only furious. 'According to you, I am miserable anyway. At least if my misguided tactics had resulted in the acquisition of a husband, I would have done my duty.'

'Your duty! It seems to me you do little else. May I remind you that you are currently saving your father the expense and inconvenience of hiring a vastly inferior governess. You are trying at some great personal cost to provide your stepmother with the company he should rightly be providing her with. You have also taken the place of your eldest sister in looking after the youngest two—another duty your father has avoided—and I have no doubt that there are a thousand other things besides. You have nothing to reproach yourself with, Cressie, but what on earth possessed you to give away something so precious to a man you did not even want to marry? That I do not understand.'

When he put it like that, she really didn't know. 'I told you, I was desperate to please both Giles and my father. You have no idea what it was like,' Cressie said wretchedly. 'Bella had just provided my father with a son, and she made it so clear that she wanted me off her hands just as quickly as possible, and back then, Papa—I mean my father, would do anything to please her. You cannot imagine how important having a son and heir is to a man like him.'

'I understand only too well.'

'I don't see how you possibly can.' She could feel the tears welling, but she was determined not to let them fall. She would not pity herself. She most certainly did not want Giovanni's pity. Cressie clenched her fists. 'I surrendered my virtue in the hope of receiving an offer.' She blinked furiously. 'I know, do not tell me because I know, that if I confessed that fact to my father, it would most likely achieve what I most desire, to be taken off the marriage mart, but I could not bear to have him gloat over my being so stupid. I, who foolishly considers herself clever. My actions have already cost me a considerable portion of my self-respect. I could not compound the felony.'

As she rested her head on the dormer window, her hair finally unravelled, tumbling down over her bare shoulders. Giovanni did not speak. The silence felt thick, ominous. In all probability, he was disgusted with her. 'Your assertion that I am unhappy would appear to be well founded after all,' Cressie said, her voice not much more than a whisper. 'But unfortunately I can see no way to improve the situation. I cannot please my father save by marrying, but I am not marriageable and even if I were...' She threw back her head defiantly. 'Even if I were, do you know, I would not! I will not give myself to a man simply to expand to the dynastic web my father is weaving. I don't want to, and I won't!'

A slow handclap made her look up. '*Bravissimo!* This is progress.'

Cressie smiled weakly. 'It doesn't feel like it.' She crossed the room towards him, the train of her mother's gown sweeping behind her on the dusty floorboards. 'Is this the part of my confession where you decide my penance and absolve me of sin?'

Giovanni shook his head, clasping both of her hands between his. 'You have already done far more penance than you deserve. I do not believe you have committed any sin, save the one of allowing people to judge you. It does not matter what they think, your father, your step-mother, that stupid oaf Giles, even your sisters. Only what you think really matters.'

'I don't know what to think any more. I will confess freely to one thing—I am thoroughly confused.'

Giovanni led her gently over to the easel. 'There, you see. This is in fact the woman you thought you wanted to be.'

Cressie was so taken aback by this unexpected revelation that it was a few moments before she could focus on the portrait. Though the lower half of the body was merely outlined, the dress to be painted in later, the face, shoulders and arms were fully realised. She stared at the woman on the canvas who was her, and yet was not. As Giovanni had promised, all the requisite angles and proportions were there. And as he had promised, she looked beautiful, somehow softer and yes, more feminine, more alluring than she really was. There was a hint of promise in her eyes, the whisper of a kiss on her lips. This Lady Cressida was the kind of woman a man would fight to marry and boast about bedding.

'What do you think?'

The tone of Giovanni's voice sounded un-characteristically uncertain. Realising with some surprise that her opinion mattered to him, Cressie eyed the portrait with renewed concentration, endeavouring to see it objectively, trying to recall the exact terms of their challenge. 'As proof of my thesis, it is well-nigh perfect. You have created beauty using nature's formulae,' she said eventually.

'But that is not what I asked.'

'I know.' Cressie peered at the woman in the portrait. 'She is beautiful, but she is not me. I don't mean the way she looks—it is a very good likeness, Giovanni, and the execution is masterful, but...'

'Tell me how it makes you feel.'

'It's strange, but it's as if there are parts of me missing. If art is truth, then this is a lie. Perhaps not a lie but a fib. You have omitted all my faults and implied characteristics I don't possess. There is very little of me behind that face. I look as if I would not say boo to a goose, as my Aunt Sophia would say, but I'm not biddable like that, nor do I recognise that sort of knowing confidence.'

'No, you are none of those things, but you are extremely perceptive. Not many people are capable of such insight. Especially in relation to themselves.'

Cressie circled the portrait, then stood in front of it again, frowning deeply. 'The proportions, the ratios, the angles, everything is perfect, but it is a lie. Mathematics is the purest of truths, its rules are irrefutable, and yet somehow you have refuted them. I don't understand. Is beauty not its own truth, Giovanni?' She whirled around to face him, her skirts catching on the legs of the easel, so that it rocked alarmingly. 'I am *not* this woman. I don't even want to *be* this woman, this simpering, pouting siren.'

'Though she is exactly the kind of woman you claimed you wished you could be, all compliance and conformity? This woman,' Giovanni said contemptuously, 'would have married to please her father without hesitation.'

'I am not that woman!'

'No, you are not. But you are not honest with yourself either. You like to think yourself a rebel, subverting the strictures of your life with little gestures, but your instinct is still to conform, to comply. This painting,' Giovanni said pointedly, forcing her to face the canvas once more, 'is not a complete lie.'

Cressie stared at her portrait afresh, her

anger dying as she assimilated the truth of what Giovanni had said, what Giovanni had painted. *'Why, I can smile and murder whiles I smile, and cry content to that which grieves my heart, and wet my cheeks with artificial tears, and frame my face for all occasions,'* she quoted ironically. *'Richard the Third,'* she added, glancing over her shoulder, to where he stood behind her. 'Apt, apparently, but hardly flattering.'

'Nor the whole truth. When I paint you as Penthiselea, I would like you to have your hair completely down.'

'So you have decided that I am to be an Amazon after all?'

He took her hand between his. 'It is certainly true that you are much stronger than you think you are,' he said, kissing her wrist.

His mouth was warm, her pulse flickered beneath his gentle caress. 'And much more inclined to self-deception, if your character assessment is to be believed,' Cressie replied, trying to ignore the way his touch made her so conscious of her body, of the proximity of his. The tension between them altered subtly, from fraught to dangerous.

'I wished to make you feel better about yourself, not worse. I know how deep go the ties that bind us to those whose blood we share. I know how strong is the urge to please them. I know how difficult it is to please oneself in the face of it.' Giovanni touched her hair, running his hand down the wild curls, to rest on the exposed flesh of her shoulder. 'I know what it is to suffer in this way, and I know what it is to escape.'

His other arm slid around her waist, pulling her to him. His eyes were dark, passionately dark, his voice low, mesmerising. There were secrets, painful secrets, hidden behind the words he used, but she was too distracted by his touch, his scent, the nearness of him, the elemental pull of him, to care. Her skin was heated. She could see the quiver of her breasts, rising and falling in the low-cut gown, as her breathing quickened.

Giovanni's fingers trailed down from her shoulder, along the lace at the neckline of her dress, the lightest and most tantalising of touches. 'You are so much more, so very much more than you think you are, Cressie,' he whispered. His lips touched hers. The slightest of kisses, the merest brush of lip on lip. 'Penthiselea, the warrior goddess. Fight for yourself.'

He dipped his head, and began to kiss his way across her *décolleté*. She moaned softly as his lips, his tongue, trailed tiny kisses over the mounds of her breasts, lingering in the depth of her cleavage. His hands cupped her bottom, his fingers kneading her buttocks. She arched against him, lifting her breasts higher for his attentions. The puffed sleeves of her dress slid off her shoulders, and the front of the gown slid over her breasts, just exactly as if it were designed to do so.

'Sei bellisima,' Giovanni muttered, and took one of her exposed tight, pink nipples into his mouth. He sucked, and a shot of pure pleasure made her jerk against him. She staggered back against the wall. He sucked again, and cupped her other breast with his hand, teasing the nipple with his thumb. Her belly tightened. An aching throb took hold inside her, an exquisite tensing of all her muscles. *'Sei bellisima,'* Giovanni said again, and she believed him. Not that she was beautiful, but that he thought her so at this moment. His tongue circled her nipple, flicking, licking, his thumb mimicking the movement on her other breast, rousing her into an agony of wanting.

His hand tightened around her bottom, pulling her tight up against him. She could feel his arousal, hard, unmistakably hard, against her belly. She wanted, desperately wanted, to feel him closer. 'Giovanni.' Her voice sounded hoarse. 'Giovanni,' she said, more insistently now. He seemed loath to lift his head from her breasts. She was loath to urge him to do so, except... 'Giovanni!'

His lids were heavy over his eyes. Slashes of colour accentuated the planes of his cheekbones even more than usual. Cressie touched his jaw, running her palm over the slight abrasion of his stubble. 'You want me to stop?' he said, his voice husky.

She shook her head. 'I want you to kiss me.'

His mouth curled into the most sensual of smiles. One hand cupped her breast, the other her bottom. *'Per fortuna*, that is exactly what I would like to do.' His lips touched hers. She opened her mouth to him.

The attic door flew open with a crash. 'Here you both are! I told James this is your secret room, but he didn't believe me,' Harry exclaimed, bursting excitedly into the room. 'You must tell him I was right, Cressie. You must tell him—Cressie, you must come at once.'

'Why? Whatever is the matter?'

'Papa is here.'

Chapter Five

❧❧❧

'That was a most meagre dinner, I must say. What was cook thinking of, sending up such a paltry selection of side-dishes? You must have a stern word with her, my dear. It is a question of maintaining standards, don't you know.'

Lord Armstrong shook out the tails of his evening coat and eased himself into a chair by the fire, opposite his wife. They had retired to the formal drawing room after dinner, a large chamber which had lain unused for several months—since his lordship's last visit to his country estate, as a matter of fact. As a result the room was chilly, the air stale. Bella had of late taken to sharing an early supper tray with her stepdaughter, before retiring to her bed almost immediately afterwards, and was struggling to stay awake. Huddled in a large cashmere shawl, obviously horribly uncomfortable in the constraints of her evening gown, Lady Armstrong remonstrated weakly. 'Had we been expecting you, my love, I would have made sure to order a more suitable and substantial dinner.'

'Always be prepared for every possibility,' her husband said bracingly, 'always stay one step ahead of the opposition, and you will never fail.'

'We are your family, not the opposition, and if you had not failed to send us a note apprising us of your imminent arrival, Father, we should not have failed to provide you with a dinner worthy of your elevated status.' Cressie, seated enough of a distance away from the fire to feel distinctly cold, was also feeling distinctly abrasive. Bella's skin had a waxy pallor, she noted. Her cheeks were also unnaturally flushed, and she knew, for her stepmother had confided in her that evening, that her ankles were so swollen as to make her slippers pinch painfully. 'Bella has been most unwell,' she said pointedly. 'She should be in her bed.'

'Nonsense. It does the circulation good to be up and about. It is good for the child too, for you to get some exercise, Bella. I am sure Sir

Gilbert Mountjoy did not mean for you to be lolling abed all day.'

'What Sir Gilbert actually said was that Bella needed to rest,' Cressie said pointedly.

Lord Armstrong, who had made a career out of turning the truth in whichever direction most suited him, waved his hand dismissively. 'She has been resting for some weeks now. As I recall, it was in order to allow my wife to rest that I sent you down here, Cressida. I wonder that it has not occurred to you to relieve her of some simple household tasks. Such as the ordering of a decent dinner.'

An angry retort sprang to her lips, but Cressie caught it just in time. It was her father's most successful tactic, to turn the tables on her, and she rarely failed to rise to the bait. But not this time. He was wholly in the wrong, would never admit to being in the wrong, and she would be wasting her time in trying to make him do so. Such a little thing it was in the grand scheme of things, to refuse to be belittled, but she did refuse, and she felt better for it. Taking a leaf from Giovanni's book, for in many aspects her father was every bit as childish as her brothers, she did not deign to reply at all, but got to her feet.

'Where do you think you're going?'

'Though it seems to have slipped your mind, Father, the main reason you *sent me down here* was to act as governess to your sons. I am going to make sure they are abed and settled. They are such very boisterous boys,' she said with a sweet smile, 'that I fear they do not always heed their nursemaid and often refuse to retire when they ought. Perhaps, now you are here, you will wish to assume the duty for yourself? In fact, I wonder it did not occur to you earlier to offer to take my place in reading them their bedtime story. My apologies. I will ensure that I do not usurp you tomorrow.'

'I have no time to be reading stories,' Lord Armstrong said, his eyes narrowing. He was not accustomed to hearing sarcasm in his own household unless it originated from himself, but if he didn't know better he might imagine that Cressida was mocking him.

'Cressie has been very good with the boys, Henry,' Bella said faintly. 'They heed her much more than they do me. Poor little souls, I was worried that I was neglecting them, for I really have been feeling very low, but they seem perfectly happy with their big sister.'

'Why thank you, Bella,' Cressie said, astonished, earning herself a tight little smile.

'Cressie has been most solicitous to me too,

Henry,' Bella persisted. 'She has taken all of
the household burdens from me, for there have
been days when I have been as weak as a kit-
ten, you know. The morning sickness is quite
debilitating.'

'Sickness! But you must be well past that
stage by now. You are what—five months
gone?'

'Indeed, for your last visit here was November.'

Lord Armstrong was rather disconcerted by
this embarrassingly personal snippet of infor-
mation. 'Nonsense, my dear, you are misre-
membering. I am sure…'

'You were present for a time on Christmas
Day. You arrived in time for church, as I recall, and left after dinner. You have not stayed
the night here since November. It is no wonder that little Freddie and George were so awkward with you this afternoon—you are quite
the stranger to them.'

Once again, Cressie stared in astonishment
at her stepmother. She had never once heard
Bella speak to Lord Armstrong in such a way.
Seeing her father's face, she realised that he
was just as taken aback as she, and hid her
smile. For the first time in her life, she felt

that she and her stepmother were fighting the same corner.

Bella, it seemed, was not quite finished either. 'You will no doubt wish to become re-acquainted with your sons, now that you are here,' she said. 'Cressie would appreciate the morning off from teaching, I am sure, if you wish to take the boys out fishing.'

First Cressida had openly mocked him and now Bella had decided to get uppity. Something was most definitely afoot, Lord Armstrong decided and he was not at all sure he approved of it. 'I would not dream of interrupting their school work. Besides, I am due back in London almost immediately. I am off to St Petersburg with the duke, you know. I may be gone for some months. That is why I am here, to ensure that the appropriate arrangements are in place before I depart.'

'Oh, I see.'

Bella wilted visibly. Had she not been paying close attention, Cressie would have missed the disappointment, so quickly was it erased from her expression. Her stepmother was hurt. It should not have been a blinding revelation, but it was. Bella actually loved her husband. Bella thought he had come to visit her, obviously hoped he had come because he was concerned about her, when all Lord Armstrong was interested in was his *appropriate arrangements*! With a shock, Cressie realised what arrangements he meant. He would be absent for the birth of Bella's child. *His* child!

Forgetting all about her strategy of indifference, she could no longer hold her tongue. 'Father! You cannot go with Wellington. I am sure he will be able to find an able replacement. Bella needs you here.'

'I beg your pardon?'

'Cressie!' Bella exclaimed.

'Bella will not say it, so I will say it for her.'

'Cressida, I beg you will not!'

'She does not wish you to travel so far beyond reach at such an important time.'

'Henry, do not heed her. I am sure I will do perfectly well on my own.'

'You will not be on your own.'

Lord Armstrong got to his feet. He rarely betrayed anger, but Cressie could see, from the rigidity of his posture, that he was having to work extremely hard to hide his feelings. Under any other circumstances, she would have been gleeful, but for now she was simply concerned with trying to make him see the utter selfishness of his behaviour. 'Father, I know it will be a sacrifice, but surely Bella is more important than…'

'How dare you! How dare you tell me what to do! How dare you decide what is important for England and what is not.' Lord Armstrong shook with rage. 'It seems to have escaped your notice that my wife has already given birth to four healthy boys without complication or drama.'

'Father, it is different this time. Bella has been most unwell.'

'And whose fault is that? I have no doubt at all that you have been encouraging her to think herself worse than she is. Mountjoy had no real concerns when he examined her, or he would have informed me of them. My wife has expressed no real concerns either, until today, and no doubt that is thanks to your encouragement. She has not once written to me of any serious complaints, have you, my dear?' Lord Armstrong demanded, turning suddenly on his wife, who seemed to be trying to bury her bulk into the depths of her armchair.

She shook her head. 'I did not wish to worry you, Henry. I know how important—'

'There, you see!' Lord Armstrong declared. The obvious note of triumph in his voice, however, made him rein in his emotions. When he spoke again, it was in his more usual tone, and most pointedly directed only at his wife. 'Despite your reluctance to burden me, I was worried, my love. Which is why I have arranged for Sir Gilbert to attend you every month until your date. Though he is almost as much in demand as I, he has graciously agreed that he will take up residence at Killellan Manor for your lying-in. You see how much of a care I have for our child.'

For our child! Not for his wife. The nuance would before today have been lost on Cressie, but Giovanni had helped her to look at her world in a very different light. She fully expected Bella to be reassured, however, and was as unprepared as his lordship for her response.

'No!' Bella struggled to sit up, casting cushions and shawls aside. 'I will not have him here. I don't want him here.'

'Sir Gilbert?' Lord Armstrong looked puzzled. 'But he has attended the births of every one of our sons. He is the best in his field.'

'*No!*' With a supreme effort, Bella rose from her seat. 'I won't have him, Henry, do you hear? I want a midwife. I want a woman. I will not have that man prodding and poking me with his cold fingers and telling me not to make a fuss in that finicky voice of his. "Come, Lady Armstrong, show a little restraint. Do you hear the cows calving in the field bellowing so loud?" I'd like to see him give birth to such great strapping boys as mine without a bellow or two. I'd like to see him managing to be stoic, faced with those dreadful instruments of torture of his. I will not have him. I shall make my own arrangements, Henry, since you will not be here, and that is the last I have to say on the matter. I am retiring to my bedchamber now. Since your visit is to be of such short duration, I will make no further calls on your time. I do not expect to see you until morning.'

With as much dignity as her rippling flesh and swollen ankles shuffling in their tight slippers could muster, Bella left the drawing room. Cressie, dumbfounded, also decided a strategic retreat was much the best tactic. It had been quite a day and she had much to reflect upon.

Cressie recounted the events of the drawing room to Giovanni the next morning. 'I feel such an idiot. I was so taken up by resenting poor Bella that I completely failed to realise that she is just as much a victim of my father's selfishness as my sisters and I. She really does care for him, and he really does care naught for her. You were right,' she whispered, for her brothers

were all four of them seated at the table working, George and Freddie on their letters, James
and Harry at their geometry. 'My father is no
more interested in what Bella wants than he is
in what I want. You should have seen her face
last night when she realised that he was only
here to make sure we all behaved ourselves
while he swans off to Russia with Wellington.
I actually felt sorry for her.'

Giovanni paused in his work, frowning over
at Freddie, whose hands he was painting. He
was finding Cressie's pacing presence far too
distracting. It had seemed only practical to
move the schoolroom to the portrait gallery,
to allow Cressie to teach the boys while he
worked, with only occasional breaks necessary
to have them in the formal pose. The arrange-
ment meant that he had made excellent progress on the portrait, sufficient to free him in the
afternoons to work on Cressie's picture without impacting on the commission. But today,
he could not concentrate.

She was different. It was as if she had changed
overnight. Having cast off her resentment, her
anger on Lady Armstrong's behalf seemed
fresher, had somehow lost its previous debilitating quality and turned into a positive force.
Penthiselea, the warrior queen. There were no

half-measures with Cressie. She was on Bella's side now, and would not waste time bearing a grudge for how she had been treated by her stepmother in the past. He wondered fleetingly what Lady Armstrong would make of this turnabout. From what Cressie had recounted of last night's denouement, it seemed that she too was beginning to resent his lordship's high-handed treatment. They would make unlikely allies, Cressie and her ladyship, but it seemed probable that allies was what they would become.

Giovanni smiled to himself. He'd like to see the outcome of the revolution in the Armstrong household that he had played a part in igniting. Sadly, it was unlikely, for this commission would take him only a few more weeks. An ache like a hunger pang gripped his belly, but he dismissed it. It wasn't so much that he would miss Cressie, it was more that he was worried he would not have enough time to finish painting her. He'd have to work like a demon.

He tried to concentrate on the work in front of him, for which Lord Armstrong was paying, but he was far more interested in Cressie's change of attitude towards her father. He doubted very much it would be so easy for her as she thought right now, to cast off the habit of obedience. He knew from his own experience that it was a durable and persistent habit which required constant vigilance to suppress. The important thing was that Cressie had made a start.

She had confided the small morsel of praise Lady Armstrong had bestowed upon her last night. The effect it had on her seemed out of all proportion, for it sounded to him like the most grudging of compliments, voiced as much to irk her sire as to bestow approval on her step-daughter.

How little Cressie required to make her blossom. It had been obvious to Giovanni, how much her brothers had come to enjoy being with her, simply by the significant decrease in disruptions to his work. Harry, in particular, had a head for numbers, and had earned James's fury by finishing the exercises in Cressie's primer well ahead of his older brother, then demanding more difficult sums. James, a boy made in his dear papa's image, had not taken well to this evidence of superiority, but Cressie had ignored his tantrum, and there could be no better tactic.

If only Giovanni could ignore Cressie, but he was horribly aware of her as she paced restlessly behind him, stopping every few moments by his easel and preceding almost every remark with 'and another thing' as she replayed last night's scene for him, or recalled another incident from her past in which her father had put his own needs over others. There were a great deal of these, a bottomless well of examples which she had obviously, unwittingly, been storing away in that clever brain of hers with every detail intact.

He abandoned his attempt to complete his depiction of Freddie's hands. The expertise with which he rendered hands was one of the things for which he was most praised, one of the techniques he had worked hardest to master, but he was not in the right frame of mind today. Picking up another brush, he began to paint in the boy's shirt instead.

'It is extraordinary how many shades you use to portray something which looks simply white to me. Watching you paint makes me realise the enormity of your skill. I cannot believe I ever suggested you were merely a craftsman.'

Cressie stood by his shoulder, gazing at the canvas. One of her curls tickled his cheek. She smelled of chalk and lavender and rather deliciously of strawberries, which Giovanni traced to the sticky patch of conserve on the sleeve of her gown where one of her brothers had grabbed hold of her. They were always grabbing hold of her. Though she was not naturally tactile, it was another change he'd noticed, her willingness to join in their rough and tumble and lately, to administer cuddles and even the occasional consoling kiss. His hand tightened on the long handle of his sable brush, thinking of those consoling kisses. He swore quietly under his breath. What, was he envious now, of a few childish kisses? Ridiculous. But yesterday, just before Harry burst in on them—that had been a kiss so very far from consoling, he'd been quite unable to think about anything else since.

He was thinking about it now, as Cressie's skirts brushed against his trousers. She was asking him about shading. He had to find something to distract his thoughts. 'Here, you can apply the next pigment. I will guide you.' He loaded his brush with lead white, and handed it to her.

'Giovanni!' She looked as if he had given her a diamond necklace—or at least, as any other woman but Cressie would look, upon receipt of diamonds. 'You can't mean—I would not dare. You saw my attempt at a horse.'

It touched him unbearably, her glowing gratitude, the genuine admiration it implied, which meant so much more than any other because there was no one else, not in England, not in Italy, who understood his work so well. So little it took to please her, and so much she deserved. If she were his to please…

He strangled that thought at birth. Cressie was staring at him uncertainly. 'I can see you've changed your mind. I don't blame you,' she said, obviously swallowing her disappointment.

Giovanni shook his head decisively. 'The beauty of oils is how easily any mistake can be repaired, for they take so long to dry. But you will not make a mistake. Come here.'

He pulled her backwards against him, holding her still with one hand on the curve of her hip, which was another piece of her anatomy which had kept him awake at night, before covering her hand which held the paintbrush with his. The nape of her neck was warm, so delicate. Her fingers trembled under his. She had been making an effort not to pick at the skin around her nails of late. He had refrained from commending her, knowing she would prefer that he didn't notice. 'Gently,' he said, meaning the reprimand just as much for himself as for her. 'The lightest of strokes, but keep the brush steady. Don't press down too hard. See.'

He guided her hand over the outline of a shirt-sleeve on the canvas.

'I'm painting! I'm actually painting. Imagine, in a hundred years' time when some expert looks at this portrait, they will frown over these very brush strokes, and wonder if you have allowed an apprentice to work with you.'

Cressie's fingers fluttered under his. Giovanni told himself she was simply nervous. And the way she was pressing her delightful bottom against his thighs, that was just for balance. He struggled against the rush of blood to his groin which was his instant response. Her breathing seemed to have quickened. Nerves again, he told himself. He would not look down over her shoulder at the rise and fall of her breasts. Such sensitive breasts, her nipples the same dark pink as one of the roses which grew in the gardens at Palazzo Fancini. He tried instead to think of the pigments he would use to create the exact shade, but it was too late. Unbidden, his hand had slid up from Cressie's thigh to span her ribcage, just under the swell of her breast. Appalled, he made to remove it.

'Don't!' Her voice was no more than a ragged whisper. 'I mean,' Cressie said, 'please do not move, lest the brush slips. I would not like Freddie's shirt to be ruined.'

He refrained from pointing out what he had already about the nature of oils. Relying on the fact that the easel and the large canvas obscured them from the view of the boys, he let his fingers drift upwards to cup her breast. She shuddered. His erection stiffened. The paintbrush wobbled. 'More,' Cressie whispered. 'I think we need more paint.'

The palette was on a side table. A stretch away. She leaned forwards, her bottom rubbing against him, and this time he knew it was deliberate, for she glanced over her shoulder at him with a smile that was both mischievous and sensual, before she loaded the brush and managed to nestle even closer against him on her return.

'Papa, have you come to see our new schoolroom?'

'Papa, have you come to look at our picture?'

'Hell and damnation!' Cressie exclaimed rather loudly. Fortunately, the scraping back of chairs and the delighted squeals of her brothers meant that no one other than Giovanni heard her.

He caught the paintbrush just before it spattered the polished oak boards of the gallery's floor with lead white. He was on the point of assuring her that her father would have noticed nothing untoward when he caught Lord Armstrong's assessing gaze and abruptly changed his mind. These last few weeks, he had come to think of the man, whom he had met only once, as an ignorant buffoon. He had forgotten the salient fact that Lord Armstrong was one of the most respected diplomats in England, if not Europe. Such a man did not achieve success without having acute powers of observation, the ability to assess a situation accurately. Judging from his expression, those powers were telling him that something was not as it should be. His eyes, which Giovanni was disconcerted to note were a faded version of Cressie's, were not focused on his sons but on his daughter.

'Why was I not informed that you had abandoned the schoolroom?'

'Come, Father, you know you have no desire to be bothered with petty domestic detail. I thought you would commend my arrangements, for they are most efficient, allowing me to teach and Giovanni—Signor di Matteo—to paint at the same time.'

Cressie was flushed, but she seemed remarkably unflustered. In fact, she seemed almost to be relishing the situation. Giovanni suppressed a smile, and made a very small bow. 'Lady Cressida is most resourceful,' he said.

Lord Armstrong's eyes narrowed. He was patently puzzled, but was fortunately so entrenched in his view of his daughter as undesirable and lacking in desires of her own that the reason his suspicions had been aroused did not occur to him. He made no attempt to return Giovanni's bow and turned his attention to the canvas. 'Hmm.'

'Signor di Matteo has made excellent progress, do you not think, Father?'

'Better part of the canvas is still to be covered.'

'Yes, but he has completed all of the faces, and most of the hands. These are the most time-consuming and important elements. They are excellent likenesses, do you not agree?' Cressie persisted.

'Yes, not too shabby,' Lord Armstrong admitted grudgingly, 'but I'd expect nothing less for the kind of fee he demands.' He turned away from the canvas after the most cursory inspection, ignoring the various pleas of his sons, now clustered around him, to agree that their particular likeness was the best. Swatting and patting indiscriminately at his offspring, for he hated to have his clothing pawed, he turned to Giovanni. 'I had hoped to be here when the portrait was completed, but that will not be possible now. I am needed in Russia on important matters of state.'

᾿ As ever when he mentioned his calling, the diplomat seemed to puff up his chest. If he had feathers, Giovanni thought, Lord Armstrong would have preened them. He said nothing, however, refusing even to pretend to be impressed, though it was his normal custom to pander to his clients' vanity.

'I shall have my man of business pay half your fee on completion,' Lord Armstrong continued. 'You will understand that the remainder will be held until I have returned, and can signify my acceptance of the piece.'

Giovanni sensed, rather than heard Cressie's protest, and quelled it with a quick shake of his head. He picked up the cloth and covered the easel and then began to gather together his brushes.

'What on earth do you think you're doing?' his lordship demanded.

'You pay me half my fee, I leave you half a painting. When you return, and are available to *signify your acceptance*, I will complete it. Until then, my work here is done.'

'I say! That is most unreasonable.'

Giovanni shrugged. Across from him, he saw Cressie cover her mouth with her hand.

She knew he was bluffing. It surprised him, that she could read him so well. He continued to pack up his painting equipment.

'You are being most unprofessional,' Lord Armstrong protested.

'We agreed on the terms of my commission. I happen to know that you—how do you call it—pulled strings—in order to gain precedent.'

'I don't know what you mean.'

'Sir Gareth McIlroy was to be my next client. He informed me that he would cede his place in my schedule to you. I know how desperate he was to have a portrait of his wife, who has consumption, completed as a matter of urgency. I must therefore deduce that the favour he owed you was significant.' Giovanni permitted himself a small smile. 'But if you wish to call a halt to proceedings I'm sure Sir Gareth would be most grateful and relieved.'

Lord Armstrong, quite disconcerted, made a show of consulting his watch. 'I cannot be wasting the morning haggling over a picture. Very well, Cressida shall authorise full payment to you when the portrait is finished.'

'Not Lady Armstrong?'

His lordship's eyes narrowed. He was fairly certain that he was being disrespected, but he had no idea how. He closed his watch with a brisk snap of the gold case and returned it to his pocket. 'My wife has more important matters to concern herself with. My daughter, on the other hand, has nothing better to do. Which puts me in mind.' He turned towards Cressie. 'I have left a list of instructions for you to follow in my absence, but there are two other things I want to mention. Firstly, Sir Gilbert. You will prevail upon your stepmother to let him attend to her when he visits. All this stuff and nonsense about midwives is just that. Secondly, Cordelia. Your Aunt Sophia is, naturally, authorised to accept any suitable proposal while I am away. She knows my preferences.'

'What about Cordelia's preferences, Father?'

'Cordelia will prefer whomever her aunt directs her to prefer. Cordelia knows her duty. Sophia knows all about the business of launching a girl, none better,' Lord Armstrong said, quite forgetting the misalliance his sister had failed to prevent Cassandra from pursuing. 'You will leave her to it, and you will refrain—*refrain!*—from interfering, do you hear me, Cressida?'

'I do, Father. Though why you should be concerned about any influence I may have with Cordelia when you are so sure that she knows her duty...'

'Impudence is a vice that is tolerable in the

very young. In a woman of your age, it is quite misplaced. I will bid you farewell, Cressida, for I aim to spend the rest of the day with my boys, and must leave before dinner. You may write me with news of my wife when her time comes.'

With a dismissive nod to Giovanni, Lord Armstrong departed with his gleeful sons. 'And I am willing to bet that within the hour he will have had quite enough of their angelic company and will be calling for me to take them back,' Cressie said to his retreating back.

Giovanni laughed drily. 'I hope that you will make a point of being unavailable, since he so summarily dismissed you.'

'Not just me. He was barely civil to you.'

'Do not apologise on his behalf. I do not care this much for the man's opinion.' Giovanni snapped his fingers to demonstrate, a gesture which Cressie thought peculiarly Italian. He began to clear away his brushes.

'Aren't you going to carry on with the portrait?'

'I find I am no longer in the mood for painting.'

Cressie picked up the brush of lead white and drew it over the back of her hand, leaving a faint trace of paint. 'Can you only paint when you feel inspired?'

'If that were true I would have produced nothing in the past decade. It is many years since I felt inspired to paint any subject. Until I met you, that is.'

'What is so different about me?'

'I don't know. It is a mystery, and therein, perhaps, lies the answer. You are fascinating, unfathomable and quite unlike any woman I have ever met. It would appear that you are also my muse.'

Cressie flushed. 'An object of obsession? That doesn't sound at all like me.'

'To obsess does not seem at all like me. And yet...'

Seconds passed in silence, the atmosphere crackled with tension like the moments before a thunderstorm breaks. What he had left unspoken hung between them like overripe fruit ready for plucking. Cressie blurted out the first thing that came into her head. 'I can help you with that.'

Giovanni stared at her in dumb incomprehension.

'The brushes,' she faltered, pointing vaguely, 'would you like me to help you clean the brushes?'

Bemused, Giovanni agreed. She followed him down a service staircase to the basement scullery which he had requisitioned for his own. A dank room no longer used by the kitchen staff, it was lit only by an oil lamp. He had left his coat up in the gallery. She watched him at the sink, admiring the lean lines of him, the way his forearms flexed as he worked his brushes free from paint.

Cressie felt restless. Tense. Exhilarated. She felt as if she were looking at the world anew, with a clarity that was almost painful. It made her want to behave outrageously, to make up for years of compliance. For the first time, facing up to her father made her feel better, not worse. She was buoyed with confidence. The way Lord Armstrong had looked at them, she and Giovanni, in the gallery, he had known that there was something amiss, but it had not occurred to him that his daughter, his obedient, mousy little daughter, could have been behaving so outrageously.

'Here, let me see your hands. You have white paint all over them.'

Giovanni pulled her over to the sink and began to wipe her hands clean with a rag dipped in turpentine. His touch was firm and sure. He had been working all morning, but his hands had barely a spot of paint on them. He was always so neat and pristine. Save for yesterday, in the attic. Remembered pleasure rippled through her, settling low in her belly. When he had touched her—heavens, the way he had touched her. And then this morning too. She really thought she might melt. He, in contrast, had been so—well, hard, there was no other word for it. Perspiration beaded in the small of her back. Really, really hard. And she had been the one who had made him so.

The turpentine-soaked rag had been replaced with a clean cloth. Giovanni seemed to be taking an unnecessarily long time to dry her hands. She watched him, fascinated by the slender length of his fingers stroking the cloth over her skin. Her heart began to thump as she caught his gaze on her, eyes dark in the dim light, but unmistakably glistening with awareness. He dropped the cloth. He pulled her to him, touched her forehead, her cheeks, her lips, as if he were painting her with his fingers. A wild excitement fluttered through her.

His kiss was darker even than his eyes, drawing her into a sultry, sensual whirlpool of emotions. Desire was sharpened by a hunger she had not known she possessed, made urgent by its newness, strengthened by its illicit nature.

Forbidden fruit. She for him, he for her. Cressie dug her fingers into Giovanni's buttocks and kissed him deeply. Mouth. Tongue. Lips. She drank him in, inhaled him, devoured him.

And he kissed her back as if it were not enough, not nearly enough. He groaned, hauling her so tightly against him that she almost lost her balance, flailing against a wooden door set low into the wall of the scullery. The latch dug painfully into her back. 'Ouch!'

'*Dio!* Every time I kiss you something or someone intrudes—what is that?' Breathing raggedly, Giovanni pulled her away from the wall. 'I have not noticed it before. Are you hurt?'

'No.' Cressie put her hand up to her hair. As she suspected, it was in a wild tangle, bits of it hanging down over her cheeks. Thank goodness the light was dim. The strength of her response to him was frightening. He would be thinking her one of those women who threw themselves at him, if she was not careful. Which was exactly what she was doing, wasn't she?

Distracted, confused, she turned her attentions to the door. 'Where does this lead to?' she asked, already lifting the latch.

'I have no idea.'

Giovanni seemed to be having as much difficulty as she in controlling his breathing, Cressie was relieved to notice. His hair was standing up in spikes. The tail of his shirt was hanging out of his trousers. Had she done that? Cressie peered through the open door. A steep set of stone stairs disappeared into the gloom. 'A cellar of some sort, it must be part of the foundations of the original house. I had no idea it was there.'

'Shall we take a look?'

Cressie looked doubtfully into the gloom. 'It's very dark down there.'

Giovanni picked up the oil lamp. 'You are surely not afraid?'

She tossed her head back and glared defiantly at him, though she knew it was exactly what he expected her to do.

'Let me go first,' Giovanni said. 'Take your time, these steps look dangerous.'

Not as dangerous as the uncharted waters she was already swimming in, Cressie thought, treading carefully down into the darkness.

They found themselves in a passageway which led, as Cressie had suspected, to the cellars of the original manor house. It was to make sure she did not slip that Giovanni held her close to him, she told herself, the same reason she clung to his arm.

There were several chambers, each with a low vaulted roof forming a shallow dome. It was surprisingly warm. 'We must be directly below the kitchens,' Cressie whispered.

Intrigued, Giovanni held the lamp high, inspecting the herringbone brickwork of the ceilings. 'The family who built this place must have been wealthy. These are almost Roman in style.'

Cressie's eyes were alight with wonder. 'I had no idea. The mathematics of the arch are most fascinating, you know. In fact, there is a most excellent work on the subject by another of your countrymen, the Abbé Mascheroni. Our own Robert Hooke explains the specific equations behind the dome at St Paul's Cathedral. I came across his work at the Royal Society.'

'The Royal Society? How did you gain entry to that august, and I believe exclusively male, bastion?'

'I...' Cressie hesitated. She had no doubt at all that Giovanni would be intrigued and amused by the story of Mr Brown, but it suddenly struck her how much more astonished he would be by the sudden appearance of Mr

Brown in the flesh. He wanted to paint the private Cressie—what better way than to have Mr Brown captured in oils? It was an inspired idea! She shook her head, smiling enigmatically at him. 'Later,' she said. 'I'll tell you later. Trust me.'

'Trust you. I cannot deny I owe you that.' Giovanni's broadest smile, so rarely seen, was all the more delightful when it appeared. It made him seem so much younger. It made her realise how stern his usual expression was. It was not that he lacked humour, but he looked at the world even more darkly than she did.

They were standing at the juncture of two of the domed vaults, by a set of supporting pillars. Giovanni held the oil lamp high, peering up at the stonework. 'Look at this, Cressie.'

Cressie. Cressie. Cressie. She jumped, startled by the sound. The echo was eerie, bouncing round the vault, as if spirits were whispering her name. 'Giovanni,' she said softly, crying out with delight at the result.

Giovanni laughed. 'It is a whispering gallery. Astonishing. In the church of Santa Maria del Fiore, when I was a child, my father—the man I called—never mind. Let us experiment.' Leaving the lamp on the floor beside Cressie, he retreated to the next gallery before crouching down in the darkness against a pillar. 'Cress-i-da,' he whispered.

She giggled. 'Gio-vaaa-ni.' She waited until the echo, which seemed to reverberate for ever, finally died down. *'Don Giovanni,'* she trilled, completely off-key, following her rendition of the line from Mozart's opera with a clap of her hands to produce a most satisfactory crack of thunder. She was rewarded with a guffaw of very masculine laughter, followed by an even more off-key rendition of the next line. 'That was terrible,' she called.

'*Si.* Now you know something else about me that no one else does. I sing like a donkey with haemorrhoids.'

The peals of her laughter rung around the room like church bells. She was becoming accustomed to the strange effect. Cressie settled down on the cellar floor. The whispers, the dark, made the mood intimate without being stifling. Dangerous. And exciting. 'Tell me something else,' she said, keeping her voice low.

'I don't like dogs.'

'I am afraid of dogs.'

'My favourite cheese is pecorino.'

'I like to eat honey from the comb.'

'Your lips taste of honey.'

'Oh.' His words gave her goose bumps. The whispering gallery brought out Giovanni's Italian accent. 'Say that in Italian.'

'*Le tue labbra sanno di miele.* You have the most delightful *fondoshiena*,' Giovanni said. 'Last night, I dreamed of your *fondoshiena*.'

The acoustics of the cellar made it sound as if he had whispered in her ear, as if his words had brushed her skin. 'Fondo...?'

'The French word is *derrière*. The English word...'

'Is bottom.' Giovanni thought she had a delightful bottom. It was a shocking thing to say, and Cressie felt intoxicated. 'Tell me,' she whispered, tempted by the dark, by the spiralling of tension inside her, tempted by temptation itself. 'Tell me exactly what it was you dreamt.'

Chapter Six

Cressie heard the sharp intake of Giovanni's breath as her question swirled around the confined space. She waited, heart pounding, for his answer. When he spoke, soft as a sigh, the words washed over her like a caress. 'In my dream, I was watching you undressing,' he said. 'You knew I was watching. As I watched, you started touching yourself.'

She slumped back against the wall of the cellar. It was cool, but her skin was burning hot. 'Where? How? What was I touching?'

'Your breasts at first. When you pulled your chemise down over them, your nipples were budded, hard. As they were when I touched them yesterday. Do you remember?'

'Yes.' She closed her eyes. Imagined and remembered. His fingers. His tongue. His lips. She slid her hands inside the neck of her dress, and touched herself, pinched her nipples, stroked them, as he had done.

'Are you touching them now, Cressie?'

'Yes.' Circling them with her thumbs as he had done. Imagining it was him, his hands. 'Yes,' she said, and the echo made her voice hoarse and guttural, which she found she liked, for it made her feel like the kind of woman who would enjoy being watched as she touched herself. A shocking, wanton woman. She wanted to know more, and he seemed to be able to read her mind.

'When you bent over to remove your stockings...' A pause. 'The line of beauty. I wanted to taste you. To kiss the skin at the top of your thighs. The softest of skin. Touch it, Cressie. Tell me, is it the most delicate of skin?'

She arched back against the wall, rucking up her skirts. She had no thought of where she was or what she was doing, lost in the intimate world of touch and sensation, no room for thinking or questioning. Parting the two halves of her pantalettes, she slid her hand between her legs. 'Soft,' she whispered. 'The softest,' she said, stroking herself, her fingers sliding of their own volition inside her, where the tension was focused. 'Wet,' she whispered, already beginning to lose herself, 'hot.'

Giovanni's voice was harsh now. 'I bent you over. I slid inside you,' he said, his words and his dream echoing what she was already doing.

She could almost feel him, feel the thick shaft of his manhood, which this morning had pressed so insistently against her. It was easy to imagine him inside her. Cressie's fingers slid over the damp hot mound of her sex. She was knotted tight. It was not the first time, but it was the first time she had imagined, wished, fantasised, that it was someone else doing the touching. 'Giovanni. Giovanni. Giovanni.' Almost unaware, she said his name to a rhythm, stroking and dipping, stroking, not wanting it to be over—another new departure, not wanting it to end. 'What next?' she panted. 'Giovanni, what next?'

'Slowly. Do not rush. I—I did not rush.'

'Slowly,' Cressie repeated but she no longer wanted slow.

'You tightened around my shaft. So tight.'

'Hard. Tight. Oh, yes. Oh, please. Oh sweet...' She climaxed with a violence that threw her, hot pulses raged inside her, twisting her, tossing her up into the air, spinning her from the inside, pulsing and throbbing, until she slumped, panting, breathing hard, cast adrift.

Slowly, she came back to herself. Blinking she saw her legs sprawled, her skirts rucked up, her hand… She peered out into the gloom, but there was no sign of Giovanni. He had not stolen up on her, though he could have. She should have been mortified, but felt only a wafer-thin floating bliss, not a release, but a shifting of her axis, as if she had shed her skin. Or another skin.

Standing up and shaking out her skirts, she called his name tentatively, but there was no reply. She didn't know whether to be glad or disappointed. What did one say on such an occasion—thank you?

Cressie struggled against a wholly inappropriate and slightly hysterical desire to laugh, but as she picked her way slowly back through the cellars to the stairs which led to the scullery, the strangeness of what had just occurred began to puzzle her. Sitting down on the bottom step, she distractedly picked at her thumb, a habit she had recently managed to cure herself of. Since yesterday, when she had finally faced the truth about herself, since last night when she had confronted her father, since this morning, when Giovanni had made his desire for her quite plain, the things which had been niggling in the back of her mind had begun to solidify. Questions left unanswered. Doors determinedly closed. Giovanni wanted to know all about her, but he gave away little about himself. There were secrets lurking there, and there was definitely pain too, she was sure of it.

Thinking right back to the first time they had met, she counted the occasions when he had deflected a question, the occasions when he had claimed to understand something but refused to explain how. For a mathematician, she had been remarkably remiss in pursuing proofs from him. For one who prided herself on her thirst for knowledge, she had been very easily rebuffed. He told her he wanted to free her, he told her he wanted to help her, but he refused consistently to tell her why.

'Damn!' Her thumb was bleeding. Giovanni, it seemed to Cressie, gave her only so much as she needed, and no more. She was grateful, but she was also insulted, for though he had helped her look anew at the world, though he had helped her take pleasure in her own body, he had remained detached even from that.

'It's all wrong!' Cressie told the oil lamp. 'Plain wrong. What the *devil* is he hiding? And as for his claim that he somehow protects his artistic integrity by remaining unengaged by anyone or anything—what is he, some sort of artistic Samson, afraid he'll lose his ability to paint if he gives up on his vow of determined isolation?' She scrambled to her feet and picked up the lamp. 'I have to make him reveal himself, just as he did me. I shall probably have to make him angry, to provoke him into it, just as he did me. Because if I don't, let me tell you,' she told the lamp firmly, 'I doubt very much he will ever be the great artist I believe he is destined to be.'

Alone in the attic studio where he had hastily retreated, Giovanni stared at the portrait of Lady Cressida and tried desperately to focus on the mundane technicalities of his craft. Background. Glaze. The hands needed some rework.

It was useless. The aching throb of his persistent erection demanding release erased any hope of concentrating on work. He had never craved a woman as he did Cressie. Had never, with any of the many women he had made love to, felt such a deep, almost tangible connection as he had felt with her. And he had hardly touched her. Though he had wanted to. *How* he wanted to.

Giovanni turned his back on the canvas. The

existence of those other women in his past, especially the circumstances surrounding those liaisons, made it impossible for him to explain to someone like Cressie. He did not want her to think of him as the kind of man he had been. He wanted her, he wanted her so much, but he *would not* destroy what existed between them. He would have to find a way, somehow, of explaining how impossible it was for him to make love to her. A way to persuade himself as well as Cressie, without poisoning her with the whole, unpalatable truth.

Posing in her evening gown the next afternoon, Cressie seemed to Giovanni quite distracted. It was as well that all he was painting today was her dress, for she seemed incapable of holding any pose, twitching the folds of velvet and gauze first one way and then the next as she fidgeted constantly.

'I cannot work unless you sit still!' He had not meant to sound so harsh, but frustration of every sort had him in its vice-like grip.

Cressie jumped to her feet. 'I cannot! I cannot sit still. I cannot hold my tongue. I cannot let another moment pass without demanding an explanation.'

'Of what?'

'Of everything!'

Under other circumstances, Giovanni would have laughed at this. Cressie had a flair for the dramatic quite at odds with the literal, logical part of her nature. The way she threw back her head, making her breasts tremble, showing off the line of her throat, she was quite magnificent at times like this—though he doubted she would care to be told so. And today, he was in no mood for drama. Yesterday he had come too close to losing his self-control to contemplate any further drama. Since he had decided, quite unfairly, that this was Cressie's fault, he resorted to icy sarcasm, even though he knew she did not deserve it. 'I am afraid you overestimate me. Even I do not claim to know everything.'

'Do not mock me, Giovanni.' Cressie stormed over to the window, leaning back against the frame. 'You have known me—how long?'

'Several weeks.'

'It is almost seven since we first met.'

'I see the mathematician is back.'

She ignored this quite unnecessary jibe. 'For seven weeks, you have made it your business to point out the error of my ways. No, do not interrupt, Giovanni, for once you will listen to me. I am not complaining. I see that you were right.

I did not want to listen, but I did listen eventually. You gave me no option but to listen.'

'Because I understand. Because I know what it is like. Because I wanted you to learn from my experience. Because I recognise in you, Cressie, a lot of myself,' Giovanni exclaimed in exasperation. 'Surely you realised that?'

'How could I when you've never told me that before. Don't you see? I cannot learn from your experience if you will not share it with me. I cannot recognise our similarities if you will not reveal them to me.'

'I have no idea what you're talking about.'

She sashayed across the room, her train gathering dust, walking just as seductively as the borrowed gown demanded. It made him wary, this abrupt change in her mood, no longer angry but very confident and very determined.

'It is time for me to know you a little better,' she said, coming far too close for comfort. 'We have established the public personas of both Cressida and Giovanni. If you wish to see the private Cressie then you must also reveal a little of the private Giovanni. *Quid pro quo*, as your ancestors would have said.'

'What do you want to know?'

'Why will you not speak of your father? Why will you not talk of your family? Blood and beauty. It is your credo. Why are you so obsessed by both? Why are you alone? Why are you so scared of the very notion of sharing human contact of any sort? Why do you dismiss my questions? Why do you close yourself off from me? You have helped me see. You have made it possible for me to view the future with hope rather than dread. I want to do the same for you.'

She recited her questions with cool calm, but he was not fooled. There was a determination in her eyes that made him very wary. 'I admit, there were things in my past—but they are exactly that, in my past,' Giovanni said.

Cressie shook her head, just as he expected she would. 'I will not be fobbed off so easily this time. You recognised my discontent, you saw the unhappiness at my core. I now see that you recognised it because you share it. You said you see a lot of you in me. You are not happy, Giovanni, are you?'

'Cressie, this is arrant nonsense. I will not—'

'Oh, for goodness' sake!' She dropped her pretended air of calm as abruptly as she had assumed it and grabbed his arm, pulling him bodily over to the easel. 'Look at that! It's damned perfect. It's a polished, technically brilliant, mathematically beautiful painting, but it's not art. You said that yourself. It's cold, it's lacking emotion and it's utterly self-contained and sure of itself. Just exactly like you.'

She was right, but no one, not even Cressie, was permitted to take such critical liberties with his art. It was the one thing to guarantee his instant loss of temper. 'How dare you to presume so!' Giovanni snarled.

She flinched, but did not turn away. 'I dare because I know you, I presume because I know you can be a truly great artist not just an extremely successful painter. You want to paint emotion. You want to capture passion. How on earth can you do that when you are so—what is it you called me?—buttoned-up! Well, you are so buttoned-up that it is just possible you will suffocate yourself.'

'You are not even making sense. What has brought this on?'

'You! Why did you kiss me, Giovanni? Why do you touch me, why do you look at me as you do? Yesterday evening, here in this very studio, you touched me, you kissed me, you were the one who started it. Yesterday morning, when you allowed me to paint with you, you deliberately provoked me into—you know what you did. And after that, in the whispering gallery. You initiated all of those things. Is it some sort of game, to show me that I cannot resist you, to prove that you can resist me?'

'Stop it, Cressie! You don't know what you're talking about.'

'You're right. In one sense I don't, because you have locked the door on me. But in another—Giovanni, if we are so alike as you maintain, can you not trust me?'

He considered it. For a few seconds, he really did think about confiding in her. But to do so would be to admit that there was just cause, that his life, which he had worked so hard for, was not as perfect as he wished it to be. He was at the peak of his profession. He wanted for nothing and he wanted no one. He need explain himself to no one! 'If you leave the dress up here, I can finish the portrait without your having to pose any further,' Giovanni said starkly, turning back towards the easel.

'You don't even need me for that, then, is that it?'

'That is it,' he replied, picking up his brush and turning his shoulder.

The door of the attic closed behind her. Giovanni dropped to the floor and put his head in his hands. He didn't want to think about what she'd said, didn't want to consider the accusations she'd thrown at him. Yesterday morn-

ing, in the whispering gallery, it had taken all
his strength of mind not to surrender to the
urge to take pleasure in her pleasure, to take
his pleasure with her. He wanted her in a way
he had not thought possible, after years of abusing his charms, the subsequent years of denying them. It would be different with Cressie,
he was sure of that, but that made him all the
more certain that it would be wrong.

It would be wrong, even though every time
he touched her it felt right. It would be wrong,
even though he could barely sleep for thinking
of her. It would be utterly wrong because he did·
not deserve her and she most certainly did not
deserve to be tainted with his past.

Giovanni rubbed his eyes with his knuckles and got to his feet. She probably hated him
now. The chances of her allowing him to paint
the second portrait were slim. She would not
be his muse, because he would not allow himself to feel the passion that smouldered between
them, but she could not see as he could, the risk
they would take if he cast off the artist and became the man.

He thumped the floor in frustration. His life
was not perfect. Even before he'd met her, the
sense of frustration, of suffocating, was there.
And almost from the moment he saw her, he'd

known. He needed to paint her. The urge was stronger than ever. He needed to reclaim himself with this painting, reclaim the artist he had buried inside the society painter. He could not bear this particular canvas to remain blank. But years of isolation, of deliberately cutting himself off, could not make him view even the smallest of explanations without a shudder of disquiet. He would have to think hard about how best to make good the damage he had done.

Cressie paced the empty schoolroom. The boys were outside with Janey. For the second day in a row, she had forced herself to stay away from the attic studio. Two days of being coldly polite to Giovanni downstairs in the gallery while she taught her brothers and he painted them. Two days, alternating between fury and frustration that she had so signally failed to break down his reserve. Two days of waiting it out in the vain hope that he would change his mind, in the slightly more likely hope that he would say he needed her to sit for the completion of her portrait.

She tried to work on her second children's primer, taking the invaluable experience she had gained in teaching from the first into account, but she could not concentrate. Work on her thesis was impossible, and even when responding to written questions raised by readers of her articles, she found her mind wandering.

There were two globes standing on top of the cupboard where she stored the boys' books, slates and chalks. One celestial, the other terrestrial, they were beautiful objects made by Carey's. Cressie's enthusiasm for the stars meant that the former was put to much more use than the latter. She rubbed at a fingerprint with the cuff of her gown. She really must persuade her father to invest in a telescope. Perhaps if she could get James to write him a letter...

'Cressida! Here you are. I have been looking all over for you.' Bella burst into the schoolroom, her face crimson.

Cressie ushered her stepmother towards a chair. Bella sank down, fanning herself with the letter she held in her hand. She was now quite pale, with perspiration beading on her brow, and looked to be on the brink of a swoon.

'Why did you not send a servant to fetch me?' Cressie asked, wondering if she dared leave Bella to search for smelling salts.

'I could not—I wanted you to see—here, read this.'

Bella thrust the letter at her. With a sinking

feeling, Cressie recognised her Aunt Sophia's spidery scrawl. 'Cordelia?'

Bella, somewhat recovered and breathing more evenly, managed to nod.

Retiring to the window seat, Cressie read her aunt's missive. Cordelia, it seemed, was setting the *ton* alight. Already, Aunt Sophia had had to reject five completely unsuitable requests for her hand. *My personal belief is that Cordelia is set upon amassing as many offers as possible*, Aunt Sophia wrote. *Rumour has it that she has actually had her name entered in White's betting book, in competition with Valeria Winwood's daughter. The scandal of such a wager pales in comparison to the very low birth of her adversary. Everyone knows exactly how Valeria Winwood acquired her husband.*

There was worse to come. Cordelia's penchant for fast company had resulted in several minor scandals, including her attendance at a boxing match of all things. Aunt Sophia, that stalwart of society, seemed to be genuinely afraid that Cordelia's vouchers for Almack's would be withdrawn. Reading between the lines, Cressie was much more concerned that her sister might, whether of her own volition or not, make a dreadful misalliance.

'She demands that I come to town,' Bella

said waveringly. 'She says that she cannot be responsible for the consequences if I do not. What am I to do, Cressida? Your father has only just departed for Russia—why did Sophia not raise these issues with him?'

Cressie scanned the letter again. It would be a mistake to underestimate her aunt, who was one of the few people capable of outmanoeuvring Lord Armstrong. Which meant that this letter was a deliberate ploy. 'I wonder,' she mused, 'do you think that my aunt simply wishes to be rid of the burden of Cordelia's come-out?'

Bella pursed her mouth. 'Sophia has the gout, and she is past sixty, for she is several years older than your father, so it would not surprise me if she was a reluctant chaperon—especially given the friskiness of her charge who, as I know all too well, would wear out a whole battalion of chaperons.'

'I must confess that I'm still surprised that Cordelia would take such advantage of the situation.'

Bella looked sceptical. 'Really? I am not.'

'What do you mean?'

'Cordelia is no more interested in marrying a man of your father's choice than any of you have been, save for Caroline. And I suppose

Celia—that foolish man who was her first husband, the one who got himself killed, he was
your father's choice I believe. But as for the
rest of you...' Bella made a sweeping gesture.
'First Cassie, then you, and it seems obvious
to me that now Cordelia too is set on defying
your poor father, though why, I do not know.'

Cressie's jaw dropped, making Bella titter.
'You think because I am fat and frumpy that I
notice nothing. You think because you are all
so clever that I am incapable of simple observation. Despite appearances, I *do* see what goes
on under my nose, Cressida. I am aware, for
example, that you are allowing that charming
and rather delicious portrait painter to take your
likeness. I hope you know what you are doing?'

Cressie was too dumbfounded to speak. Her
cheeks flooded with colour. She was mortified,
not that she had underestimated her stepmother,
but that she had judged her so callously, and
had indeed assumed her foolish as well as fat.
'I did not know—we did not mean—indeed,
Bella, it is simply...' She stuttered to a halt
under her stepmother's critical gaze.

'Let us at least have some truth between us,
Cressida. We will never be bosom friends, and
I have no interest in playing the mother to you
any more than you are interested in allowing

me to. It would suit me very well to have every one of you married and gone, for then perhaps your father would pay a little more attention to me and my boys. I don't care who you marry. I don't give a fig whom Cordelia marries either, so long as you both marry.'

'And if I don't choose to find myself a husband?'

Bella shrugged. 'Then choose to find a way of quitting my household.'

'Would you support me if I asked my father for an annuity?'

'My dear Cressida, you may play the bluestocking spinster with my blessing, but you must know how little real influence I have with my husband. He wants nothing from me save a succession of sons. You will have to find your own way of persuading him, if that is the road you choose to take.'

Cressie examined her ragged thumb. Deciding it was quite bloody enough, she tucked her hand out of reach under her skirts. Her stepmother's candidness had excused her from some of the guilt she felt, for she knew deep down that not even a desire to make amends would bring about a genuine attachment between them. It was a relief to know that Bella felt the same, though not such a relief as to make her feel anything other than dreadful about her own behaviour over the years since her father's second marriage.

She got to her feet, folding her Aunt Sophia's letter up. 'I am glad we had this talk, Bella.' Cressie kissed her stepmother's cheek. The skin was cool, with some of the bloom of youth upon it still. Bella was not so very much older than she. Lost somewhere in the layers of fat and insecurity, there must be a Bella who regretted what she had become, who perhaps longed for escape, just as Cressie did. 'You look better today,' she said. 'Has the sickness eased?'

'Not really.'

Bella placed a hand on her stomach which, Cressie noticed, was not nearly as distended as it had seemed a few days ago—nor nearly so swollen as it ought to be. From the very earliest days of her previous pregnancies, Bella had been vast. 'You know that my father has insisted that Sir Gilbert Mountjoy visit?'

'I shall not see him, and your father is not here to make me do so.'

'But perhaps—forgive me, Bella, I know very little of these matters, but surely you should not still be so sick?'

'It is a girl, that is why. Everything about this confinement is different, and I am sure it is because it is a girl.' Bella heaved herself to her feet. 'What am I to do about that letter?'

'Obviously, you cannot go to town. I believe my aunt exaggerates matters in order to try to goad you into action. My father has only recently left London. If Cordelia really had been so outrageous, he would have heard about it. I shall write to my sister and demand the truth from her. Until we hear back from her, I think the best thing we can do is ignore this.'

'Very well, but if something happens in the meantime...'

'It shall be on my head,' Cressie said with a wry smile. 'I have nothing to lose in terms of my father's goodwill, but you do. I understand that.'

With a satisfied nod, Bella sailed out of the schoolroom. Left to her own musings, Cressie stared out of the window, where her brothers were fishing from the bridge. She would write to Caro as well as Cordelia. Since her marriage, Caro had become quite withdrawn, visiting Killellan Manor only rarely, London even less. But of the five sisters, Caro was the most intuitive. It would be interesting to read her views on Bella's revelations.

She must have drifted off to sleep, perched on the window seat with her cheek resting on the pane, because Cressie woke with a start, to find Giovanni standing in the schoolroom doorway, a most forbidding expression on his face. She jumped up, automatically putting a hand to her hair, which was pressed flat on one side, a tangled mess on the other. 'You startled me. What do you want?' Her voice was flat and unwelcoming, to compensate for that unchecked moment of being pleased to see him.

'I came to apologise.'

It was as she expected—he wanted to finish his painting, nothing more. 'This is quite a day for unparalleled events,' Cressie said coolly.

Giovanni flinched. He was, as usual, dressed entirely in black, save for his white shirt and a waistcoat of alternating navy and sky-blue stripes. 'I was unforgivably rude. I lost my temper. I said things I should not have—I am very sorry, Cressie.'

'What you mean is, will you please still pose for me.'

'That is not what I mean. I want to explain why it is so crucial to me to paint you,' Giovanni countered. 'Will you listen?'

Cressie sighed. He seemed genuinely contrite, and she was genuinely pleased to see him. The silence between them these last two days had made her realise how much conversation they normally shared. She'd been lonely without him. 'Yes, of course I will. Indeed, with the ample evidence I have just been given of my lack of perception and quickness to judge, I would be happy to listen. No, don't ask for I have no intentions of explaining right now.' She sat back down on the window seat and patted the cushion beside her.

Giovanni, however, chose to remain standing. He seemed unsure of himself, less composed than usual. And now that she looked at him closely, which she had not permitted herself to do since their quarrel, she saw that there were dark shadows under his eyes. 'You have been working too hard.'

'Not at all.' His denial was automatic, but he caught himself almost immediately. 'Yes, I have. I often work at night when I cannot sleep. I have been trying—experimenting with form.'

'Thank you. For not brushing me off, I mean.'

'You are welcome. You see, I do listen, but it does not come naturally to me, the urge to explain.'

Cressie laughed. 'Nor to me, as you well know.'

As he sat down beside her, she was granted one of his rare, true smiles. 'I did not mean to be so—overbearing. I must have seemed to you every bit as much of a tyrant as your father at times, trying to browbeat you into my way of thinking.'

'Good grief, Giovanni, please, you are nothing like my father.'

'I am extremely relieved to hear you say so, but…' He took her hand in his, and kissed her wrist. 'I am sorry. I wanted only to help you.'

His lips had the usual effect on her pulse. Only now that he was here, actually contrite, did Cressie allow herself to admit how upset she had been by their disagreement. 'You have helped me, but now you must allow me to help myself, if I can.'

'And to help me too, if you will. I want to prove that I can produce something more than just a *polished, technically brilliant, mathematically beautiful painting.*'

'Did I say that?' Cressie made a face. 'Sorry.'

'It is the truth, that is what I do paint, but I am capable of more. With your help.'

Giovanni leaned over to touch her face, tracing the line of her forehead, her cheek, her throat. Such a familiar touch, one she had not thought she'd feel again. It made her skin tingle, it roused memories of all the other times he had touched her, and it brought with it too a melancholy, a prelude of the time when he would not be here, when her portrait would be done, and Giovanni would be done too, with her. But for the moment, he was still here. And that was enough. 'When will we start?'

'You are still willing to sit for me, Cressie?' She laughed at his eagerness, at the way he clapped his hands together and leapt to his feet. 'We can begin tomorrow. I have finished the other portrait, the first one, save for the final glaze.' His smile faded. 'But I need to tell you first—explain something.'

Frowning, Giovanni began to spin the Carey globes, just as she had done earlier, first one then the other. 'You asked me why I must always retreat from you, why I am so buttoned-up, as you put it. You've awoken in me what I thought was dead, Cressie, the desire to create, to paint from the heart. You have rekindled my passion. And the reason I cannot—the reason I will not—I am afraid. No, I am terrified that if I allow myself to...'

He spun the terrestrial globe so viciously that it rocked on its stand, then turned to face Cressie square on. 'I am afraid that if I allow us to become close, if we make love, I am afraid it will destroy the magic between us. I am afraid it will prevent me painting you. I don't want to destroy what I have only just rediscovered. Do you see?'

She saw that his words were irrefutably from the heart. She saw that he believed them, though she could not understand why. Cressie was afraid to speak, lest she say the wrong thing. 'Thank you. For explaining. For trusting me with your—thank you.'

He seemed both relieved and just a little bit uncomfortable. Was he still holding something back from her? She agreed to sit for him the next day. It was only later, as she lay awake in her bed replaying the conversation, that the exact words he used tempered her euphoria. *I don't want to destroy what I have only just rediscovered.*

He had once had another muse. Of course he had, and it was a very stupid and illogical thing to be jealous of her, whoever she was, especially since she was obviously no longer in Giovanni's life. Had he made love to her? Certainly. Had he loved her?

'That,' Cressie told herself, laying aside her translation of Legendre's *Exercices de Calcul Intégral*, 'is absolutely none of my business.' But logic and emotion were, she was discovering, rarely in alignment. The idea of Giovanni in love sat very ill with her.

* * *

'You are late.' Giovanni was standing in front of his easel, his drawing board covered in charcoal sketches, when he heard the door slowly open. 'I have been working on some ideas, but I am not sure—aren't you coming in?'

Cressie hovered in the doorway of the attic, clutching her mother's evening cloak around her. 'Have you set your heart on Penthiselea?'

He scored his charcoal impatiently through something. His cravat dangled over a chair, on which were also his coat and his waistcoat. He had a smudge of charcoal on his forehead. She could see a smattering of hair peeping out from the open neck of his shirt. Cressie's throat went dry. The light in the attic was bright, with the sun shining directly through the dormers. Through the billowing folds of his cambric shirt, she could quite clearly see his nipples, could see that the hair arrowed down towards the dip of his belly. She shouldn't be looking but she couldn't drag her eyes away. She reminded herself that in order to inspire him she must allow him to keep his distance, but what she wanted was to rip the shirt clean off his back and run her hands over the lean, hard muscles she was certain were underneath, to feel the contrasting roughness of his hair and smoothness of his skin, the sinew and tendon ripple as she touched him, to hear him groan as she tasted him. She wanted to…

'Cressie, are you coming in or not? Why are you wearing that cloak?'

She closed the door behind her, and leaned against it. 'I had an idea. It is a surprise.'

He was looking at her now, no longer distracted by the drawing board. 'I don't, as a rule, like surprises. I rarely find them to be pleasant.'

She didn't want to let Giovanni see how nervous she was, for it would quite spoil the effect. It had seemed such an inspired idea but now that it came to it her resolve began to falter. Would she look preposterous? Would he ridicule her? Standing up, she began to unfasten the cloak, her trembling fingers fumbling with the clasp. 'Turn around,' she commanded. 'Don't look until I say so.' She dropped the cloak to the ground and slipped the hat she had been hiding beneath it on to her head. 'Giovanni?'

'*Si?*'

'You can turn around now. I want you to meet…'

'Penthiselea,' he guessed.

'Mr Brown.' Cressie swept her hat back off

her head in a movement she'd practised for hours last night in front of her mirror, and made a bow she was rather proud of.

She was rewarded with an astonished bark of laughter. 'What on earth...?'

'You remember you asked how I managed to attend meetings at the Royal Society? Well...' Cressie did a little twirl, her coat tails flying '...this is how. You were right, I would never be admitted as a female, no matter how impressive my scientific achievements, but some of the great minds of the age lecture at the Society and I go to great lengths to hear them.'

Giovanni laughed again. 'I never doubted your passion for your studies, but this is something else entirely. Am I to understand that you actually travelled about London dressed in these clothes? Did they know, the august members of the Royal Society, that a woman had penetrated their hallowed rooms, disguised as a man? They must surely have guessed, for you seem to me a very feminine man.'

'Do I? I am not aware that my disguise was detected. Save by Mr Babbage, of course. A friend, who facilitated my attendance.'

'And has Lord Armstrong met Mr Brown?'

'Good heavens no! No, no, he must never

know. No one knows, other than Mr Babbage. And now you.'

'I am honoured. And really very impressed, Cressie. But why did you take such enormous risks? Were you discovered, the consequences could be catastrophic.'

'I know, but not so catastrophic as never being able to—can you not see, Giovanni, how stifling it is to be a mere woman? I cannot deny that each time Mr Brown and I go out into the world I am in a constant state of terror, but it is also so—exhilarating. Such freedom as these breeches give me. And I must admit, there is too a certain *frisson* in knowing that I am fooling the world. Is that so very difficult to understand?'

'Not so very difficult, knowing you. You are a remarkable and very brave young woman, Cressie.'

'Young man, if you please, just at the moment,' she replied with a toss of her head.

Once again, Giovanni laughed. 'Mr Brown, it is a genuine pleasure to make your acquaintance,' he said, bowing extravagantly. 'I kiss your hand, Mr Brown—you are quite, quite perfect.'

And he did kiss her hand, his mouth lingering on her palm, though he dropped it immediately at the resultant *frisson*, making a show of inspecting her costume. 'Well?' Cressie demanded. 'Will you paint me as my alter ego?'

'I can think of nothing better. So very delightfully seditious, you look. There is something about the clothes which brings out all of your curves. I cannot believe that any red-blooded man was taken in by you. Your English intellectuals must all be blind.' He had been circling her, but now he stopped in front of her. 'This is wrong,' he said decisively, pulling out her hair pins and casting them carelessly onto the floor. 'The trick will be to show you as Mr Brown and Cressie at the same time.' More pins flew in all directions until her hair tumbled down over her coat. 'Now, put the hat back on so—but at this angle, like a coquette. Yes. And the coat like this. Yes, yes. Once more I commend you, Cressie—this is inspired.'

Giovanni kissed her hand again. Cressie closed her eyes, the more to relish the touch of his lips, and wondered how much more of this she would be able to endure without losing her self-control. He stood her on a box and paced around her, adjusting her clothing, her hair, her breeches, her boots. He smelt of charcoal, turpentine and linseed oil, faintly of sweat and overlaying it all, something definitively male

and quite definitely Giovanni. Was there such
a thing as eau de Cressie? She tried to distract
herself, wondering what it would be. Chalk
definitely. Her soap, which was scented with
lavender, that was good. Jam or chocolate or
barley sugar, depending upon what particular
treat her brothers had been indulging in—not
good, but not so bad. The other day, though,
Freddie had spilt the contents of a whole jar of
dead frog spawn over her. She hadn't smelled
very nice at all then. One of the pigments
Giovanni used smelled rather like that, now
she came to think of it. Which colour was it?

'You can stand down now. I think we should
try another pose.' Giovanni pulled a gilded
chair into the middle of the room. It was Egyptian in style, rosewood inlaid with brass, the
legs turned and fluted, the black velvet seat
saggy and faded.

'Oh, I remember those chairs. There was a
full set and a table to match in the small din-
ing parlour. My mother loved everything Egyptian. She was prone to saying that she'd liked
to have been Cleopatra.'

'Your mother does not sound at all like the
kind of woman your father would have married.'

'You'd think not, to see him now, but I believe in the early days, when they were first married—well, you've seen the kind of dresses she wore.' Cressie giggled. 'At least, I assume she wore them for my father. Oh, that is a terrible thing to say.'

'But you wish it was a little true, no?'

'A little. I mean no! We are discussing my mother, for goodness' sake, Giovanni.'

'Motherhood does not automatically invest a woman with virtue.'

'Well, no, of course not. In fact, motherhood is often the result of a lack of virtue,' Cressie agreed, 'but I have no cause to think that *my* mother—I mean, they are all so alike, my sisters—except for me, and—Giovanni! Do you think that is it? Do you think perhaps I'm not my father's child?'

She didn't mean it. Much as she hated to admit it, Cressie could not deny the resemblance between herself and Lord Armstrong, especially around the eyes, but she was in a skittish mood, and dressed as Mr Brown she felt a reckless confidence, quite freed from normal proprieties. She had meant it as a joke, but her jest had somehow gone awry. 'Giovanni? What have I said?' He had been smiling, teasing, light-hearted but at the same time wholly focused on her guise, on his painting. Now his face was dark, his brows drawn tight together. His satyr look.

'It is nothing.'

'I thought we were going to have no more lies between us.'

'I do not lie.'

'Not lies, then. Avoidance of truth. Stop prevaricating. What on earth have I said to upset you? I did not mean it, about my mother playing my father false, that is.'

'I do not care one bit for what your mother did or did not do. I want you to sit in this chair sideways, like this.'

Cressie suffered him to adjust her, crossing first one leg then the other, facing one way then the other, resting her chin on her hand, clasping her hands, with her hat on and with her hat off, while all the time trying to pinpoint the exact part of the conversation where his smile had turned sour. Not the first mention of her mother. Nor at the shocking notion of her possibly having an *affaire*. But after that. Something about motherhood. That was it! 'I said motherhood is often the result of a lack of virtue,' she exclaimed. 'Do you—were you...?'

Giovanni threw himself away from her. 'Always you must pick and pick. I feel sometimes as if I have no skin left. Yes, I was referring to my own mother. Now you have your answer, can we please concentrate on the task in hand?'

'Yes, we can,' Cressie agreed. Partly because his tone brooked no argument but mainly because she had just managed to breach, ever so slightly, the walls he had built around himself, and she did not want to press her luck too far.

'Mr Brown awaits Signor di Matteo's pleasure,' Cressie said. Which on reflection was probably an unfortunate turn of phrase.

Chapter Seven

It had been Cressie's idea for the boys to build a kite, the notion being spawned after reading of the American Benjamin Franklin's use of them in his research into the nature of lightning. Unfortunately, Mr Franklin did not see fit to explain the method of construction, and Cressie had only the vaguest idea of the practicalities. Having fired up her brothers' imagination with the project, she was at a loss as to how to progress it until Giovanni stepped in. With a few rough sketches, he explained the mechanics and sent the four boys off, with James in charge, in search of the various components.

Cressie was astounded when they returned, all four of them in unusual harmony—though when she thought about it, she realised that they did argue a lot less these days. Only when their father was at home had their bickering and jostling for position resumed, their individual demands for attention and precedent, which her father seemed to relish, in the manner of a king and his fawning courtiers. James, Harry, George and Freddie treated Giovanni as if he were not their king but their general, jumping to obey his every order, anxious to execute it to the best of their ability, quietly pleased rather than gloating when they earned his praise. Which Giovanni gave unsparingly, but justly, as he did his reprimands.

Unlike Lord Armstrong, who tended to blame whoever was convenient, or whoever was his current victim of choice. There was one particular time, when Cressie was twelve or thirteen. Caro it was, who had broken the Chinese figure which had been a gift to their father from the British Ambassador to that far-off country, but it was Cressie who was sent to bed for being discovered in the same room as the pieces, despite Caro's noble protests of guilt. Caroline, their father had insisted, was simply trying to cover up for her clumsy sister.

The memory was startlingly vivid. There had been many of these little pastiches of recollection popping into Cressie's head these last few days, long-forgotten, usually trivial things, which caught her by surprise with their freshness. Had she tucked them away because they were too painful, or because they would have made her attempts to conform too painful? Both, most likely. The surprising thing was that they didn't hurt now. They made her sad, often wistful, but neither regretful nor resentful. There was no point in railing at her past, and now that she was starting to understand herself more, she could see that each memory was part of her, and each one could be turned to a more positive effect. It might be fanciful but she felt as if she were evolving and in doing so growing stronger.

Her brothers had scorned Cressie's inept attempts to help them build their kite, demanding Giovanni's assistance instead. She'd been happy to step out of the fray and more than happy to watch the kite take shape under Giovanni's expert guidance—though he disguised his efforts so well, her brothers were convinced the finished product was entirely their own work. He was patient when it came to decorating the kite too, sketching in fantastical Chinese dragons and samurai warriors for the boys to colour, making sure that none of them were aware when his quick hand fixed their childish mistakes.

It was a blustery day, and perfect for the first launch. Cressie perched on the stone wall of the field, watching Giovanni instruct her brothers in the art of kite-flying, another subject about which she had been clueless. The breeze blew the skirts of her emerald-green pelisse around her legs. She wore no hat, but had tied her hair back with a green silk ribbon, which seemed to be holding for the moment. The skirts of Giovanni's coat flew out behind him, giving her tantalising glimpses of long, muscular legs clad in his customary tight trousers. He wore boots today, black of course, and highly polished, though now spattered with mud, which he didn't seem to mind at all.

The boys were taking turns with the kite in pairs, James with Freddie, Harry with George. 'Your turn to launch her,' James said, handing the kite carefully over to his youngest brother. 'Here, hold her high above your head by the struts.'

'Like as if she is a fluttering butterfly,' Freddie shouted encouragingly at his twin. 'You have to be careful not to tear her wings, doesn't he, Gio?'

'A fluttering butterfly,' George shouted delightedly, 'a buttering flutterby.'

'A buttery, fluttery, utterfly.' Freddie clapped his hands together gleefully, jumping up and down, spattering his nankeen breeches with mud.

'Watch out—it's trailing in that puddle.' James grabbed the beribboned tail, catching it up and gathering it carefully together before handing it to Harry. A few weeks ago, such a silly thing would have resulted in a fight and a broken kite, Cressie marvelled.

'Ready, Harry?' Giovanni asked.

'Ready,' the boy replied solemnly, taking the spool as if it were the crown jewels.

'Do I run now, Gio?' George shouted.

'When Harry gives the order. Harry, you must remember to feed out the line slowly.'

Frowning hard, Harry did as he was told. James, the veteran of one successful flight already, impatient as usual to show his superiority, made to shout out instructions, only to find himself silenced by Giovanni's hand over his mouth. He looked so surprised that Cressie couldn't help laughing. For a moment, James looked upon the brink of a tantrum, but a quirk of Giovanni's eyebrow stopped him in his tracks.

Harry called out the command to launch. George ran as fast as his chubby legs could carry him across the field. Unfortunately, he was so intent on holding the kite aloft that he first splattered himself with a wet cowpat, then tumbled head first over a large boulder. Boy and kite went flying, the one down the other up. A gust of wind yanked the kite high, and would most likely have lifted Harry off his feet had not Giovanni lunged and caught him just in time.

Cressie ran to George, who was lying flat out on the grass, but by the time she reached him he had staggered to his feet. 'He's just winded,' Freddie assured her solemnly.

'And smelly. What on earth...?'

'I smell like a cow's bottom,' George announced.

'You always smell like a cow's bottom,' Freddie said with a snigger.

'Never mind that—look!' George exclaimed. 'Up, up, up high. Higher than yours.'

'Not higher.' Freddie frowned up at the kite, which was soaring above their heads, the rich colours of the dragons and the warriors like exotic jewels against the blue English sky. 'Well, perhaps *as* high.'

Harry was struggling to control the kite

with the whole string played out. Bright red in the face, his fair hair blowing wildly, cap askew, the tail of his shirt hanging out like a flag where it had come loose, he really looked as if he might take off himself.

'Harry's going to fly, Harry's going to fly,' the twins called, holding hands and spinning round and round, their ecstatic faces turned to the sky. 'Gio, Gio, Harry's going to fly.'

'Giovanni, I think he might need some help.'

'What do you think, Harry? Can you hold her?'

Harry said something that sounded like a strangled affirmative. Cressie, now thoroughly concerned, protested. 'He's not a baby,' James said, jumping to his brother's defence. 'Why do girls always fuss, Gio?'

'I think your sister is jealous. I think she would like to fly the kite for herself, wouldn't you, Cressie?'

She would. He knew she would, but one look at her brothers and she knew she could not spoil their fun. 'I am not nearly strong enough,' Cressie said graciously, though she would dearly have loved to have flown the kite, Giovanni standing close behind her, guiding her hand just as he had done when he allowed her to paint a little of the canvas.

She retreated to the wall once more, contenting herself in her role as spectator, watching a very different Giovanni from the one she knew, laughing, entirely at ease. He was every bit as athletic as she had imagined him as he ran across the field with the boys and the kite, his lean body showing to admirable effect as he hoisted James into the lower limbs of a tree to free the flapping toy.

'So this is the kite I have been hearing so much about.' Bella, in a claret pelisse topped with a Paisley shawl, picked her way carefully towards Cressie. 'I heard the boys' shrieks from the salon window. I don't think I've ever seen them laughing so much. Look at Georgie, waving his hands like a windmill. And James. I had not noticed how tall James had become these last few weeks. Why, his breeches are several inches too short for him.'

'Janey has let the seams out several times, but I fear he is about to burst out of them,' Cressie said, smiling.

'They seem to bicker so much less these days. Henry—your father—told me that it was in a boy's nature to fight constantly. "It's how the lads assert themselves," he said. "Encourages their competitiveness," he insisted.'

Taken aback, not so much by the accuracy

of Bella's mimicry as by the mocking tone behind it, such a contrast to the tender way she had spoken of her sons, Cressie was forced to laugh. 'My father believes that competitiveness is one of the ultimate virtues. For a man, that is.'

'Your father loves to compete provided he can be sure to win. I meant what I told him, Cressie. You have been a very good influence on my sons.'

'Thank you. You will not take offence when I tell you that your compliment means all the more, coming from you.'

Bella laughed. Not her usual tinkle, but a gurgle which sounded positively girlish. 'Because it is so grudgingly given, you mean.'

'Because you are such a stern critic, is how I would have worded it.'

'Same difference.' Bella leaned her bulk against the stone wall, shading her eyes against the sun. 'Signor di Matteo is quite the most beautiful man I have ever seen, I must say. Not handsome, but beautiful. I confess, I thought him a cold fish, but one would not think so, seeing him like this. I saw the drawings he did for the boys. He understands them very well. Unlike...'

Bella trailed off into silence, looking suddenly older and sadder. Feeling uncomfortably as if she were intruding, Cressie returned her attention to the kite flyers. James was helping Freddie with the spool now, Giovanni standing with his hand resting casually on Harry's shoulder, the pair of them laughing at some private joke. She hadn't seen Giovanni with his guard so completely down before.

'He would make a good father, though I doubt he will ever choose to become one.' Bella too was watching Giovanni. 'For all his attractions, he is a man who avoids human contact. Yet he obviously likes my boys. Perhaps it is because they are no threat to him.'

'What do you mean?'

'Ask yourself why a man who could have any woman, if his reputation is to be believed, chooses to have none. It is not that he is the type who likes men, that much is obvious— though it is obvious too that men of a certain sort would find him most appealing.' Bella smiled her tight little smile. 'I may live out of the world, but I once lived very much in it and I still keep up with the latest gossip, Cressida, do not look so shocked.'

'Gio—Signor di Matteo—I believe he was in love once.'

Bella snorted. 'Is that what he told you? I

doubt it is true. Or if he was, it was more likely a hundred times than once. Poor Cressida, I detected you had developed a fondness for him but I had not realised things had gone so far. Take my advice. Do not set your heart on a man like that. He will freeze the life out of you, for he has not a heart to give you in return. Trust me on this, I know about these things. Now, I think I have had my annual allocation of fresh air and exercise. It certainly makes one peckish. I hope cook has been baking today.'

With an airy wave of the hand, Bella began to pick her way delicately back across the meadow. As she watched her go, Cressie decided that Bella was wrong on any number of scores. For a start, Giovanni was not in the least like Lord Armstrong. It was merely that Bella was hurting, and wished to lash out. You only had to look at the way Giovanni was with Freddie, George, James and Harry, to see that he was not the selfish, self-centred man her father was.

Bella was simply jealous. And she was wrong about Giovanni's reserve too. It was nothing to do with him being cold. Quite the reverse. He had been hurt, hurt so badly that he had lost his muse. And yes, perhaps his decision to turn his skill to commerce was a cold and calculated one, but what was wrong with that? He was the best—he deserved to be recognised as such.

But the thing Bella was most wrong about was her assumption that Cressie—Cressie!— could possibly be imagining herself in love with Giovanni. The thought hadn't even crossed her mind. Would *never* cross her mind. She was the muse he had lost. She was proud to be his muse, and honoured, and in addition, it meant that she could see at first hand whether she had been wrong about art and mathematics and beauty and—and all that stuff which was important, very important, even if she had lost sight of it.

Cressie jumped down from the wall and ran over to join the boys, who were gathering in the kite, flushed from their exertions. 'If you could capture them like this,' she said to Giovanni, 'it would make a painting much more like the truth than the one in the gallery.'

'And far less valuable, sadly. I could sketch them for their mother, though, if you think she would like it?'

'I think she would adore it. That is very thoughtful of you.'

'They are actually quite nice boys, when you get to know them.'

Giovanni handed the kite to Harry and picked up Freddie, throwing him over his shoulders, much to the little boy's delight. 'Gee gee, Gio is a gee gee,' he giggled.

Cressie lagged behind, watching Giovanni gallop across the meadow with Freddie on his back. Bella was right about one thing—he would make an excellent father. It took her by surprise, the sadness that gripped her. Thinking that she would never marry was one thing. Realising what she would be sacrificing, that was quite another.

Giovanni had finally settled upon a pose. Cressie sat sideways on the Egyptian chair, her breeched and booted right leg crossed over her left, one arm resting casually on the chair back, the other on her crossed leg. She looked full on at the painter, her beaver hat provocatively tilted over one eye, her hair wild and hanging free. The tails of her coat hung down almost to the floor, her neckcloth carelessly tied, the buttons of her waistcoat undone.

'I don't look a bit like a man,' she said, when he showed her the preliminary sketches.

'Do you wish to?'

She twisted a strand of hair around her finger, her latest attempt to stop herself biting her fingernails. 'I thought I did. I thought I wanted to *be* a man.'

'I remember you told me you wished just that.'

'But I don't now. I think I like this. It's…'

'Subversive, I hope. I want to show you peeping out from your disguise. You have a very mischievous sense of humour. I want to demonstrate that. And I want to use the clothing to show—I am not sure how, but I want your man's clothes to show more of the woman.'

Cressie giggled. 'Perhaps if you combine Mr Brown with Penthiselea you can achieve that effect.'

'That is it!' Giovanni threw down his charcoal and threw his arms around Cressie. 'You are a genius!'

Smiling and shaking her head in bewilderment, Cressie tried not to notice the instant response of her body to his. 'I am more than happy to be called a genius but I have no idea why you do so. I meant it as a joke.'

'But no, it is perfect. It is outrageous. It will be…'

He kissed his fingertips. The gesture was so dramatic and so typically Italian and so untypically Giovanni that Cressie laughed. 'I don't understand. How can it be so outrageous? Oh!'

As realisation dawned, her smile faded. 'You mean that I will have to…'

'Bare your…'

'Breast.' Cressie swallowed. Her throat was dry. She licked her lips. She looked at Giovanni to find that he was staring at her chest.

'You have beautiful breasts. Speaking as an artist, that is,' he added quickly.

'Do I?'

'Si. Bellissimo.'

Colour slashed Giovanni's cheeks, emphasising their sharpness, giving his face a hungry look. He led her back over to the chair. 'Let me show you. It can be done tastefully.' She sat statue-still as he arranged her coat and waistcoat, as he untied her neckcloth. His fingers were cold, shaking slightly as he undid the six little pearl buttons on the bib of her shirt. She wore only her corsets underneath. When his fingers brushed her skin, she breathed sharply in.

Giovanni loosened the laces. His hand hovered over her breast. Her nipples hardened in anticipation. She could see, from the angle at which his head was bent over her, that his hair grew in a little circular whorl at the back of his head. Heat radiated, from him, from her, from both of them. Her skin was on fire. Sweat prickled at the base of her spine.

Giovanni stood up. 'Then—when we come to paint—then we will...'

Disappointment made her rash. Cressie dragged her corset down, twisting the open neck of the shirt so that the vee shape where the buttons stopped supported her bare breast. 'There, is that what you meant?'

Giovanni simply stared. Her nipple looked a much darker pink against the white of the man's shirt. Cressie hadn't really paid much attention to her nipples before. It seemed to her that it was defiantly pert. She straightened her back. She felt defiantly pert herself. She placed her open palm over her breast, cupping it lightly, shivering as her fingers grazed her aching nipple. His breath came out in a low hiss. His eyes went dark. He was swallowing repeatedly. Desire and power surged together. 'What do you think, Giovanni?'

'I think...' It was his dark smile, the one that made her feel as if she were being twisted tight from the inside. 'I think,' he said, 'that you know perfectly well what I think, Lady Cressida. I just hope you can hold the pose.'

She could not decide whether to be glad or sorry when he disappeared behind his easel again and began to sketch. He drew no grids this time, his movements seemed freer, his concentration much fiercer than before, as he sketched and muttered and scored lines through what he'd drawn, tearing page after page of drawing paper from the board and casting it on to the floor.

It felt like a day had passed, it might have been as little as an hour, when he looked up and smiled triumphantly. 'I have it.'

Her nipple was stiff with cold and nothing else by now. She had no thought but to move before her muscles seized altogether, and to cover herself. 'May I see?'

She hadn't expected him to agree, but he beckoned her over, another change from the previous portrait. 'Well?' he demanded impatiently.

Cressie shook her head in amazement. 'You don't need me to tell you.'

'I do, Cressie.'

'Giovanni, it's brilliant.' She grinned as she stared at herself, roughly outlined in charcoal but nevertheless fully realised. There was no careful symmetry evident in this portrait, though she could see that the angles, of her face to the front, of her body in profile, were quite deliberately chosen. It was the contradictions which she liked best though. A female in man's clothing. A manly pose and a womanly breast. Her face, serious and yet mischievous. And the overall effect, it was strangely sensual, though she could not say how. She looked out from the drawing defiantly, confidently, herself, but not as she had ever seen herself. 'It is—confusing though. I don't know what to think.'

Giovanni smiled with deep satisfaction. 'That is it exactly. Confusing. Inflammatory. Anarchic. Not one thing or the other.'

'It doesn't—I mean I can see that there are some rules, but it seems to me that you have quite deliberately broken many.'

'Poor Cressie, what will your theory say of this painting?'

'I really have no idea.'

'I will prepare the canvas tonight. We can start painting in oil tomorrow. No more today, you must be tired.'

'I was not the one who spent all morning running about with four obstreperous boys. You must be exhausted.'

Giovanni shook his head. 'I enjoyed it, to tell the truth. I had forgotten how exhilarating it is to be young and carefree. I envy them their innocence.'

'Watching you all today—I have achieved at least one of the things I hoped from my time here. I have come to love them for themselves, and not because they are my brothers.' Cressie picked up her cloak and began to smooth out the folds. 'I ought to go and write to Cordelia now. I promised Bella I would, but I confess I have been putting it off.'

'Why?'

'My Aunt Sophia wrote—oh, it's complicated. You wouldn't want to know.'

'Sit down. Tell me about it, I do want to know. Cordelia is the sister who is in London, yes?'

Giovanni took the cloak from her and placed it on the Egyptian chair, guiding her over to the window, where he had placed a rather tatty *chaise-longue* in the embrasure for him to rest on between bouts of painting. 'I am all ears,' he said, 'as you English bizarrely like to say.'

It was a relief to pour out her concerns, and a relief to laugh too, for it was true, Cordelia might lack judgement, she was rash and un-thinking and often very selfish, but she was always amusing company, she had a knack for making sure no one could ever be angry with her for too long, and really some of her exploits were very droll. 'Though why she should wish to watch two men beating each other up with their bare fists, I cannot imagine,' Cressie finished. 'I will have to find a way of making her heed our aunt before she puts herself beyond the pale, though I have no idea how.'

'From what you have said, Cordelia will do exactly as she wishes, whether you intervene or not.'

Cressie smiled. 'You are quite right, and I can't help but admiring her for it. She is like a cat, my youngest sister. You can throw her from the highest of windows and she will always land on her feet.'

'You love your sisters very much.'

'Yes, I do. We are all so different, but I never doubt they would come to my aid if I really needed them. Perhaps it is a result of growing up without Mama. When we were younger and all living here at Killellan, we were very close. Now—well, you know what the situation is now. But I wouldn't be without them. Or my brothers. I can't imagine what it was like, growing up an only child as you did.'

Giovanni shifted uncomfortably. He had become used to suppressing the unwonted urge to confide in Cressie, accustomed to reminding himself that the past was in the past. But the more he denied himself, the more he had begun to realise how isolating was his silence. It was not so much that he wished to talk about it, more that he wished Cressie to know him better. He found he wanted to share some of himself with her. It mattered that she understood him, even just a little. And sitting here so comfortably in the privacy of their studio, with the daylight waning, and the outline of what he hoped would be his magnum opus on the drawing board, with Cressie so relaxed and at her ease sitting beside him, he would never get a better opportunity. Her remark, that their relationship was entirely one-sided, had hit home. It had just taken him a long time to acknowledge that fact.

'You have that look.' Cressie was managing to frown and smile at the same time. 'The look that tells me I've said something you don't like, and you're not going to tell me what it is.'

'You are wrong this time. I am going to tell you. I was just—steeling myself.'

Cressie had kicked off her top boots. Now she folded her legs up underneath her and turned side-on to face him. 'Is it so bad?'

'I do have a family, many sisters and brothers, though none of them are full-blood. Some are known to me, some not, and those who are known will not acknowledge me for the same reason that my mother will not acknowledge me and why my father had me raised by a fisherman's family until he needed an heir. The man who fathered me is Count Fancini. An ancient and extremely wealthy family, with a bloodline which can be traced back until before there were records. I am Count Fancini's bastard. Illegitimate. His baseborn son.'

Cressie actually reeled with shock. Her eyes were huge as she covered her mouth with one hand, the other reaching for his. He ought not to allow her to take it, he did not need the words of pity which she was obviously trying to swallow, but he twined his fingers in hers all the same, and it felt—right. Not pity, but sympathy—he could bear that.

'Oh, Giovanni, how awful.' She was blinking furiously. 'I cannot imagine—I shall never, never complain about my family again. No wonder you were hurt when I joked about wishing my father was someone else. I am so, so sorry. Did you say that your father—your real father—he had you adopted?'

'*Si.*' Giovanni tightened his clasp on her hand. 'For twelve years, I thought myself the son of a fisherman. My father—the man I thought was my father—was a rough man, but kind. He—it was he who took me to Santa Maria del

Fiore. You remember I told you, the church with the whispering gallery? And he taught me to swim. And of course to fish. I was teased by the other boys in the village for the way I look.' He winced, and smacked his forehead. 'This face, it was not at all like the face of the people I called *Mamma* and *Papa*, but I never questioned, and they never breathed a word, my parents. I thought they loved me.'

'Giovanni, of course they did.'

It was like a weight around his heart, this truth. Like a heavy stone he never tried to move, for how could he when the facts were so clear? 'They handed me back to him, Cressie. I was just a child and they gave me back without protest.'

'No. I am sure—that cannot be true, Giovanni. No one who has raised a child as their own could simply hand them over. It would be too painful. Your memory must be playing tricks.'

'I was twelve years old. I remember it perfectly, as if it was yesterday. I remember they made no move to hug me when the carriage came to take me away. I remember the one answer to all my letters was a request to stop writing. My father—my real father—told me he had been paying them to look after me.' Giovanni swallowed, but the lump in his throat would not budge, the stone in his heart seemed heavier than ever. No matter how many times he told himself it didn't matter, he could never quite make himself not care. He dug the knuckles of his free hand into his eyes so hard that he saw red. It didn't help.

Cressie shuffled along the *chaise-longue* and put her arm around his shoulders. She stroked his head, a strange little movement, as if she were trying to tuck a lock of hair he didn't have behind his ear. It was intensely comforting. 'You told me once,' she said softly, 'that what we think and how we feel are often quite different things. You said there was a big gap between logic and instinct. I remember it so well because it struck a chord with me. I know you think you ought to hate them for giving you away, those people. But for twelve years, the better part of your childhood, you thought they were your parents. It would be quite unnatural for you not to love them, even if they did hurt you. Look at me, for goodness' sake. I don't respect my father, I don't like him, there are times when I hate him, but I still love him, and I know that won't ever go away, no matter how hard I try. I've stopped trying to hate him. It is a relief, I promise you.'

Cressie kissed his temple, then resumed her

rhythmic stroking. She was warm against him, soft and pliant, contradictorily more feminine than usual in her man's clothing. Giovanni allowed himself to relax against her, just the tiniest bit. It felt good. 'I don't hate them,' he said. 'They were poor people, they needed the money. I understand that.'

'That's just arrant nonsense.' Cressie stopped her stroking and put her face up so close to his that their noses almost touched. 'You loved them. You were obviously happy with them. They clearly loved you—your father did not have to teach you all those things, swimming and the like. He did not have to take you to that church with the whispering gallery. They cared for you and you loved them as all children love their parents. It must have been awful, beyond awful, for all of you, when they had to give you up. At the very least, you must feel hurt. Your real father is obviously a man of great influence. If he desired your return, I doubt there would have been much to be done to stop him. I am sure they did not abandon you, Giovanni, though I can understand it must have felt like it. I can see why you think you hate them.'

Cressie's truths had always been uncomfortable. Her way of seeing through things to the nub of the matter, it was one of the things he most admired in her, but it was painful to be on the receiving end. Such clarity of thought made it impossible to avoid confronting the truth. And how much worse would it be if he told her the whole unadulterated truth? *Never!* Giovanni pushed her away gently. 'I don't hate my parents,' he said, which was true.

He could almost see the wheels and cogs in Cressie's mind working. He saw the very moment when she decided not to pursue the matter. For a split second, he was relieved. 'Then tell me about your real father,' she said. 'The one you really do hate.'

He was forced to laugh, a hollow sound which made Cressie shiver. 'Blood. My real father is the man who taught me the significance of blood. He is the reason I understand you so well. He is very, very like your own father in character.'

Cressie shuffled back along the sofa and nestled up against him. 'Tell me the whole story,' she said, draping his arm around her shoulders.

Her curls tickled his chin. 'It is a sad story. The sort of story someone else would have turned into a fairytale. I have never told it before.'

'I have often thought fairytales tend towards the tragic. Celia used to read us *Cendrillon*, it was Cassie's favourite story. She loved the romance of a poor little ragged girl marrying a prince, but I always thought what Cendrillon would have preferred would be to have her mama back. We didn't have a wicked stepmother ourselves at that point, of course,' Cressie added with a grin. 'I think Bella would have put quite a different slant on that story. But I am interrupting yours. Please, go on.'

He couldn't think with her so close. Giovanni untangled himself from her embrace and laid his head back against the *chaise-longue* and closed his eyes. 'Once upon a time,' he began, for it was easier to think of this as a story than to relive it, 'there was a rich Italian count. His name was Fancini.'

Cressie shifted round on the seat, the better to watch his face. Shocked beyond measure by what he had thus revealed of his childhood, she could now see quite clearly why Giovanni appeared so cold. To have been abandoned not once but twice—no wonder he was determined no one else would hurt him. As for that woman who had been his lover and his muse—how could she have hurt him when she must have known—no, she did not know, for Giovanni said he had never told anyone. Cressie was to be his first and only confidante. That counted for something, even if he didn't love her as he

had the other woman. Not that that was relevant
in any way. She was not in love with Giovanni.
The very thought of it was—was—not to be
thought of!

But she did find herself thinking of just that
as she listened, wrapping her arms around
herself, mostly to stop herself wrapping them
around Giovanni. She could not possibly be
in love with this man. This strange feeling, a
sort of tightness, a dawning awareness like
a light flickering in the dim recesses of her
mind, waiting for her to turn the corner and
discover—no, that wasn't love. And the ache
in her heart, that was sympathy for the pain he
had suffered, nothing more.

'Count Fancini was of impeccable birth,'
Giovanni continued, 'from a long line of blue-
blooded Tuscans and who counted the Grandu-
cato di Toscana amongst his closest relatives.
The count has a child from his marriage, that
all-important thing, a male child, a son and heir
to the vast country estates and the palazzo in
Florence. The Countess Fancini produces many
more children, but all die or are still-born. The
count, a man of lustful appetites, has several
more healthy children, born, as they say, on
the wrong side of the blanket, but all are females and therefore unworthy.' He opened his

eyes momentarily. 'You see,' he said with a wry smile, 'it is the same the world over.'

Cressie touched his hand briefly, but said nothing. He closed his eyes once more, speaking as if he were far away, talking of another world, of other people, as if none of it were connected to him. Which was completely understandable. How many times had she herself escaped into the fantasy life of Mr Brown? How alike they were in their experiences. An affinity, that was what they had. That was *all* they had. She smoothed her waistcoat down over her shirt. Affinity was a most logical explanation. She couldn't understand why it felt such an unconvincing one.

'One day,' Giovanni was saying, 'Count Fancini met a girl, a beautiful young lady in actual fact, as well born as he, quite a different sort altogether from his other amours. Though he had no business wooing her, being a married man, woo her he did. And Carlotta, for that was the young lady's name, most foolishly imagined herself in love. Her parents had the highest hopes of her making an excellent match—blood and beauty again, you see. These hopes seemed dashed when Carlotta discovered herself with child, but between them, her parents and the father-to-be, Count Fancini, hushed up what could have been a major scandal. Carlotta gave birth in secret. Six months later, still apparently fresh and virginal, she was married off. The boy—for it was, unfortunately, a boy—was given to a childless family of humble origin as their own, and thus, the story ended. Or so thought Carlotta and Count Fancini.'

'And then?' Cressie asked with a sinking feeling. This was a fairytale without a happy ending.

'And then,' Giovanni said, his voice becoming icier in his efforts to maintain his air of detachment, 'the count's only legitimate son tragically died. And the count was by now, for reasons associated with his having been so eager to indulge his lustful appetites, unable to father another child of either sex...'

'Let me guess,' Cressie said fatalistically. 'The count decides an illegitimate son is better than no son at all and has him summarily recalled from his foster parents.'

'Exactly.' Giovanni's smile faded, to be replaced by his satyr look. 'Like your Cendrillon, who in Italian is known as Cenerentola, our poor little fisherman's boy was granted great riches. He was given the best of tutors, taught how to fight with a sword, how to converse politely, how to bow and how to eat with his mouth closed. He was taught how to be a gentleman. He worked hard at his studies, he wanted very much to please his most intimidating and most powerful new father, but the count was a difficult man to satisfy. Giovanni was forbidden all contact with the people he still thought of as his real family. Their names were beaten out of him, and—as I said, finally he was given proof that they had no wish to see him. He knew he ought to be happy living in such luxury, but the truth is that he was lonely. He was still much too rough around the edges to be exposed to society, and he was not permitted to find friends among his father's servants and tenants. Where once he had had the run of the village and the freedom of the sea, now he was confined to the family estate. Beautiful as it was, Giovanni came to think of it as a prison.'

'I don't know what to say.' Cressie was struggling not to cry, all the more so because Giovanni was so determinedly unemotional. Whereas she was feeling—what? She didn't know what to think either. She couldn't allow herself to think. Not about that. Not about him or her feelings for him.

Oblivious of the turmoil raging in her heart, Giovanni shrugged her hand from his arm.

'There is nothing to say. I was never hungry. I had an excellent education. I was still a bastard, but I was as close to being a legitimised bastard as it is possible to be. My father formally recognised me and had his will changed. I should have felt privileged.'

'But?'

'I tried, just as you did, Cressie, to do what was expected of me. I tried to be grateful, I tried to pay back what was being given with obedience. I was miserable.'

'Which is why you recognised it in me?'

'Exactly. Like you, I fooled myself into thinking that if only I tried harder I could want what my father wanted for me, but I could not. The one thing I had of my own was my art. I'd been drawing since before I could read or write. When he saw how much it meant to me he had my paints taken from me. Drawing, you see, is a hobby for women. Painting is carried out by artisans. Neither are acceptable activites for the son and heir of a count.'

'Like mathematics for the daughter of an earl,' Cressie said. 'At least my father merely discourages me. I shall never think of him as a tyrant again.' She uncurled her legs and wriggled her toes to rid herself of the pins and needles which had taken hold. 'Was it then your mother, Carlotta, who encouraged you to paint?'

Giovanni swore. 'I met her only once. She did not want to know me. Her reputation was of far more import than her first-born. It was when Count Fancini decided to send me off to the army to finish my education that I finally rebelled. He said he would cut me off. I told him I could make my own way in life without him. He told me I would return with my tail between my legs. I have not seen him since. It has been fourteen years.'

This last part of his story was told in a flat voice, without pretence of distance or objectivity. Giovanni looked drained and horribly close to defeated. It was clear there was more, much more, that he had not told her, but to ask him now would most likely send him into the darkest of tempers or the deepest of depressions.

'So you cast off your blood and made a living out of beauty,' Cressie said.

She could restrain herself no longer. Jumping to her feet, she pulled him with her, putting her arms around his waist and resting her head on his chest. She could feel his heart beating, slow and steady. Her senses were alight, attenuated, alive with an awareness of him. She couldn't fool herself any longer. This wanting, this dragging, drugging insistent wanting, she ought to have known it could be nothing else.

She reached up on tiptoe to smooth his hair, unable to stop herself fluttering kisses over his forehead, his eyes, the sharp planes of his cheeks. 'I'm so sorry, I'm so sorry,' she whispered over and over. Sorry for him. Sorry for her own stupid self. 'Sorry,' she said, pressing herself more tightly against him, as if burrowing into him would bring comfort, telling herself that was all she wished, while at the same time her hands stroked his head, his neck, shoulders, and her mouth sought his and her heart wished for so much more.

When their lips met, she felt his resistance. She closed her eyes and pressed tighter into him. Kissing. Little tiny kisses to comfort and reassure and to take away the pain. Kisses that soothed, then kisses that slowed as he began to respond. Kisses that became a kiss. Her lips clung to his as tightly as her hands, her body. She felt as if she were pouring her heart out in her kiss. And it was that, not the salt taste of her tears, which made her stop lest she betray herself.

'I'm sorry. I'm so sorry,' Cressie said, tearing herself free. 'I doubt you feel better for having unburdened yourself right now. My own experience with such confessions as you have drawn from me is that all you will feel is exhausted. But you will feel the benefit of it soon, Giovanni, and see things more clearly.'

Loath as she was to leave him, she knew him well enough. He would not like to have the details picked over or analysed. Besides, she needed time alone with her own thoughts, time to reconcile herself to *that* thought. She touched his cheek, almost overwhelmed by what she was feeling, desperate now to get away before she broke down. 'You will create a new sort of beauty here, with me as your model, yes? I must go and write to my sister now. Thank you for trusting me with your story.'

She kissed his other cheek, then draping her cloak around her made for the door. Giovanni stood still, his eyes blank. Cressie felt as if her heart were being squeezed, seeing him so. She loved him so much. There, it was said.

Chapter Eight

'I categorically refuse to see him. You have to get rid of him, Cressie, I beg of you.'

Bella gripped at the sleeve of her stepdaughter's dress plaintively. Pink silk striped with grey, the gown had a plain round neck, puffed sleeves which tapered to end just past the wrist and a pretty design of scrollwork around the hem in the form of waves. It was one of Cressie's favourites, but it crushed very easily. She tried to unpick her stepmother's fingers, but Bella refused to let go.

'Sir Gilbert has travelled all the way from London; surely you can at least grant him a short audience. It would be a most sensible precaution. You must think of the health of your unborn child. There is no disputing he is considered the pre-eminent man in his field.'

'No!' Bella threw herself across the salon and dropped dramatically on to a sofa. 'No, no, no! I told your father, I was most plain with him. I simply will not have that horrible man touch me again. His fingers are like—like frozen twigs. And his nails are far too long for his calling. They are positively sharp, Cressie. You cannot imagine.'

Cressie could, unfortunately, imagine very well thanks to Bella's graphic description. She shuddered and pressed her knees together. 'Could you not simply consult with him, discuss your symptoms without subjecting yourself to the rigours of an examination? You have been quite unwell, after all.'

'Because this child is a girl. I have been sick, that is all.'

Bella folded her arms protectively over her stomach. Her really very small stomach. In fact Bella herself, Cressie thought, seemed to be shrinking. Was she losing weight?

'Please, Cressie. Don't force me to see him. His head looks like an egg peeking above a bird's nest. He has one eyebrow permanently raised and a way of looking at one—he makes me feel as if I have committed some sort of heinous crime. And his voice. It is cadaverous, all whispery and monotone and cold. I tell you, he would not look out of place in a graveyard. He makes me feel as if *I* shall not be long in taking my own place there. As for his hands—but I have told you about his hands.'

Bella was now wringing hers together tragically. Her feet, no longer swollen but clad in blue satin slippers, were dancing a frantic little two-step, thanks to the way she was jiggling her legs, something of which she seemed to be wholly unaware. Why, if she disliked the surgeon so much, had she allowed him to attend her at all three of her confinements? Cressie rolled her eyes. The answer was obvious. Lord Armstrong must have insisted. It was wrong of her, but she couldn't help thinking that it would be gratifying to help thwart her father just once. Telling herself that she did so only for Bella's sake, Cressie nodded. 'Very well. I am sure you exaggerate—the poor man cannot be so grotesque as you describe but I will send him away. I have to admit that you are looking much improved these last few days.'

'The sickness has gone, certainly.' Lady Armstrong sank back on to the sofa with a huge sigh of relief. 'Thank you, Cressida. I very much appreciate this, I truly do.'

The words seemed to be genuinely heart-felt. Cressie was touched and rather pleased at this latest development in their relationship. As Bella said, they would never be bosom companions, but there was honesty and an understanding between them which meant they could exist, if not in harmony, then at least in peace. Even the two oldest boys seemed to have noticed the thaw in their relationship. James and Harry rarely played the obnoxious brat when in their mother's and Cressie's company, whereas before they had misbehaved terribly, feeding off the enmity between the two women. Which meant that Freddie and George no longer followed their lead with their own childish tantrums. Rarely did Cressie wish, as when she first took on her role to teach them, to tie them up and gag them, or to run screeching from the room tearing at her hair in frustration. Her brothers would never be angelic but they were nearly always biddable, and indeed likable, these days. She supposed that Harrow would soon change all that, if her father and the excruciating man he called his friend, Bunny Fitzgerald, were anything to go by.

She paused in front of a looking-glass in the hallway. Her hair was a mess, as usual. She had stopped pinning it up during the day, for she had to take it down each time she sat for her portrait, and so instead tied it back with a ribbon. Today's was dusky pink like her gown. Giovanni said she suited this particular colour but should never wear a paler shade. She could sort of see what he meant when she saw how well this gown suited her, but she had no idea why.

The ribbon dangled from her fingers as she stared at her reflection. It had been almost a week since she'd started posing for the Mr Brown portrait. Almost a week since Giovanni had told her the story of his past. And almost a week since she'd realised that she was in love with him.

She'd hoped the feeling would go away of its own volition. Melt away in the same way as it had crept up on her. The wild elation she felt every time she looked at him, the warmth that enveloped her when she thought about him, the ache in her heart when she reminded herself that every day that passed was another closer to him leaving. But she didn't really wish it would go away, and it had not. The opposite in fact. Every time she saw him, it seemed to expand, this feeling, filling her with a longing which was physical and more. Each moment she spent apart from him was a moment lost.

Each little fact she managed to extract from him was a treasure, to be stored up and added, like pieces of tesserae, to complete the mosaic of him. Not that she believed she'd ever have the complete picture. There was no time, and in any event, Giovanni was a man who would never give all of himself to anyone. That he had given her so much already, so much more than he'd ever given anyone before, that was one of the things which made it easier for her to bear the thought of his absence.

She loved him. In one sense it made no difference at all. There was no point in contemplating any sort of future with him. She knew for a fact that Giovanni had no interest in any sort of alliance, sanctified by the church or not. Of her own wishes, she was not so certain, but she was beginning to conclude that marriage, even if it was to a man of her own choosing rather than her father's, was one of the things she'd been silently rebelling against all her life. She didn't want to be someone's wife. She wanted to be herself. She still had no idea what that meant, but she did know it didn't require a change of name.

In another sense, though, being in love changed everything. Time took on a strange quality. When she was with Giovanni it accelerated, the hours flew past unnoticed. When apart it slowed inexorably, almost seemed to stop altogether. The relationship between love and time. Maybe she could occupy herself with a new theory in the long endless days after he was gone, she thought wryly.

For the moment, everything had taken on a new meaning. She saw and heard things differently. Her mood swung wildly from exhilaration to despair in seconds. The stupidest things made her cry. Or laugh. She was in a constant state of awareness. She wanted, passionately wanted, to have everything and all of Giovanni that she could. She wanted to know him inside and out. She wanted him. She really, really wanted him. But ever since he had begun on this second painting, ever since he had named her his muse, he had steadfastly refused to surrender to the smouldering tension which fired each portrait session. He would not make the first move for fear of breaking the spell. Cressie was certain that the chemistry between them could only enhance it. Which meant she would have to make the first move. And so far, she had been unable to pluck up the courage to do so.

A solicitous cough behind her made her jump. 'Sir Gilbert Mountjoy wishes me to inform Lady Armstrong that he must leave for another urgent appointment in fifteen minutes, my lady,' Lord Armstrong's butler said. 'I informed her ladyship, but she said that you had the matter in hand.'

'I do.' Cressie hurriedly tied her hair ribbon. 'Lead the way, Myers.'

'I tell you, Giovanni, I had been convinced that Bella's unflattering description of Sir Gilbert could only be much exaggerated,' Cressie exclaimed an hour later, sitting in the attic studio, 'but in fact it was nigh on perfect, possibly even understated. He is a veritable death's head of a man. I cannot blame her at all for fleeing from his ministrations. He really does have fingers like icy twigs. I shuddered when he shook my hand. Why any woman with child would let that walking cadaver anywhere near them is quite beyond me.'

Giovanni smiled over the top of the easel. 'So the venerable surgeon has been despatched, never to return. What will Lord Armstrong make of that, I wonder?'

'I could not care less,' Cressie said impatiently. 'Bella has an excellent point. If my father cannot make the effort to be in attendance, he has no right to dictate arrangements for the birth. After all, *he* is not the one who has to suffer the privations. Do you think she is looking better, Giovanni?'

'I think she is certainly looking thinner. Has she ceased to devour half a patisserie shop each afternoon?'

'She's not eating much at all, but she seems to be much the better for it.' Cressie lapsed into silence. She loved to watch Giovanni at work. He had a special painting frown which was not at all like his satyr look. When he was happy with something, he smiled lopsidedly and tapped his brush on the edge of his palette three times. When he wasn't happy, he pressed his thumb hard into his forehead. For some reason known only to himself, he had abandoned his normal custom and was painting this portrait in his shirtsleeves, discarding his waistcoat as well as his top coat. As a result he had managed to get paint or oil or pigment or charcoal, sometimes a mix of all, on his shirt by the end of each session. When she suggested a smock he laughed scornfully. He seemed to have an infinite supply of snow-white shirts anyway, for he turned up each morning to paint her brothers looking as immaculate as ever. Only here, in their attic studio, did he relax both his dress code and his behaviour.

* * *

'I had a letter from Cordelia today.' Cressie rolled her neck and stretched her legs as they took a short break, an hour or so later. 'She says that Aunt Sophia is exaggerating matters. She denies any knowledge of a wager on the number of her suitors, and informs me that there is absolutely and positively no need for either Bella or myself to come to town. Were it not for that last remark, I would be a little reassured.'

Giovanni stood frowning at the canvas, obviously unhappy with some element of the painting. 'But you are not reassured?'

Cressie wandered over to stand beside him. 'I think Cordelia is scheming. I suspect all these silly things my aunt has herself in a tizzy over are a ruse to deflect attention from Cordelia's real indiscretions, and I think Cordelia knows perfectly well that I would smell a rat the moment I saw her. What I don't know is what I should do about it.'

'You said yourself that your sister will do as she wishes whether you intervene or not,' Giovanni said distractedly.

'Yes, but...'

'I think it is the hair. I cannot capture the exact way it falls over your eye just here.' Giovanni swept a long curling tress of her hair over her forehead. 'I wonder if you tilted your head a little more like this—so. Or tucked your hair behind your ear, perhaps. Let me demonstrate, if I may.' Cressie stood quite still, concentrating on breathing. 'Yes, that is better,' Giovanni said. 'If you had perhaps a pearl earring that would be...yes.'

His fingers were tangled in her hair. His thumb caressed the lobe of her ear. Did he realise he was doing it? She could feel his breath as he leaned towards her. His fingers were stroking in delicious little circling movements, the area just behind her ear. Was it accidental, this feather-light touch in this most sensitive spot, or was he just thinking about the painting? She risked a glance. Dark eyes. *That* look, the flaring-heat one. Not the painting then. The knot of excitement which was permanently present when she was with him, when she thought of him, which was only temporarily unravelled when she touched herself at night in the dark thinking of him, the knot began to tighten.

'I have a pearl drop,' Cressie said.

She meant an earring. It didn't sound as if she meant an earring. It didn't look as if Giovanni thought so either. His eyes flickered closed. 'You have a pearl drop,' he said softly, making the words sound even more erotic.

His mouth hovered over her ear. His fingers played up and down the line from her ear to her neck, threading and unthreading through her hair. Though she had pulled her shirt closed when he had called a break, she had not bothered to pull her corsets back into place. The cotton of her shirt was abrasive on her nipples. They were stiff and engorged.

Giovanni kissed her earlobe, taking it gently into his mouth and sucking. He licked his way around the contours of her ear, as if he were painting it with his tongue. His thumb stroked the pulse at the base of her throat. His other hand crept around her waist and slid down to cup her bottom. She knew he would come to his senses any moment. She knew that if he did, she would most likely lose hers. She had to find the courage. Cressie slipped her arms around Giovanni's waist and lifted her head up to kiss him full on the lips.

He did not resist. She slid her arms up his back, flattening her palms along the ridges of his muscles, feeling the heat of his skin through his linen shirt, opening her mouth to him, silently pleading with him not to stop.

He didn't. His kiss was languorous, his lips

clinging to hers, not with a violent thirst but drinking from her as if she were nectar. Slowly, his tongue licked across her bottom lip. She dug her fingers into his back and arched into him, flattening her breasts against him. His kiss deepened. His fingers tightened on her bottom. His breath was warm on her face as he kissed her, and kissed her, and kissed her.

Slowly, like a dreamer awakening, he stopped and began to disengage himself from her embrace. What to do? She didn't know what to do. And then she did. For they were the same, she and he. That's what he had said. Kindred spirits. 'I dreamt of you last night, Giovanni,' Cressie said in the barest whisper.

Her words instantly arrested his retreat. 'What did you dream?' he asked. Her words from the whispering gallery. He understood. And now she must turn his words into hers. 'I was watching you undressing. You knew I was watching.' She hesitated. 'I was touching myself.'

His pupils were huge. She had his entire attention, fixed unwavering on her. But he did not move towards her. 'Cressie…'

'Like this,' she said, pushing back her coat and waistcoat, sliding one hand inside the open neck of her shirt, cupping her breast. Her heart was pounding. She was hot, but she was not at all embarrassed. 'I was touching myself like this, Giovanni.'

He moaned. A low guttural sound, it found an echo in her own sigh as she circled her aching nipple. His hand reached for her breast then dropped. He stared as she touched herself, fascinated. It was empowering and extremely arousing, the way he looked at her, the way she could make him look at her.

'I dreamt you saw me,' Cressie whispered. 'You were pulling your shirt over your head, and you turned around to look at me. I dreamt that when you saw me, you called to me. "Help me, Cressie," you said. And I did.' She let go of her breast and pulled his shirt from his trousers. Up slid her palms on his skin, finally on his skin, as she pulled the folds of his shirt until he tore it off and threw it across the room.

His skin was not tanned but a beautiful olive colour. The dip from his ribs to his abdomen was clearly defined, almost hollow. Black hair ran in a thin line up from his navel spreading out over his chest. His nipples were dark brown. She touched them, rubbing her cheek against the rough hair of his chest. Don't say beautiful, she told herself, don't say it. But he was. Truly beautiful.

'What happened next, Cressie?' he said, his breathing shallow.

He seemed mesmerised by her. He would do as she bid, but only if she bid him. He wanted her, though he was terrified to break the artistic spell. But he wanted her to break it. She could see that, in the way he looked at her, in the tension which made him seem coiled, every muscle tight, poised. *What next?*

Echoes in the whispering gallery. She dragged her shirt over her head, mirroring his movement. 'You touched me here,' she said, taking his hands and laying them on her breasts, which had escaped from her corset. 'You touched me.'

He did. As he had before, as she had imagined that day, and each night since. He cupped her breasts, lowering his mouth he hungrily licked around their contours. He sucked hard on each nipple then circled with his tongue. Heat, fiercer than any she had felt before, engulfed her. Every part of her seemed to be connected. Her nipples, her fingertips, her ears, her toes. Even the backs of her knees tingled. *What next?*

'The softest of skin,' she whispered. 'I wanted you to find the softest of skin.'

'Softest,' he repeated, slipping his hand inside her breeches.

There was not enough room. Hurriedly she undid the buttons. His hand found the gap between the legs of her pantalettes. Cressie gasped. How could his touch be so different from her own? She had imagined him touching her there, but she had never dreamed it could be like this. The way he touched her, so gently, like the fluttering of a feather over her skin, and yet it seared.

'What next?' he asked, his voice ragged against her ear.

'I needed to know if we were the same,' Cressie answered. 'I needed to touch you. "Let me touch you," I said. And you unfastened your trousers. You took my hand, and you guided me, you taught me.'

She prayed that he would, since she was beginning to lose confidence, and her prayers were for once answered. Giovanni took her hand and slid it inside his trousers. Soft hair at the top of his thigh. Then rougher. His groan was louder and less restrained when she cupped him. Heavy. Warm. He contracted in her hand.

'Cressie. I don't think…I can't think. Cressie, what next?'

What next? 'Show me,' she said. 'I asked you to show me how to touch you. And you touched me too. Show me, Giovanni, show me

now as you did in my dream. Show me how to
do to you what you did to me in the whispering gallery.'

She could sense his hesitation. He knew she
was playing an erotic game. This was no mere
recounting of a dream but a form of seduction.
He lifted his head to look at her, tilted her chin
to look deep into her eyes, searching. She did
not know what he found there, only that it was
pivotal. The shift was almost tangible, from
doing her bidding to his taking control.

Giovanni's smile was entirely sensual. 'In
the whispering gallery,' he said, 'I have never
so much in my life wanted you to touch me.
Wanted it to be me touching you.' He was kissing her neck now, his fingers stroking her thigh,
with his other hand easing her breeches down.
She had taken off her boots when she broke
her portrait pose. 'In the whispering gallery, I
wanted to be with you like this,' Giovanni said,
lowering her to the floor, quickly kicking off
his shoes, discarding the rest of his clothing
to kneel before her, between her spread legs,
completely naked.

'I wanted to do this.' When he leaned over
her to kiss her, her breasts brushed his chest,
the most delightful *frisson*, but not nearly
enough. His mouth was hot, his kisses dark,

drawing the tension up from deep inside her like water from a well. 'You were aflame in the whispering gallery,' he said, 'you were slick and wet, weren't you?' His fingers slid slowly inside her, and Cressie gasped. 'And I was hard,' Giovanni said, his voice so low it vibrated. 'Feel how hard I was, Cressie.'

He took her hand and wrapped it around his erection. She couldn't help noticing how different he was from Giles. Darker skin. Thicker. When she clasped her fingers around him, he pulsed. When he slid his fingers deeper inside her, she cried out.

Her cry released any vestige of restraint in both of them. Giovanni pulled her hard up against him and began to stroke her, his fingers sliding over her, circling her, slipping into the heat of her then back over, sliding, sliding, like his tongue sliding inside her mouth now. She knew she should be returning his touch, but it was all she could do to hold on to him as he touched her, fingers and tongue, her mouth, her sex, bringing her to a height she had not thought possible to climb, pushing her mercilessly on until she climaxed, feeling as if she were splitting, pulsing around his fingers, her mouth pressing hot, wild kisses into his throat, his shoulders, his heaving chest. But it was not enough this time, her own completion. Not nearly enough. She wanted to share it with him. 'Show me,' she insisted, 'Giovanni, tell me what you want, show me.'

She thought he would resist her. She saw the effort there in his eyes. Then she began inexpertly to stroke him, and he arched his back, his hand sinking into her flank. 'Like this?' she asked. He muttered in Italian. Something that sounded like a plea. Then he kissed her again, putting his hand over hers to slow her, showing her how to hold him. 'Like this?' she asked again. But even as she did, she felt him tighten, felt the pulse of blood and the rush of seed, and heard him cry out, a painful cry as if she had released the very devil, as he spent himself over her hand.

The speed of his climax, the unstoppable nature of it, swept Giovanni into a strange vacuum, a world where he floated in wholly unaccustomed bliss for the longest, sweetest moment. It was not that he had forgotten, he was certain of that, even though it had been years. This felt different. Completely different. Apart from anything else, he had never, in the past, had any difficulty in controlling his release, for those women he had pleasured had expectations. Expectations he had not only met, but surpassed.

His face was buried in Cressie's hair. Her breasts were pressed against his chest. He could feel her heart racing. His own was pounding heavily. He ran his fingers down the perfect curve of her spine. The line of beauty. He should be ashamed by how quickly he had unravelled, of his lack of restraint, but he was not. He felt none of the things he had felt before— no ennui, no sadness, no sense of emptiness nor even the slightest hint of the disgust which had seized him when he had been forced to sell himself in order to survive until his artistic success made it no longer necessary. It had become a habit, performed like the most perfunctory of tasks. But this, this was very different.

Cressie's arms were wrapped tight around his waist. The salty, musky scent of sex mingled with the familiar smell of her, lavender and chalk and freshness. Her face was pressed into his chest. Her breath was soft on his skin. It only now occurred to him how bold she had been. She was no experienced woman seeking amusement, nor was she one of those women seeking the relief of a fresh male body from the tired, familiar one of her husband. But she had been determined, nevertheless, despite her very limited experience, to seduce him. Not for her own pleasure, but for his.

It was that, Giovanni realised, which made it so very, very different. She wanted to please him. Her pleasure was in pleasing him. She had given herself to him unselfishly, encouraged him to take what he wanted and demanded that he show her what he desired. No woman had ever done that before. All they had been interested in was what his body could do for theirs. Cressie wanted him for himself.

As if he needed further proof, she stirred and sat up, smiling shyly, blushing, as she pushed her hair back from her face. 'I hope my lack of expertise did not spoil things for you.'

Giovanni winced. 'Rather it was my lack of control which—Cressie, why did you do that?'

'I wanted to show you that surrendering to passion will make you a greater painter not a lesser one.'

'So you did it to prove a point?'

Cressie dropped her eyes and tugged self-consciously at her corset, pulling it back up over her breasts. When she looked at him again, her blush had deepened. 'That is not the real reason. I—after the whispering gallery—I needed to know, Giovanni, that it was not just me who felt—this. To prove something to both of us, I suppose.'

Disarmed by her frankness, he was also uneasy, for he sensed that she was nevertheless holding something back. Giovanni got to his feet, pulling her up with him, and picked her shirt and breeches up from the floor, hastily pulling on his own trousers. The sense of euphoria which had thrown him high in the air vanished, dropping him abruptly back down to earth like a kite which suddenly loses the wind. Angry with himself for having even half-formed the thought that he would give anything to be able to make love to Cressie properly, for even starting to imagine her response, Giovanni grabbed his own shirt and pulled it quickly over his head. She was sitting on the Egyptian chair pulling on her boots and looking horribly forlorn. The twisting in his gut warned him too late what he had risked. That she had risked so much more, and all for his sake made him feel quite sick with guilt. Yet he could not make himself regret it. That feeling, the aftermath of his climax, that feeling of bliss, of real ecstasy, of completion, he would not regret that.

Dio, what a self-centred bastard he was. As if anything was possible between them with his

past. As if he would ever inflict his sordid self
on such a unique creature. He did not deserve
to even fantasise about her. He had to put an
end to this somehow, without hurting her feelings and without revealing the shameful facts
behind the necessity to end it. He had nothing
to offer Cressie save her portrait. It sickened
him, knowing how close he had come to ruining her. The taste of what might have been
was bitter, but he swallowed it down as he knelt
in front of her, taking her hands between his.
'I say nothing because I don't know what to
say,' Giovanni said, trying for once to speak
as candidly as she deserved. 'I have no words
to thank you for being so—so brave and so—
to take such a risk—you have great courage.'

'Giovanni, I have not—'

'No, let me speak. What you did for me,
it was beautiful, but I cannot allow it to happen again. It was my fault. No, I will not let
you take the blame, Cressie. I knew exactly
what I was doing. I could have stopped, but I
did not—do not pretend that you think differently.' He touched her forehead, the soft plane
of her cheek which he loved for being so very
different from his own, the sweet curve of her
lips which from the moment he saw her he had
wanted to kiss. 'Despite your years, you are

an innocent. And I am not. It is not right, for me to take what you offer. Not for any reason, and especially not in the name of art. I will not pretend that I will find it easy, but I won't take advantage of you. You deserve far more, far better than me.'

'You're not taking advantage of me.'

'Are you angry?' Giovanni asked, puzzled by the mulish note in her voice.

'I won't be patronised.' Cressie pushed his hand away and got to her feet. 'You're not using me. If anything, I was using you. I wanted to see what it would be like, and now I know. Perhaps now that we have brought this—tension—between us to some sort of conclusion, we will be able to focus on the task in hand. Which, I may remind you, is the completion of our little experiment.'

'You think I was patronising you? In what way was I patronising you?' Giovanni asked, struggling to understand her sudden change in mood. How could she have misconstrued what he said?

Cressie strode over to her favourite position at the window. *'It is my fault. I will not let you take the blame. You deserve better.'* She threw herself down on the window seat, and almost immediately jumped back up again. 'I

am six-and-twenty years old. I am an intelligent woman and contrary to what you said, not
without experience. I knew perfectly well what
I was doing, Giovanni, and if—and I say *if*—I
chose to do it again, then it would be because I
wanted to, and not because you have somehow
put me under your spell. I can make up my own
mind, as you have spent the past two months
telling me.' She strode over to him, standing
with her hands on her hips, her eyes bright with
temper. 'If you wished to put your mind at rest
as to my expectations, you had only to ask.'

'Cressie, that is not—'

'Take your hands off me!' She pushed his
chest so forcefully that he staggered back. 'Did
you think that one touch from the Adonis of
the art world would make me fall at your feet
as no doubt hundreds of other women have? Or
worse, being your muse, did you worry that I'd
fall in love with you? Well, I've done neither
of those things.'

She dashed a hand over her eyes and took
several deep breaths. Her hair covered her face.
Her shoulders were hunched. She was obviously
trying hard not to cry. He wanted to put his
arms around her, but suspected she would strike
him if he did. *Inferno! This is what he got for
attempting to be honest!* His conscience pricked

him. Not wholly honest. Nowhere near wholly honest, but he could never sully Cressie's ears with the unadorned, unpalatable truth.

She had pushed her hair back from her face again. Her cheeks were streaked with tears. He hated to see her cry, knowing how much she hated it herself. 'Cressie, I swear, it was not at all my intention to upset you. I only wanted...'

'To warn me off.' She sniffed. 'There was no need, Giovanni. You have made it absolutely clear that you have no wish to share your life with anyone, and my own plans for the future don't include any man,' she said with a toss of her head.

It was ridiculous, but it was as painful as if she had stabbed him. 'You have plans? You haven't mentioned any plans.'

'Why should I? You form no part of them, nor wish to.' Cressie took a deep breath. When she continued, the hard edge had disappeared from her voice. She looked deflated. 'That was unkind of me, Giovanni, I beg your pardon. I did not tell you my plans because they are only half-formed. I am thinking of writing to my sister Celia in A'Qadiz. She has established a new system of schooling there, which educates girls as well as boys. For some time she has been endeavouring to increase the number of schools but has been struggling to find suitable teachers. I believe I have a talent for teaching. I have come to enjoy it, and I think that in A'Qadiz Celia would give me the freedom to experiment with new methods. I don't know what she'll say, but if her reaction is positive—well, it means that I am no longer dependent on my father. And it means I could have finally found my true calling.'

'Arabia! That is halfway round the world. Could you not teach here in England?'

'In a ladies' seminary you mean? I cannot embroider, you know I cannot draw, and I have no wish at all to spend my days beating the basics of arithmetic into the heads of a clutch of girls who see its only application in calculating the annual income of their future husband.' Cressie clapped her hand over her mouth. 'Now *I* am being patronising, but even if there are young women out there who wish to learn what I can teach, they will not be permitted to do so. In A'Qadiz, Celia's husband, Prince Ramiz, is very forward looking and wants the best for all his people. He supports Celia's desire to see girls educated in the same subjects as boys. It is revolutionary, and in some parts of their kingdom it is being resisted, but—you see what a challenge it would be?'

What he could see was that the evangelical sparkle was back in her eyes. He could see that she meant it when she said she hadn't considered him at all as part of her future. Which was exactly what he wanted. So why did it hurt? 'I see that it is a challenge you would relish,' Giovanni said tightly.

His own contrariness angered him. He'd thought his future perfectly mapped until he met Cressie. He wandered across the room to stand in front of the easel. Mr Brown peered out at him from the canvas, mischievous and sensual and subversive, just as he'd hoped. The colours were vibrant, the brush strokes clearly visible, the portrait itself less defined, more like a sweeping impression of Cressie than a precise mirror-like representation. It would not sell. It was too different. He thought it was good, he thought it was innovative, but he'd been wrong before. If this was his future, then his future was going to be a struggle.

A struggle he would have to make alone. How ironic. Alone, free of demands and obligations, free of the need to sell himself for his art, that was what he'd dreamt of back in the early days. Alone. The word took on a different meaning now that he had surrendered himself to passion. Alone meant being without Cressie.

Alone no longer meant safety, security, success.
It meant loneliness.

What an idiot he was! He should be glad
that Cressie had her own plans. Glad that she
was looking forwards to a future of her own
choosing, glad that she saw no place for him
there. It was a mistake to imagine what had
happened between them was in any way pro-
found. A release of pent-up desire, that is all it
was. And this absurd wish to divest himself of
all his secrets, to confess all—what the devil
was he thinking?

'What about you, Giovanni? What does your
future hold?' Cressie stood at his elbow. How
many times had she stood there beside him, inspecting his canvases, speaking her thoughts
which were almost always a reflection of his
own, and even more often taking him aback
with her insights, for she seemed able to see
behind the paint to his intentions. Would he be
able to develop this new di Matteo style without her? He had no option.

'I will finish this portrait of Mr Brown,'
Giovanni said brusquely, 'and that is the only
part of my future you need concern yourself
with.'

Cressie picked up her cloak. Giovanni clearly
wanted her to leave, no doubt already wish-

ing what had passed between them undone. She would not allow him to spoil it for her. For those precious moments, he had been hers and hers alone. For those precious moments, she had allowed her heart free rein and given him all of herself. But he didn't want her, and now she ought to be very glad indeed that she had not betrayed herself. She would not add her broken heart to the burden he already carried around with him. Wrapping the cloak around her, she managed a bright and completely false smile. 'Very well. Since you have no need of me, I shall go and progress my own plans.'

Closing the door of the attic behind her, Cressie bit the inside of her cheek hard. She would write to her publisher. Mr Freyworth could not fail to be impressed by the results she had achieved with her brothers. And if he was not, she would find another publisher. That, at least, was something she could control. Her stupid, contrary heart, now that was something else entirely.

Chapter Nine

It was a beautiful English late-spring day, the sky cobalt blue, the hedgerows bursting into life, studded with cow parsley, celandine and campion. Primroses huddled in bright yellow clumps in the lee of the stone walls which bordered one side of the road. The woodlands were bright with bluebells, fluffy white lambs gambolled in the rolling fields and the trees were awash with fresh green foliage. 'It is as perfect an English idyll as you could wish for, if you were that kind of artist,' Cressie said, glancing over to Giovanni, who was sitting beside her on the gig.

'Thankfully I am not. Flowers tend to be painted by flowery painters,' he replied witheringly.

Cressie smiled. 'I can think of no adjective less applicable to you than flowery.'

Giovanni bowed. 'I will take that as a compliment. Tell me, why are you so eager for us to take tea with your neighbours today?'

'Aren't you tired of being cooped up at Killellan?' In fact, it was she who was feeling claustrophobic. In the aftermath of what might well be her one and only experience of making love to the man she loved, even if they hadn't technically made love, Cressie had discovered yet another example of logic and instinct being at war. There could be no future for them, that was plain, so it would be futile to waste any more time being in love with him. Except she was in love with him, and she couldn't persuade herself not to be. He kept his distance, as promised. She kept hers. Except that every time they were alone together the distance narrowed to nothing in the glances they exchanged, the looks quickly disguised, sometimes just in the way they talked to each other. It hung there, unacknowledged but palpable like a spectre at the feast, the attraction between them. Giovanni at least had the diversion of his painting to occupy his thoughts. Cressie—Cressie was plain frustrated most of the time. She'd thought getting outside, away from the studio and the portrait and all the attendant emotions and memories, would dissipate the tension. But it was still present in the way he sat as far away from her on the bench of the gig as possible, in the way his hand seemed always to be in the process of avoiding her.

Cressie forced her attention back to the road, though the horse was so familiar with the journey, on account of Lord Armstrong's housekeeper being the daughter of Lady Innellan's butler, that she really had no need to do more than keep a loose hold on the reins and point him vaguely in the right direction. 'You have barely been over the door since you arrived, save that one day kite-flying in the park with the boys,' she prompted Giovanni, who seemed distracted, lost deep in the recesses of his complex mind. 'I thought you might appreciate a change of scene.'

'I will have a change of scene soon enough when I return to London,' he replied tersely.

He'd been mentioning his departure more and more. Was he managing her expectations, or his own? Cressie wondered. One positive effect it had. The desire to tell him how she felt was well and truly under wraps. She would be horrified if he guessed the depth of her feelings for him and therefore made every effort to ensure he did not, sometimes wittering inanely for hours about Celia and teaching, even though it was much too early for her letter even to have reached A'Qadiz, far less for her sister to reply. 'I have a confession to make,' she said with forced brightness. 'I accepted the invitation to tea not just to get away from Killellan. I had another motive.'

'That sounds ominous.'

'It was meant to be a surprise, a nice surprise, for you. Don't spoil it by making me tell you.'

'Cressie, I have told you before that I don't like surprises. I have had enough of them in my life and none of them have been remotely nice. Which is why I cannot abide surprises.'

'Oh very well, then.' Cressie sighed. 'I discovered from Bella that one of the Innellans' guests is someone I thought you might be very interested to meet.'

Giovanni frowned. 'Why?'

Cressie hesitated, wondering if she had been a little rash. After all, Giovanni had not actually said he intended to paint anything other than this one portrait in his new style. But he was so passionate about it, he surely could not mean to return to his perfect pictures, even if they did earn him pots of money. Could he?

'He is apparently something of an expert on the latest vogues in art,' Cressie confessed in a rush. 'I thought you might like to talk to him about—about your new—I thought it might be useful if you—talked to him,' she finished lamely, for the satyr look had given way to something quite thunderous.

'And what makes you think you have the right to take such a liberty with my work? Do I send off your mathematical primers to a publisher and tell them perhaps he might like to print them? Would I have the temerity to write to your sister in Arabia and suggest she offer you a post in one of her schools?'

'They're not all schools as such. Some of them are no more than glorified tents. But I take your point,' Cressie said hurriedly, for Giovanni looked as if he might throw her out of the carriage. Or more likely himself. 'I'm sorry. I didn't think it was taking a liberty. I thought that if you could speak to him, explain...'

'Explain what, precisely?' Giovanni cursed. 'One portrait, Cressie. I have painted one portrait—and that unfinished. I don't even know myself what I think of it. And besides that, are you sure you would wish me to be displaying it to all and sundry, given the subject matter?

Do you wish the world to see you dressed as a man and baring your breast?'

'I hadn't really thought of that.'

'No, you hadn't really thought at all, had you?'

'But I would do it, Giovanni,' Cressie said, rallying, 'if it meant...'

'That I was provided with the means to expose myself to ridicule for a second time.' Giovanni dropped his head into his hands.

The horse, spooked by their angry tones, encouraged by Cressie's unwittingly tightened grip on the reins, lumbered into a trot which went quite unnoticed by the carriage's occupants. 'A second time?' Cressie repeated slowly. 'What do you mean, a second time?' she asked with something much worse than a sinking feeling. Drowning?

'You think I always intended to paint the depictions of perfection that made my reputation?' Giovanni said bleakly. 'I started out believing in inspiration, in creativity, in truth. And that is how I used to paint, from the heart. But my muse deserted me, I told you that.'

Belatedly reining in the horse, who took another unnoticed liberty and pulled over to crop at the verge, Cressie thought she might actually be sick. 'I remember,' she said miserably, 'the woman who broke your heart.'

'What woman?' Giovanni stared at her, dumbfounded. 'You think that a woman—that I had a lover...'

'She was your muse, this woman. And then she left you. And you were devastated and couldn't paint properly any more without her in your life. Until you met me that is. And obviously,' Cressie said, sensing his bafflement, her face burning with mortification, 'I got completely the wrong end of the stick. Oh God!'

It would be no exaggeration to say that Giovanni looked as if he was wearing a thunder cloud as a cloak. Rage and something darker, more dangerous, emanated from him in waves. The last thing he would welcome was further questions, but she had to ask them. She would not allow him to make her afraid of him. And besides, she had meant well. Plus, he had an incredible talent, even she could see that. 'Giovanni, what did you mean, a second time?'

He was staring at the floor of the carriage. The planes of his face were stark, his skin pale, the coldness of his expression stripping him of his beauty. He took a deep breath and spoke in a monotone. 'When I walked out of my father's house, I became an apprentice to one of the Ital-

ian masters and began to learn the skills which
would eventually bring me fame and fortune.
But at the same time I was also trying to create a style of my own. Something unique and
revolutionary. I was so excited when some of
my work was chosen for an exhibition. It was
savaged by the so-called experts. A humiliating
and very public failure which naturally came to
Count Fancini's attention. *You will come back
with your tail between your legs. No one will
buy those pretty jottings of yours. Mark my
words, you will be back. And I will be waiting.*
Those were his last words to me when I left. I
have never forgotten them—they are seared on
my mind. I knew he was patiently waiting for
me to fail, but I would not allow him to win.
That is when I decided to make a living out of
the depiction of beauty and to defy my blood
heritage. My father killed my muse, not some
woman.'

His words had knocked the wind out of her.
Cressie hated the unknown Italian count for
his mindless destruction of the son he was so
reluctant to acknowledge and so determined
to bend to his will. And she was furious at
Giovanni for being so very blind. 'You said
you would never allow your father to win. But
by sacrificing your artistic integrity for com-

mercial expediency, Giovanni, you are doing just that. You are letting him win. You told me you painted in order to prove to your father that you could succeed on your own terms. But you haven't succeeded on your own terms, you've succeeded on his. When will you have earned enough money to be free of him? When will you have produced enough of those mathematically perfect portraits of yours to finally return to your true calling? I'm guessing never.'

A long silence greeted this tirade. Cressie was crying, the tears blinding her eyes. When he tried to hand her his handkerchief, she shook him off, wiping her eyes with the backs of her gloves, fumbling for the reins, which she had dropped on the floor of the gig.

'What are you doing?' Giovanni asked as she set about, most ineptly, trying to turn the horse and carriage around.

'Taking you back to Killellan.'

'No.'

'You have a portrait of my brothers to finish. You have to go back.'

'No, I mean don't turn around, Cressie. Take me to this tea party of yours.'

'What?' Cressie let the reins fall again. The horse, the most even-tempered of beasts under normal circumstances, snorted and tossed his head in frustration.

'You are right,' he said simply. 'About all of it. You are, unfortunately, in the right of it. You have a way of presenting the facts with the precision of a mathematical instrument,' Giovanni added with a ghost of a smile. 'For some time now, I have been ignoring this feeling of...' He gestured with his hands, something like a shrug, which made him seem very Continental. 'I don't know the word. I wasn't unhappy, but I knew there was something wrong. I was beginning to hate every blank canvas, could see nothing of interest in the people I painted because I had stopped looking. I was arrogant, but I told myself that I had the right to be. Like my father, you will tell me.'

His expression was stark, lost, uncertain. He was looking at her as if she had all the answers he sought. Cressie was overwhelmed with love for this man. A tearing tenderness, a fierce, visceral reaction gripped her, to gather him to her, to keep him safe, to tell him it would all be fine, all of it, even though she had no idea what she was talking about. 'Giovanni, you're nothing like your father.' She shuffled over the seat and took his hand between hers. Long fingers, immaculate nails, not a trace of paint. She couldn't resist the most fleeting of kisses. 'We really are very alike, you and I, trying to play our fathers at their own game, and not realising what we actually need to do is break free from them. You don't have anything to prove to Count Fancini, but you have a lot to prove to yourself.'

He laughed. 'You see. Like a precision instrument.'

He touched her forehead. She knew before he did that his fingers would move on to her cheek, her throat. Cressie closed her eyes, trying to memorise the way his touch made her skin tingle, her muscles clench in anticipation. She could not bear for there to be a time when she would have to imagine and not experience. When his lips met hers, she was so surprised that she almost flinched. He had been so very careful to keep his distance. His kiss was the gentlest of touches. His lips were like silk. His hand cupped her jaw, his thumb stroking her throat. She thought she might truly melt, had barely slipped her arms awkwardly around the bulk of his greatcoat, when he let her go.

'*Grazie*, Cressie. I am sorry I lost my temper. What you have done—it was—*grazie*.' He picked up the reins and handed them to her. 'I will miss you when it is time for me to go,' he said, 'but in future, when I am in any doubt about something, I will say to myself, what would Cressie think, and I am sure you will keep me on the right path. What is the name of this expert that I am to attempt to impress today? Is it Granville? Sir Magnus Titmus perhaps?'

'I don't actually know. All Bella could tell me was that he was from the Continent and was the up-and-coming man. Which was why I thought—but there's no point going back over all that again.'

Cressie took up the reins once more and coaxed the patient horse back into a plodding walk towards the Innellan estates. For a wild moment she'd thought that kiss had signified a turning point, for if Giovanni could finally shed the shadow of his father, perhaps he could also make room in his life for her. For a few heart-breaking seconds, she'd thought she could even in time make him love her. She bit the inside of her cheek hard to stop the foolish tears from flowing, telling herself it was enough that she had helped him, a blessing that she had not blurted out her feelings and turned him from her for ever.

'Lady Innellan seems to have invited half the county,' Cressie said, surveying the packed drawing room. 'Those who are not in London for the Season, that is. Her son, Sir Timothy Innellan, has just returned home from the Continent to claim his title, as I told you. Rather belatedly, in fact, for his father passed away over a year ago.'

She nodded over at the prodigal son. Giovanni saw a heavily bearded man dressed in a flowing robe and turban with a crescent-shaped sword dangling from his waist, holding court in the middle of the room. 'Goodness,' Cressie muttered, muffling a giggle, 'one must assume that his travels have taken him to Arabia.'

'What dangers do you think he fears to encounter in his mother's drawing room?' Giovanni asked, also smiling, though rather at Cressie's face than the new baronet with the bayonet.

'Scheming dowagers with marriageable daughters for a start,' she replied promptly. 'I am glad my father is not in the country. I am sure he would have no qualms in throwing me in Sir Timothy's path. "Take her with my blessing, even if you have the look of a Whig,"' Cressie said in a very fair imitation of her father's pompous mode of speech. 'Though actually, Sir Timothy has more the look of those strange men who stand guard outside the harem in Celia's palace. I saw them when I visited. Most intimidating. Now I come to think of it, Celia told me that traditionally they were *castrato*. I wonder how far Sir Timothy has taken his admiration of the East.'

'I wonder what his mother would say if she discovered you were speculating about such matters in her drawing room while taking tea,' Giovanni said. 'You have a most unconventional sense of humour.'

'My Aunt Sophia is always telling me to put a guard on my tongue.'

'Don't ever do so on my account.'

There was no time for Giovanni to dwell on the dwindling number of days left for her to heed his words, for Lady Innellan descended upon them at that precise moment. A stately woman who had, according to Cressie, worn her blacks dutifully and cast them off promptly a year to the day upon which her husband had departed this earth, she was an old friend of the Aunt Sophia Cressie was so fond of. Her first words following her introduction to Giovanni were to enquire after the aforementioned lady. 'For I believe that her health is somewhat in decline,' she said to Cressie. 'She is bringing out your sister Cordelia, is she not? Quite a charge, for a woman of her years. I am surprised Bella did not take on the responsibility. How is your stepmother, by the way? I have not seen her in an age.'

'Unfortunately she too has been unwell, though she is a little better now.'

'Do not tell me she is increasing again! Does your father intend to match every one of his daughters with a son?' Lady Innellan asked with a titter.

Giovanni watched with amusement as Cressie struggled between a desire to ridicule her father by agreeing, and the urge to defend Bella. The grudging respect she had for her stepmother clearly got the upper hand. The smile Cressie returned was just as false as the one her hostess had given. 'Oh, I think my father is more than content with his four boys. An heir and several spares, as they say. It is a pity that not everyone can be in such a fortunate position.' She looked pointedly at Lady Innellan's single heir. 'Bella wishes for a daughter this time. I am sure she will be up and about directly, when you would be most welcome to call, but in the meantime I shall pass on your good wishes, shall I?'

'I wonder that you are not in town with your sister, Cressida. Your father must be most eager to see you suitably attached. It has been— what—eight seasons now?'

'I am needed at Killellan,' Cressie said, and Giovanni noticed her hands curled into fists beneath the long sleeves of her pelisse.

She did not need his protection, she was more than a match for Lady Innellan, but he couldn't help standing a little closer all the same. 'Lady Cressida is taking her brothers for lessons while her stepmother finds a suitable new governess,' Giovanni said. 'I have been commissioned to paint the boys' portrait and thanks to Lady Cressida's extraordinary ability to control her brothers, the task of taking their likenesses is proving surprisingly straightforward.'

Throughout the conversation, Giovanni had been pointedly ignoring the fact that Lady Innellan was batting lashes like a hummingbird's wings at him, casting him smouldering sideways glances. Now, he saw with resignation that the smile she turned on him was very different from the one she had bestowed upon Cressie. 'Your reputation precedes you, *signor*,' she said. 'It is quite an honour to have you here in my modest provincial drawing room, for you are quite the recluse, I believe. There are several of my guests most eager to make your acquaintance.'

Several ladies, no doubt. He saw that thought

flit across Cressie's mind too, as she glanced around the room, smiling wryly over her shoulder in recognition of the coyly admiring looks being cast his way. 'I begin to understand,' she whispered, 'what you mean when you say that beauty can be a burden. Shall I make our excuses?'

He was tempted, but her earlier challenge would not allow him to turn away. *You don't have anything to prove to Count Fancini, but you have a lot to prove to yourself.* She was right. He would have to face the bastions of the art establishment at some point. Why not make a start with this newcomer? Giovanni shook his head and turned to Lady Innellan. 'I am told that you have an art expert visiting you. Will you be so kind as to introduce me to him?'

'Indeed. My son met him on the Continent where it seems they became very good friends,' her ladyship replied, reluctantly ceasing her blatant inventory of his person. 'Where—oh, there he is, hugging my son's side as ever. They are very good friends indeed, you know. Quite inseparable.' She raised a beckoning hand.

As the man picked his way daintily across the salon in answer to Lady Innellan's summons, Giovanni felt a sick feeling of recognition.

'Signor di Matteo,' Lady Innellan said, 'may I present...'

'Luigi di Canio,' he said heavily. 'We are already acquainted.'

'Well, well. If it isn't the illustrious Giovanni di Matteo.' Luigi's smile dripped with a venom many years in the fomenting. 'How very—interesting—to find you here.'

Luigi had been a well-built youth, but now he was inclined towards the corpulent. His hair was still the colour of ripe wheat, but it was receding from his high brow at a rate which he was obviously self-conscious about, for he had attempted to disguise it by having it combed out, Giovanni noticed. Vain and extremely effete were the first impressions he projected, with his thinly sneering mouth and his ridiculous pointed beard. His clothes had all the flamboyance one would expect from an Italian artist too. A bottle-green coat, a waistcoat embroidered with pink cabbage roses and a cravat tied in a monstrous bow. He looked rather like a precocious over-large child, though Giovanni was not fooled. Luigi's grip was limp, his palms damp but his pale blue eyes were extremely astute and cold, like the eyes of a reptile.

As Luigi bowed low over Cressie's hand, it was no consolation to Giovanni to see her repress a shudder. Nausea gripped him, and fury, though it was directed more at himself than at Luigi, that vindictive, malicious figure from his past who would not be able to resist making trouble. And Luigi could make plenty trouble, for he had observed Giovanni's rising star with the meticulous attention of one whose own star was falling. Luigi, that most expert bearer of grudges, would be unable to resist dropping enough hints to reveal the truth in the most tarnished and tawdry of ways. The truth that Giovanni should have told Cressie himself.

He gave himself a shake. They were in an English drawing room taking tea. Luigi was an honoured guest. Why would he sully the occasion with the past which did neither of them credit?

But his unease refused to be calmed by logic as Luigi began to inspect Cressie from head to foot in a way which made Giovanni's hackles rise. 'Lady Cressida,' he said. 'Charmed. You must be the latest subject of Giovanni's attentions.'

Cressie was on her guard, and rightly so. Giovanni would not trust Luigi any further than he could throw him which, looking at his ample girth, would not be far. 'I beg your pardon?' she said.

Luigi tittered. 'In oils, my dear. In oils.'

'Oh, I see,' she said, looking unconvinced. 'No, that privilege falls to my brothers.'

Cressie knew something was awry. Giovanni wanted to drag her away from the polluted air around Luigi. He wanted to wrap his hands around the salacious slug's throat and throttle him. He knew, with sick certainty, that what he ought to have done was told Cressie the whole truth. He knew too that the truth Luigi would imply would be much, much worse than the reality. He had to get out of here. Yet still he did nothing, frozen into inaction by their surroundings, by the vain hope that he had underestimated his fellow Italian.

'How do you come to know Signor di Matteo?' Cressie was asking now.

'Luigi and I were apprenticed at the same studio,' Giovanni intervened curtly.

'You are a fellow artist?' The disbelief in her tone would have been amusing under any other circumstances.

'Sadly,' Luigi said with a bitter little smile, 'I found I did not possess enough talent to earn the right to call myself that, unlike my friend Gio here. But I do find, dear Lady Cressida, that a little practical knowledge is most helpful in my current calling as an arbiter of taste.

As such, I would have to admit that our man here has done very well for himself. Have you not, Gio? After that—debacle?—yes, I fear it really was a debacle. Did he tell you, Lady Cressida? A most unfortunate exhibition, as I remember...'

'I know all about it,' Cressie interrupted.

Luigi raised his brows in surprise. 'He told you, did he? How interesting.'

It was her obvious dislike which sealed Giovanni's fate. Cressie had no other intention than to defend him, he knew that, but her words had implied too much between them. He had always thought it a lie, what they said about drowning men's lives flashing before them, but that is exactly what seemed to be happening to him. He saw a montage of beautiful faces, and floating sneeringly above them all, his Nemesis.

Luigi was unable to disguise his delight at having discovered what he undoubtedly thought was an *affaire*. He had a nose for scandal and a taste for revenge which he would not be able to resist. Giovanni clenched his fists, but made no move to use them. A part of him was resigned. A part of him thought he deserved his fate. A part of him wished desperately that he could undo the past. Cressie was looking distinctly upset now. She wanted him to speak. She wanted him to explain. But how could he?

Luigi too was eyeing him askance, but he would not give him the satisfaction of showing how he felt. 'You really do surprise me,' he was saying to Cressie. 'That is not the sort of thing one confides in just anyone. Though perhaps you are not *just anyone*. Giovanni's taste in women, like his taste in art, has changed significantly, if that is the case,' he added with a waspish smile. 'Back in the old days, our Gio was really rather more renowned for the beauties he bedded than his paintings. So eager those ladies were, to lend both their faces and their fortunes to help a poor starving artist on his road to success. Though of course, Lady Cressida, you will know all about that particular aspect of our Gio's success too, since he has taken you into his—er—confidence.'

Giovanni's muscles tensed. Finally he spoke, his voice a menacing growl that didn't sound at all like his own. 'I warn you only once, Luigi. You will mind that vicious tongue of yours, or tea party or no tea party I will...'

'You will beat me with your fists for my insolence, the way you used to when we were apprentices.' His eyes alight with malice, Luigi tossed his head disdainfully and turned to

Cressie. 'Gio never could endure being teased about his many lady friends.'

'Giovanni has painted many beautiful women, that is no secret,' she responded. Her voice was flat as if she didn't believe her own words. 'I don't know what you are implying, but...'

Luigi laughed, a brittle little sound like the crystals from a chandelier tinkling in a draught. 'He did a lot more than paint them, my dear. How do you think he survived, in those years when he scrabbled about for commissions? I concede he possessed a raw artistic talent, with the emphasis on raw. He did not leap, fully-fledged, from that tragic exhibition to the higher echelons of portraiture in a matter of days. Or even months. But our friend has more than one string to his bow, as you already know, I am sure. This beautiful face, this so very, very attractive body of his, they were quite an asset back in those days when he was struggling in his artistic garret.'

'Stop it!' Cressie pleaded. 'Stop saying those wicked things. You say them only because you are envious of his talent.'

Luigi simpered. 'Oh, I do not deny I am envious, my dear Lady Cressida. Back in the old days, I would go so far as to say that I was even just a tiny bit jealous. I am not short of personal

charm myself even now. As a young man—
well, I considered myself at least as worthy
of Gio's attentions as those ladies, and Gio—'

'Stop!' Cressie reeled as if he had brought
her world tumbling down, though Giovanni
knew it was rather his own which crumbled.
You deserve better, he'd said to her. Now she
could see that he had been right. He was aware
of her drawing Luigi a look of disgust before
bestowing upon him something more forlorn.
He was aware of Lady Innellan making her
way towards them, her son in his ridiculous
outfit in tow. He was even aware of the look Sir
Timothy bestowed on Luigi di Canio. Not of a
friend but that of a lover. He saw Cressie recognise that too. On the way back in the carriage,
she would have enjoyed speculating about that
look. But now she picked up the skirts of her
pelisse and ran for the door.

It was Giovanni's cue. With a vicious snarl,
he smashed his clenched fist smack into the
middle of Luigi's astonished face.

Cressie had the gig halfway down the carriageway of the Innellans' manor house, sob-
bing, almost blinded by tears, and tempted to
try the unlikely feat of urging the horse into a
gallop when Giovanni leapt into the carriage.

He looked every bit as devastated as she felt. Cressie steeled herself. She would not allow herself to feel sorry for him. She would not speak. She would not utter a word. The one thing she had not done was give herself away completely, and she absolutely would not do that now!

'Cressie.'

'I don't want to talk about it.'

'*Si.* I understand.'

He lapsed into silence. The air between them had the heaviness of a pending thunderstorm. Cressie focused hard and quite unnecessarily on the road ahead, which the horse took at his usual sedate pace. The hedgerows were still in full blossom. The trees were still luscious green. The bluebells were still blue. Not just blue. Cerulean? Too dark. Cornflower? Not pink enough. Lilac? Teal? Cobalt? 'Oh for goodness' sake, who cares!' she exclaimed.

'I do.'

'I wasn't talking about you,' she snapped.

'Cressie...'

'How could you! How could you, Giovanni? How could you *sell* yourself in such a way. Why, you are nothing short of a *gigolo*!'

He flinched, but did not deny it, which made her feel much worse instead of better. 'The first time you kissed me I remember wondering if seduction was part of your technique. When I got to know you better, I felt guilty for having thought so.' Cressie attempted a derisive snort. It sounded pathetically like a sob.

'I have never kissed you for any other reason than that I could not resist you.'

'Very good, Giovanni, that is excellent. If you would relieve me of the reins I would applaud you. The fact is that you *did* resist me, despite my attempts to throw myself at you.' And the fact was that this was the most mortifying thing. All those women, and Giovanni had made love to them casually, easily and regularly! So many others he had made no effort to resist, yet he had gone out of his way to resist her. 'What is wrong with me?' she demanded, too hurt and too angry to care at how needy she sounded and how pathetically jealous. 'Why not me?'

Once again he flinched. Did he turn paler? It looked as though the blood had drained from his face. But she would not feel sorry for him. And she would not feel sorry for herself either! 'Do you know, I was actually envious when I thought you'd had another female muse,' Cressie continued remorselessly, determined to whip her anger into a fury lest she break down

into hysterics. 'What an idiot I am. I didn't realise you'd had hundreds. I didn't realise I was
just the latest in a very, very long line. Who
will be next, I wonder? Lady Innellan? A little
old, perhaps, but she is very wealthy and made
her interest in *you* obvious enough. Though
perhaps you are more fussy these days, now
you are in such high demand.'

'Enough!' Giovanni grabbed the reins and
pulled the horse over to the side of the road.
A pulse beat at his temple. 'I told you, I have
not been with a woman in years. I do not lie,
Cressie.'

'But you are obviously very sparing with the
truth, Giovanni.'

'*Si.* That is true. But I have never lied to
you.'

He dug the heels of his hands into his eyes.
His shoulders were hunched. The sound he
made was very like a dry sob. Was he crying? It took everything in her to refrain from
touching him. She couldn't bear it, to see him
so dejected. If only he could explain. Mitigate.
Make it not true.

'There were not hundreds, but there were
many.' Giovanni sat up, holding himself rig-
idly. He had himself under control again. And
he was not avoiding her eye. She could see the

resolution written in the stark planes of his expression. The stripped look she'd seen on one occasion before today. The look that told the blunt, unvarnished and horrible truth. She didn't want to hear it, but she knew she had to. Cressie gripped her fingers together tightly.

'It is as Luigi implied. I was desperate, not so much for success at first, as simply to prove my father wrong. I would make my art pay. I knew I had the skill, but I needed time and I needed willing subjects and they needed to be…'

'Beautiful.'

'I could not make my name painting anything other than perfection. At least, not the name I wanted to make.'

'I know how it is,' Cressie said dully, 'you don't need to explain.'

'It was easy. Far too easy. This,' Giovanni said, pointing at his face, 'this face, this body made it easy. I knew it was wrong, but to me if felt so much less wrong than forcing myself into the mould my father had created for me. I told myself that at least this way I could use my talent. And I was not wholly lacking in morals. I took only what was offered freely. And I did not take from those…' He swallowed several times. When he spoke again, his voice was low, filled with self-disgust. 'There were men as well as women willing to pay.'

Cressie stared at him in horror. 'You mean they—did Luigi?'

'Once again, I commend your perception. As you saw, he is not someone who takes well to rejection, of any sort. You have to believe me, Cressie,' Giovanni said earnestly, 'I never—not with men, not with any woman who wanted more from me than a few afternoons' pleasure. They paid what was at the time an inflated fee for their portraits. I asked nothing more. But I will not deny it, I sold myself. My performances—for such they were—were polished, skilled, technically brilliant but emotionless. Just like the paintings I produced.'

'And when your portraits began to be in demand, you no longer needed to sell your body, is that it?' Cressie said tightly.

'That is it. I will not pretend that it disgusted me at the time, Cressie. What young man would find taking a beautiful woman to bed a chore? It was only afterwards that I began to find myself repellent. There is a pleasure, a different kind of pleasure, to be had in sacrifice, in cleansing. Until I met you, that too was easy. Since I met you—but what is the point in talking about it? I will not taint you with my sordid past. You...'

'Deserve better,' Cressie finished for him quietly. 'So you said.'

'And meant it.'

Giovanni made to take her hand, but stopped himself. She should have been glad he did so, but it was this simple gesture which nearly broke her. He would always stop himself. And though his revelations were appalling, what was even more appalling was that she still loved him. 'Will Luigi talk?' Cressie asked.

'Not for some time.'

'What do you mean?'

'When I last saw him he was flat out on Lady Innellan's drawing-room rug with a small crowd gathered round him. He seemed to be missing some teeth and there was, I confess, some blood on that ridiculous bow of his.'

Cressie put her hand over her mouth. 'You should not have,' she said, though actually, she could not pretend to be anything other than glad.

Giovanni shrugged. 'You can take the boy from the fishing village, but you cannot take the fishing village from the boy—or so they say. I expect I have created quite a scandal. I am sorry for that.'

'I am sure Lady Innellan will be secretly delighted. Notoriety is the next best thing to popularity. Besides, the incident will be put down to the tempestuous nature of Italian artists. Giovanni, are you sure that Luigi will not make mischief?'

'He has much more to lose than I. His reputation is still relatively new and he knows I could easily ruin him if I chose to reveal some of what I know about his own sordid past. He will also know that if he did so, I would hunt him down like a dog. Not that I care. I am done with living my life this way, Cressie. You are right. I must make my own way on my own terms.'

It was small comfort now, but it would feel more significant in the future. Right now, she was completely drained. It felt as if her bones had been removed. She wanted nothing but to lie underneath her bedclothes in the dark and howl. Resolutely, she picked up the reins.

'There is just one more thing.' Giovanni touched her arm, snatching his hand back immediately. 'It was different with you. I want you to know that. When I told you I was afraid of the passion between us, I meant it. I was not just afraid that surrendering to it would destroy what inspired me to paint you, I was afraid I would destroy you. I have never before been with a woman who cared for how I felt. When you touch me, it is as if no woman has ever touched me. You always ask me for proof. I can provide none but it is the truth none the less. It was different with you. You will simply have to trust me on that.'

Tears clogged her throat, but she was too raw to do any more than nod and set the horse in motion. 'Thank you for being so honest with me but I can't talk about this any more, Giovanni. I just can't.'

They completed the short journey in silence. Cressie held herself in, gathering tightly together, counting the minutes until she could be alone. The one thing she didn't feel was disgust. Stealing a glance at him, sitting ramrod straight, staring sightlessly ahead, obviously lost inside the morass of his jumbled thoughts and emotions, she knew that the one thing she did feel was love. Despite all, she loved him and was resigned that she always would.

Chapter Ten

'I'm afraid her ladyship requires your presence urgently, Lady Cressida. She is most anxious to speak with you.' Myers's words of greeting were the last thing Cressie wanted to hear as she pulled the gig up at the front door. 'I'll have the carriage taken around to the stables, my lady. Lady Armstrong awaits you in the small salon.'

The image of the sanctuary of her darkened bedchamber which had sustained her during the last few miles of the drive home, vanished in a puff of smoke. What else could go awry on this most inauspicious of days? Cressie jumped down from the gig, brushing away Giovanni's proffered helping hand, and wearily trudged through the reception hall.

Bella was lying prostrate on her favourite *chaise-longue*, her sal volatile in one hand, an ominous-looking missive in the other, but upon Cressie's opening the door, she scrambled to her feet. 'This came by express not long after you left for Lady Innellan's,' she said, waving the letter in the air. 'I wanted Myers to send someone to fetch you straight away, but he managed to convince me it would be futile since it would be too late by the time you returned for you to leave for London tonight. Only if you wait until the morning I fear it will be too late. According to this letter, it is already too late. I told you, Cressida, I told you it was on your head if anything happened, and now—what are we to do? Your father will *kill* me.'

Cressie took the letter, eased Bella back on to the *chaise-longue* and waved the sal volatile under her nose. 'I can think of nothing less likely than my father turning to murder. Do not be ridiculous, Bella, and I pray you please do not work yourself up into hysterics. It cannot be good for the baby, and if something happens to that…'

'There you are wrong. This baby is a girl—your father will not care one way or the other if anything happens to her,' Bella replied tartly, patting her stomach.

Which was probably, sadly, true, Cressie thought abstractedly, dropping into a chair opposite her stepmother. She had already noted that the hand which had written the letter belonged to Aunt Sophia. She was already, following receipt of Cordelia's last missive, prepared for bad news. Her aunt's frantic note confirmed the worst. Cordelia had apparently eloped, though with whom and whence were details conspicuous by their absence. 'I should have known. I suspected all along that Cordelia was leading my aunt and everyone else up the garden path with her wild behaviour,' Cressie explained in answer to Bella's questioning look. 'A ruse to mask a far deeper game, and it seems I was right. Though what my aunt expects you to do about it, I have no idea.'

'Me!' Bella shrieked, dropping the bottle of smelling salts.

'The letter is addressed to you.'

'Cressida Florence Armstrong, you know perfectly well that we agreed...'

'Stop! Bella, please stop. It was an attempt to lighten the mood. A feeble attempt at a joke.'

'Very feeble.'

Cressie rubbed her brow. 'I suppose I must go to London to see what can be done to retrieve the situation.'

'You do not look well, Cressida. Is something amiss?'

'I have a headache.'

'You never get headaches.'

'Bella, it's been a long day, and I'm tired and the very last thing I wish is to go traipsing off on a wild goose chase after Cordelia, who is very likely hiding out somewhere not too far away laughing up her sleeve at the chaos she has caused.'

'How went your visit to Lady Innellan? Did you make the acquaintance of that man you seemed so keen on introducing Signor di Matteo to?'

Cressie winced. 'The only way to describe the tea party is that it was unforgettable.'

'I am not surprised,' Bella said with a hungry look in her eye. 'I had heard a rumour that her ladyship had recently appointed, at great expense, a London cook.'

'I was not referring to the food. There was an altercation between Giovanni and his fellow-Italian art expert over... It does not matter. You will no doubt hear a wildly exaggerated version of events once the servants start talking but for the record, Giovanni was much provoked.'

'I cannot say I am totally shocked. Your father says the Latins, despite their bold claims about being the cradle of civilisation, are the most obstreperous, ill-disciplined and rash nation on earth. He says he would rather deal with a Berber horde than mediate between two Italians with a grievance. He says—'

'Lady Innellan was asking kindly after you,' Cressie interjected, unable to listen to another syllable of her father's guide to diplomacy.

'What was the son like?'

'Let us say that there is absolutely no chance of him being interested in becoming a candidate for my hand.'

'Aye, his tastes do not run in that direction,' Bella said with her sharp little smile. 'I'd heard that too.'

'Did you? Goodness, I had no idea you were so very well informed,' Cressie said tartly. 'It is a pity your contacts cannot give us some clue as to the whereabouts of my sister.' She thumped her forehead with the heel of her hand. 'I beg your pardon, that was quite uncalled for.'

'Are you sure it is a headache you are suffering from? Has that man been taking liberties? I warned you about him, Cressida.'

'You did, and let me assure you again, Bella, that you need have no fears in that direction. None whatsoever.'

Bella pursed her lips, noting the catch in her

stepdaughter's voice. 'This trip to London may have come at timely juncture, it seems to me. A little distance will bring some perspective.'

'I suppose I must go.' Cressie got to her feet. Her legs felt like lead. 'I think after all it would be best if I left straight away. The days are getting longer. We may get as much as halfway there before nightfall.'

Bella got to her feet looking remarkably recovered, Cressie thought uncharitably. 'You will take two of the stable boys as outriders as well as the groom. And your maid, of course. Myers will arrange it all. I will call for him forthwith.'

Less than an hour later, Cressie was seated in the Armstrong travelling carriage on her way to the capital. She had not seen or spoken to Giovanni, not even to explain her sudden departure. There had been no time, and it was probably for the best. When she returned, when time and distance had placed some perspective on today's revelations and she had perhaps made a start on the dismantling of her love for him, then she could finish sitting for him, for she was determined that he would complete the portrait. Else all would indeed have been lost.

* * *

Giovanni stood in front of the two portraits of Cressie. Thesis and antithesis. The public Cressie and the private. A representative painting and an interpretive one. The former was classically beautiful and highly polished. Lady Cressida, totally lacking in any of Cressie's real character. Mr Brown, Cressie's alter ego, on the other hand, was a rougher piece of work all together. This version of Cressie had her fierce intelligence, her impish sense of humour and a hint of her sensuality. This version was subversive, an image intended to unsettle the viewer, but looking at it now, it still did not seem to be exactly the Cressie that Giovanni had wished to depict.

There was something missing. Or lacking. An authority, a certainty. Art as truth, that's what he wanted to paint, but this did not represent the whole truth. This was a painting which spoke as he had—in half-truths, to disguise the reality. Truth was not one but two-sided. It showed not just the truth of the sitter but the truth of the painter. The emotion which was missing was not Cressie's but his. There was no avoiding it. Giovanni dropped on to the bare boards in front of the portraits and groaned, slumping back against the wall and banging his head heavily in the process. If he could bang it a little harder and achieve blessed oblivion, then he would be happy.

He cursed inwardly. Who was he trying to fool! He would never be happy. Not with his work, not with his life. Something was missing. Lacking. And the source of that void was the same as the missing element in the portrait. Cressie.

Giovanni swore again, this time in the guttural dialect of the fishermen among whom he had been raised. He was in love with Cressie. That was the truth lacking in the Mr Brown portrait. He had not acknowledged his love for her and it showed in the work. The empty space in his heart which he had become accustomed to think would never be filled was now overflowing. He was in love with her. Cressie had taken up residence there.

Giovanni pulled his drawing board towards him and began to sketch quickly. The forms took shape almost unbidden. Cressie laughing. Cressie furiously biting back the tears. Cressie beaming with pride at some minor accomplishment of her brothers. Cressie frowning over one of her mathematical tomes. Cressie, eyes closed, head thrown back, back arched in ecstasy as she climaxed under his touch. He wanted to paint all of those Cressies, a portrait of a woman with every one of the elements which made her so essentially her, the woman he loved and whom he had lost irretrievably, thanks to the many he had not loved who had gone before her.

If he could only reclaim his innocence. If he could only undo the past. As his hand raced over another blank sheet of paper, he remembered something she had said to him. Something about the past being the thing which made her herself. All of it, she'd said, describing some trivial incident which she'd only just remembered—*if I undid any of it I would be a different person.*

Would he undo his past if he could? Giovanni's hand stilled. He remembered a summer morning, a sea the colour of Cressie's eyes. He was four, perhaps five years old. He remembered the fish, a large coral-pink snapper, far too heavy for his line. He remembered being determined to haul it into the boat without his papa's help. He stood up to heft the line and fell head first into the sea. He remembered the water closing over his head, and then a pair of arms around him, the feeling of safety, of sanctuary. Papa. The swimming lessons began the next day. He remembered Mama smiling with pride the day she watched him swim from the boat to the shore for the first time, with Papa by his side, under solemn oath not to help him.

It was a cliché, but it was also true. Like a floodgate opening, the memories tumbled their way into his mind, bright with primary colours, warm as the heat of the Tuscan sun, silly things long forgotten. He *had* been happy. He *had* been loved. It was because it had been so that it had hurt so much, the forced separation. Might it have been because it would have been too painful for them that they had severed contact with him so brutally, his adopted parents? Too late now to discover that truth. That memory was in sepia, of his return to the village by the sea, the year he left Italy for good. They were both dead. Papa's boat lost in a storm. Mama lost to a cancer left too long untreated.

He had run out of drawing paper. The light was fading when there was a cautious tap at the door. Giovanni jumped to his feet, trying to smooth down his hair with his hand. Cressie. He reminded himself that it was hopeless, but still he hoped. Foolish, foolish, foolish, he told himself as he turned the drawing board with its revealing sketches to the wall. She must not see those. They said something she must never hear. She had most likely come to tell him she would not sit for him again. It would be like her, not to leave things unfinished between them. Cressie liked her facts straight and ordered. But still, as he hurried over to the door and turned the key in the lock, Giovanni's heart gave a strange little leap.

'Harry told me I'd find you up here.' Bella's face was flushed with effort. 'I need to talk to you, Signor di Matteo.'

Bella swept past him and into the room, stopping dead in her tracks in front of the two portraits. Her face, as she stared at first one and then the other in a bizarre reflection of the stance Giovanni himself had taken a few hours before, was comical in its variety of expressions. 'Does my husband know about this? I cannot believe that he actually commissioned these—these images of his daughter.'

'No commission. I have been painting them for my own pleasure and entertainment.'

Bella nodded. 'I am sure you have derived much pleasure from painting them, Signor di Matteo. What is the meaning of this one, if you please?' she asked, pointing to the unfinished portrait.

She knew nothing of Mr Brown, of course, and Giovanni was not about to enlighten her.

He shrugged. 'I thought it would be amusing, to depict Cressie—Lady Cressida—dressed as a man. Given her interest in mathematics,' he added disingenuously.

'A semi-naked man, in point of fact. I would like to hope that at least some elements of this portrait stem from your vivid imagination and are not representative of reality, *signor*.'

'As you say, Lady Armstrong. I have taken some artistic liberties.' One of those half-truths at which Cressie said he was too adept, but in this case he could see no alternative.

It seemed to have the desired effect. Bella pursed her mouth but did not challenge him. 'What do you intend to do with these canvases? The first, I will grant you, is a very pretty piece. I am sure Lord Armstrong would be happy to find a space for it with the family collection, were you to present it to him. But the other—there is something lascivious about it. Real or imagined, I cannot permit you to expose my stepdaughter to public ridicule.'

He had never intended to exhibit it, had never intended to show it to anyone, no matter what Cressie said, but Giovanni was not inclined to have Lady Armstrong dictate to him. 'That is Lady Cressida's decision,' he said stiffly. 'I painted it for her. The painting is hers to do with as she wishes. I will let her decide.'

'That may be problematic.'

'Indeed. Why so?'

'Because she has gone.'

'Gone?' Giovanni repeated stupidly.

'To London. She was summoned there on urgent family business.'

Cressie was gone. She had left without telling him. She could not have made her feelings clearer. 'By family business you mean Lady Cordelia, I assume,' Giovanni said dully.

Lady Armstrong narrowed her eyes. 'What, may I ask, do you know of it?'

'What? Nothing, save that Cressie—Lady Cressida was concerned her sister would act rashly.'

'It is a pity, then, that Cressida did not choose to act more pre-emptively herself, and thus spare us a very embarrassing situation. Your discretion, *signor*, I assume I can count on it?'

'In every respect, my lady.'

'Which brings me to the point of my expedition all the way up here, Signor di Matteo. Cressida will be detained in London for at least a week. It looks to my untutored eye as if my sons' portrait is nearing completion. You will oblige me by making every effort to finish it before she returns.'

'You wish me gone?'

Lady Armstrong tittered. 'You Italians, why must you be so dramatic. I have no wish to cast you from my door, I merely desire you to complete your commission as quickly as possible.'

'Before Cressie returns.'

Her ladyship smiled at this slip. 'Indeed,' she said, 'before *Cressie* returns.' Her smile faded as she made her way across the attic to the doorway. 'Let us call a spade a spade, *signor*. Despite what she may claim, Cressida is no woman of the world. I, on the other hand, am precisely that. I strongly suspect you have been taking liberties. Indeed, anyone would, who saw these paintings. And one merely has to see the way that Cressida looks at you, hear the way she speaks your name, to know that she is setting herself up for a fall. I am not her mother, but nor am I the wicked stepmother she and her sisters labelled me. I would not like to see Cressida hurt any more than she has been already, Signor di Matteo, and if you remain here then that is almost certainly what will happen. Do we understand each other?'

'Well enough, Lady Armstrong.' The whole truth this time. Giovanni nodded curtly. 'If it is any consolation, hurting Cressie is the last thing in the world I would wish to do.'

'It is no consolation, *signor*, for the deed is already partly done.'

Without giving him time to respond, Bella swept from the room as suddenly as she had entered it. Sick at heart, overwhelmed by the cascade of harsh truths which had flowed his way today, Giovanni lit two oil lamps and arranged them on the table by his easels. Removing the completed canvas from one, he replaced it with his drawing board and studied his sketches of Cressie. Later, he would stretch a new canvas. Tomorrow he would begin the third painting. If he worked at it day and night, he could complete it and be gone before she returned. A triptych—Lady Cressida, Mr Brown and Cressie. 'Three Aspects of Lady Cressida,' he would title it. An arc that encapsulated her. He was so inspired by the concept he had to force himself not to start painting straight away.

In the days which followed, night blurred into morning and into night again. Giovanni worked furiously. The portrait of the Armstrong boys required only the final touches and the glaze. The boys were subdued in Cressie's absence. He took them out each afternoon, to

fish and to climb trees and to fly their kites—
for they had each one of their own now.

There were moments, usually in the smallest hours, when he stood before the third part
of his triptych, his eyes gritty with the oil light
and lack of sleep, when he asked himself if it
would not be possible for them to forge a future
together. As the painting took shape, all the ar-
guments against this possibility solidified. He
took to reciting them in an effort to dispel the
most foolish of hopes before it could take a grip
of him and torture him.

Though he had from the first been at pains
to help her free herself from her father's tyr-
anny, Giovanni was not so cruel as to wish
Cressie to become estranged from her family.
Despite all, she loved her father, and though it
was a love that would likely grow stronger the
more distance she put between herself and Lord
Armstrong, he had no doubt that the diplomat
would make every effort to ensure that she suffered if she went so spectacularly against his
wishes by taking up with Giovanni. He would
be apoplectic, and would undoubtedly extract
revenge. He could probably not tear the sisters
asunder, but he could make sure that Cressie
never saw her brothers again, nor her home,

nor indeed the mysterious Aunt Sophia whom Cressie seemed so fond of.

Giovanni's past lovers and his abuse of his own body, he saw as such an obvious barrier as to be barely worth mentioning. The look of disgust on Cressie's face when she called him a gigolo was something he would never forget. He would not inflict such a man upon her.

As if this was not enough, there was the simple fact that she was not actually in love with him. She was not the type to become infatuated, but she did not talk like a woman in love. She talked, on the contrary, like a woman with very clear ideas about deciding her own fate. *I've finally found my calling*, she had said to him. She was excited about the future—she must be, for she talked about it all the time. Her future lay in a far-off land where she could be with her two dearest sisters. She had no thought of making a place for him. She didn't love him. How could she?

The third painting was almost complete. It was like nothing he had created before, the brush strokes wild and instinctive. In places he had resorted to using a palette knife to apply the pigment directly to the canvas. The lines of the figure blurred and seeped into each other as did the colours. The background was almost organic, a part of the subject rather than an accessory. Nothing about it was clearly defined. Yet as Giovanni looked at it in the grey light of dawn, he knew finally he had created something true, something from the heart. This was how he would paint in future, and damn what anyone else thought of it. Cressie, his muse, his heart's desire, had given him back his calling. That was her parting gift to him. This painting would be his to her.

Giovanni lined up the three portraits to form the triptych, Cressie in the middle, flanked by Lady Cressida and Mr Brown on either side. Who knew, he might in time become a true artist and not a mere painter. Here was the map of his progress. Here, in the centre, was the pinnacle of his art to date, the foundation for his future.

You are letting him win. Giovanni caught himself looking over his shoulder at the door, then gave himself a shake. Too many sleepless nights. Cressie was not here, only her words whispering like ghosts in his head. He had spent the last ten years painting the kind of work whose success he thought his father would admire to prove him wrong. But as Cressie had so rightly pointed out, by doing so he was allowing his father to control his actions even now. Ever since he had been lifted from his life with Papa and Mama, he had been fighting Count Fancini in one way or another. He had not seen his father for fourteen years, but still he knew the count was waiting, patiently—or more likely impatiently—waiting. Giovanni's failure to confront the man had prolonged that game, allowed the illusion that he might return to be maintained. Perhaps even given his father hope.

To make a fresh start, he must lay his demons to rest. It seemed so obvious. He would cancel all his commissions and return to Italy *pronto*. Giovanni put down his palette and pulled a large cloth over all three paintings: Lady Cressida, the last of a kind; Cressie, the first of a kind; and Mr Brown, the pivot. Making his way down to the scullery to clean his tools, he could not pretend that leaving without seeing her again filled him with anything other than misery. He loved her, would always love her, and would never love another woman. But she had given him the gift of his art. He would not repay her generosity by abusing it again. And that required an audience with Count Fancini.

'I fear there is nothing more to be done, Aunt Sophia.' Cressie sat carefully down on the chair beside her aunt's day bed, for the skirts of her new gown were much fuller than she was accustomed to wearing. It had been delivered by the modiste this morning, and she had been unable to resist trying it on. Cream silk striped with the shade of dusky pink Giovanni most admired her in, the dress had puff sleeves with long under-sleeves in soft pink wool. The neckline was trimmed with pink velvet, as were the three flounces which formed the hemline, and though the dress hung straight at the front from her waist, at the back it was pleated and swung out behind her when she walked. She was pretty certain that Giovanni would like this effect, for it emphasised the curve of her bottom—something she had ascertained after much squinting over her shoulder and contorting in front of the mirror.

'Henry will have to be informed.' Aunt Sophia spoke in a pale imitation of her usual stentorian voice. Cressie had been dismayed to discover her so frail-looking. If they ever did recover Cordelia, along with her reputation, it was inconceivable that Aunt Sophia could continue to act the chaperon. Like it or not, Cordelia would have to cut short her Season and return to Killellan until next year, when

Bella would be well enough to bring her out herself.

Cressie pressed her aunt's hand, the skin dry and papery. 'I shall write to my father myself, Aunt, do not fret.'

'If we could but find a clue. It is the not knowing that is the worst. For all we are aware, Cordelia may be dead.'

Cressie chuckled. 'Now I know that you must be much more seriously ill than you appear, Aunt Sophia, for that is the most ridiculous thing I've ever heard you say. If Cordelia were dead, her body would have been discovered.'

'Not if she were at the bottom of a cliff. Or tied up in an attic. Or...'

'What about bricked in behind a fireplace? You sound just like Cassie.'

'I most certainly do not.' Lady Sophia struggled upright. 'Did I tell you that I saw that poet of hers recently? Augustus St John Marne, that was his name. Didn't speak to the man, of course. Quite down in the mouth he looked too, wandering in the wake of that carrot-haired wife of his and a clutch of brawling brats.'

'Thus are the mighty fallen,' Cressie said. 'Cassie had a lucky escape.'

'You may not remember, but he more or less

abandoned her at the altar. She had not the sense to realise—but she was ever a flighty piece. I fear Cordelia is another such. Have you really been unable to find any trace of her at all?'

'She took a hackney carriage when she left Cavendish Square, but she took care not to let her direction be overheard. I don't know how many hacks there are in London, but short of interviewing every single driver—it would take months, and goodness knows how much in bribes, by which time I am very sure Cordelia will have informed us herself of her fate, one way or another.'

'You do not hope this will turn out well for her, Cressida?'

'No, I don't, Aunt,' Cressie said gently, 'and I think you are far too sensible to rely on hope either.'

'No, I do not. I am feeble of body but not yet of mind,' Aunt Sophia said with a glimmer of her customary wit. 'You should return to Killellan, Cressida. It has been more than a week—Bella will have need of you. There is nothing more we can do until your sister shows her hand.'

'I am more concerned about my brothers' lessons. I suspect they will be making hay in my absence,' Cressie replied, forcing a smile.

Her aunt drew her a piercing look. 'You do not fool me, Niece. Something is amiss with you. You are quite—changed. Were it anyone else, I would say there was a man behind it, but in your case—what is it, Cressida?'

'Nothing.' Cressie caught herself just before she began to pick at her thumb.

'Rubbish. You think because I am sick and abed that I need to be mollycoddled, but I know there is something wrong, and I am sure I can help. Is it Bella?'

'No.' Cressie opened her mouth to deny once more that anything was amiss and faltered under her aunt's gimlet stare. 'It is nothing for you to worry about. Trust me,' she said, borrowing Giovanni's words.

Aunt Sophia did her the honour of heeding her wishes, though her parting words were to reassure her of her support should Cressida require counsel. Sitting in the carriage a few hours later, dressed in a comfortable travelling gown with her new purchases safe in her portmanteau, Cressie heaved a sigh of relief at having to no longer put up a front, and gave herself over to her anxieties.

She missed Giovanni terribly. She had not thought herself lonely when he came into her life, for she had Cordelia. But Cordelia, she now realised, was as self-contained in her own way as Cressie. Six years between them, and Cressie having assumed the position of elder sister when Cassie married, meant that there would always be a distance between them. And besides, Cordelia had never understood her quite as Giovanni did. No one had.

'He sees me as no other does,' she recalled Celia saying of her husband. Cressie hadn't understood that until now. 'And I see him in the same way,' Celia had added. That hateful little man Luigi di Canio had forced Giovanni to strip himself bare. The revelations had been so shocking that Cressie had for the first few days when she arrived in London been unable to think beyond the hurt they caused. That he could have so carelessly given himself to those other women. *Sold* himself. The very thought of it made her shudder. Shamefully, shudder not so much with disgust, as with simple jealousy, for he had given them so easily what she had never had from him.

It was a conversation with Aunt Sophia, a discussion of all the prospects which Cordelia seemed to have thrown away with her mysterious elopement, which had given Cressie pause for thought. Was not her own father in the business of selling his daughters, trading their bodies and their bloodline in order to achieve what he wanted, what Cressie called his dynastic web? For Lord Armstrong, his daughters were a means to an end. Truly, was this so very different? Or perhaps even worse, for at least Giovanni sold his own flesh and blood to his own advantage, not someone else's.

It amused her to imagine having that conversation with her father. Cressie smiled bitterly out of the window of the coach as the countryside flashed by. Was she so desperate to persuade herself that she could accept Giovanni's past, that she was resorting to sophistry? That was what Lord Armstrong would accuse her of.

Sophistry or not, what mattered was whether she could come to terms with those other women in Giovanni's past. Asking herself this question made Cressie realise she had already decided that she wanted to. Which raised the question of what Giovanni wanted. She had no idea how he really felt about her, and had given him no chance to tell her after Luigi di Canio had put his vicious spoke in the works. Loathsome man. She was glad Giovanni had punched him. She would like to punch him herself. Better yet, lock him in a room with the worst possible art she could find and force him to look at it every day until he begged for mercy.

Through the window of the coach, the countryside was becoming familiar. 'Not far to Killellan now, my lady. No more than an hour,' her maid said.

Cressie nodded distractedly. An hour, not much more, and she would see Giovanni again. She would tell him—no, not that she forgave him, it was not her right to forgive. Actually, now she came to think about it, it was Giovanni who was far more disgusted than she by his past. Sordid, he'd called it. He hated his body, the instrument of pleasure he had sold. It was different with her. He'd said that too, but she had been so angry and so hurt. *It was different with you. I want you to know that.* He thought he was so tainted he would destroy her, but had he not also implied that she could remake him?

When you touch me, it is as if no woman has ever touched me. Cressie shivered. He had not once mentioned Giles, never reproached her for her lack of innocence. That too had not occurred to her until now. It was not the same, but it was not so very different, her giving herself in return for a name, a position, for the sake of her father's approbation. When she had confessed this truth of her past, Giovanni had been angry, not *at* her but *for* her. He had not judged her. He had made her see that she must stop judging herself. It was not the same, but it really was not so very different at all.

When you touch me, it is as if no woman has ever touched me. Yes, that too was the same. He made her feel as if he were the first. Was it too fanciful to imagine that they could start anew? If he loved her as she loved him, she had no doubt they could. But did he? As the coach trundled up the carriageway to Killellan Manor, Cressie allowed herself to hope. Not for the conventional happy ending of orange blossom and blessings. She had no interest in either. But for something new, something which she and Giovanni could create together. And the first step was to see him, talk to him, tell him.

She sprang out of the carriage before the footman had a chance to let the steps down, and was in the reception hall struggling with the ties of her bonnet when Bella opened the door of her salon. 'No news,' Cressie told her stepmother hurriedly. 'No trace of Cordelia. I will write to my father tonight, but first I must— forgive me, but I must see Giovanni. Do you know where he is?'

It was the expression on Bella's face rather than her words which stopped Cressie in her tracks. Pity. 'Gone?' she repeated, trying to take in the meaning of the word. 'Gone where?'

'Italy, apparently,' Bella told her.

One's hopes being utterly dashed was actually akin to being flayed alive, Cressie discovered as she dropped her bonnet on to the marbled floor. She felt like a child, opening the wrong present on her birthday. Or no present. Or—for God's sake, what difference did it make how she felt! Cressie ran up the stairs at full tilt, hurled herself into her bedchamber, locked the door behind her and howled like a baby in an agony of pain and frustration.

She did not discover the portraits until the next day. Bella it was who told her to look in the attic. 'He left them for you.'

'You've seen them?'

'What were you thinking, Cressida? I cannot believe you allowed things to go so far.'

'Things did not go far enough, as far as I am concerned,' Cressie replied, too worn out and depressed to prevaricate. 'I love him, Bella. I love him.'

If she was in search of comfort, she was to be disappointed. 'More fool you,' her stepmother replied. 'Did I not warn you about such men?'

'You said he was heartless, but he is not.'

'Did he compromise you, Cressie? Because if you are with child, I can help. I believe there might be a way—are you with child? All those headaches you have been complaining of lately, I was thinking that was a sign that you might be—are you?'

Confused by the change, the strange note—was it eagerness?—in Bella's voice, Cressie did not answer directly. Bella had lost more weight since she last saw her, she noted. In fact, the amount of weight she seemed to have lost these last few weeks was quite dramatic. The voluminous flowing gown she wore made it difficult to tell, but if she did not know for certain that Bella was increasing she might think... *Did* she know for certain? 'When you first told my father about your pregnancy, he said Sir Gilbert Mountjoy had examined you,' Cressie said.

'That man!' Bella waved a dismissive hand. 'I told him about my sickness. He told me to rest.'

'So he didn't actually examine you?'

Bella was beginning to look uncomfortable. 'There was no need.'

'Are you really expecting, Bella? Is there a child?''

Her stepmother took a faltering pace backwards, clutching at her stomach protectively. 'If it is your father you are worried about, you need not,' she said. 'He won't be back for many months. By the time he next deigns to pay us a visit, you would have already given your baby over to me. It's bound to be a girl. Both Cassie and Celia had girls first. Henry would never know the difference.'

'Bella, what on earth are you talking about?'

'I saw the paintings, all three of them. After he'd gone, I went up to the attic to take a look. There is no way he could have painted you like that unless you had—but it doesn't matter.' Bella stretched out a pleading hand. 'It doesn't matter, Cressie. I will take your baby. Your little girl. I'll take her as my own and I'll never tell, I promise you.'

'Bella, I'm not with child,' Cressie said gently, 'and I don't think you are either, are you?'

A large tear rolled down Bella's cheek. 'I thought I was, I truly did. All the signs were there. My courses stopped. Then there was the sickness, all the time the sickness. And my stomach swelled. And my breasts. And you saw my feet, Cressie.'

'I did.' Cressie put her arm around Bella's waist and steered her towards the *chaise-longue*. 'I did see.'

'I wasn't lying.'

'No. No, of course you were not.'

'Only it all stopped. And then my courses started. And I feel so empty. So very empty. But she was never there, my little girl. Janey said—she said that I—she said that sometimes when a woman wants something too much, that she can imagine it is true. I couldn't contemplate telling your father the truth—you can imagine his reaction—so I just sort of carried on pretending and hoping, not knowing what else to do.' Tears trickled down Bella's rouged cheeks.

'Please don't cry, we are all of us capable of deluding ourselves by wanting something too much,' Cressie replied gently, thinking of the clearly misplaced hopes and plans she had concocted in the carriage, remembering with fresh pain that Giovanni was gone. Gone!

'I thought if you had been so foolish as to allow that man—are you sure, Cressie?'

'Bella, I wish I had been so foolish. Truthfully, I would gladly have been so foolish if he had allowed me. But it was Giovanni, not I, who would not—not—he would not.'

'Oh.' Bella's fingers tightened around Cressie's. 'I know it's a terrible thing to say but I confess I wish he had.'

Cressie laughed, a bereft little sound. 'Not as much as I wish it.'

* * *

She handed her stepmother over to the tender ministrations of Janey, eventually. The nurse-maid took her aside to apologise. 'I wanted to say something, my lady, but I did not quite know *what* to say.' Telling her not to worry, Cressie asked Janey to take good care of Bella, and made her guilty escape.

Three paintings. Bella had said three paintings. She eased open the door of the attic, holding the oil lamp high, for it was past dusk. No easels. No palette. No brushes. Only the smell of linseed oil and turpentine hung faintly in the air. Giovanni was not there. Of course he was not, but it took her a moment to stop looking for him.

The paintings stood in a row along the *chaise-longue* by the window. True enough, there were three canvases. *Lady Cressida*, the printed label by the left-hand painting said. *Mr Brown*, read the label on the right-hand portrait. The finished painting had a wittiness to it she had not noticed while it was a work in progress. It made her smile, and it set her off balance ever so slightly. So many contrasts, the portrait asked far more questions than it answered. How could she have been so pompous as to think she knew anything about art?

Her stupid theory, so logical and so precise, explained nothing about how real art played on the emotions.

Turning to the middle portrait, her visceral reaction felt like a punch to the stomach. *Cressie,* said the label. Just Cressie. Stretched quite naked, gloriously and provocatively naked, across the canvas, her arms over her head, making no attempt to hid her breasts, her sex. Her smile was all the more wicked for its being shameless. *Cressie.* Simply Cressie, revealed and naked. This was how Giovanni saw her, defying every rule, and innately beautiful in a way she could not explain but did not need to. The truth. The unadorned truth. And it was beautiful, *she* was beautiful.

She understood finally, staring at herself as she had never seen herself before, but with a recognition that was incontrovertible. Giovanni's art showed the truth about her, the sitter, and about himself too, the painter. He could not have been clearer if he had written it in bold capitals. This, Giovanni was saying, is the woman I love.

Chapter Eleven

Firenze was as beautiful as he had remembered. Giovanni walked along the banks of the Arno as the setting sun cast a warm glow on the soft stone of the impressive buildings on the river bank opposite, light and architecture combining to dazzling effect. The jewellery shops lining the Ponte Vecchio were closed for the evening, but the sun's dying rays caressed the old stone, mellowing it from ochre to burnt umber. The reflection of the arches on the water was so crystal clear it could be another bridge, upside down and quietly drowning. It was a melancholy thought, but he shook it off. He had no intention of quietly drowning, not any more. He had come here, to Florence, to ensure just that.

He had tried to paint this scene many times, but his work had always lacked lustre. Beautiful as the city was, he was never going to be a landscape artist. It was people who interested him, not places. And at this moment, as his feet found their way of their own accord to the Palazzo Fancini, one person in particular.

The palace, built by the Fancini family during the Renaissance, was modelled on the palazzo built by the notorious Medicis. Roman in style, it was classically proportioned, presenting a stuccoed frontage to the street, facing on to beautiful gardens to the rear. The servant who opened the vast oak door to him was unfamiliar. The ring of Giovanni's footsteps on the cloistered inner courtyard as he made his way to the count's private apartment was, on the other hand, only too familiar. He could hear the echoes of his boyhood self playing alone here. He could see the ghost of his adolescent self too, sheltering from the heat of the summer sun with his drawing board perched on his knee, his concentration almost comic in its intensity.

Count Fancini's rooms opened out one from the other, presenting a series of salons of increasing grandeur. In the old days, the count had told him, the status of a visitor was easily demarcated by the progress he made through the various echelons towards the inner sanctum. *In the old days.* Giovanni's father was wont to speak as if he himself had lived through the Renaissance, had had the ear of the Medicis, had wielded influence and the power of life and death. Which he did, which he had, over his son, until the day Giovanni had left the palazzo for ever.

No, that was a lie. Count Fancini's grip had remained tight around his son for all the years he had thought that he was free. Cressie had been right about that. Today that state of affairs would end.

As the servant threw open the last of the double doors, the ones leading into the grandest of the salons where the ceilings were embossed with gold leaf and the tapestries which covered the vast space of the walls had been embroidered many centuries ago, Giovanni halted in his tracks. Memories assaulted him, brutal in their clarity. Beatings and tears, then as he grew older and his resentment and stubbornness grew, beatings stoically endured dryeyed. Punishment and reward was his father's credo. He had tried. Despite the resounding sorrow of his forced separation from Papa and Mama, Giovanni had tried to please his father.

But nothing he did had ever been good enough for the count, and there is nothing like repeatedly telling a boy he is a failure to make a rebel of him.

The servant coughed politely. Giovanni stepped into the salon. Count Fancini was seated at the far end by the window which overlooked the gardens. He did not rise, but as he approached, Giovanni saw that this was due to infirmity rather than lack of inclination. The old man sat in a wheeled chair.

'*Conte.*' Giovanni bent over his father's hand. It was liver-spotted, the veins knotted through the translucent skin.

'*Mio figlio.* So, you come at the last. They told you I was dying, I suppose.'

'*No, padre.*' Though it would have been obvious to even a casual observer. Giovanni took the seat opposite his father. The count had always been a robust man, as tall as Giovanni but much more heavily built. The old man before him had the gaunt, wizened look of one close to death. He could not feel anger towards a man so tragically reduced. All the things he wished to say, the recriminations and accusations, all fled from his thoughts. What was the point? It had happened. It was part of him. It was over. Giovanni took his father's hand. 'I came to say goodbye, *padre*,' he said gently. 'Not because you are dying, but because I must live.'

There was to be no tender death-bed reconciliation. The count was too stubborn and too accustomed to having his own way for that. There could never be love between them, nor even affection, but a mutual parting was finally, reluctantly, agreed. The papers which would free Giovanni from his heritage would be drawn up the next day. The count refused to discuss who would inherit now that Giovanni had confirmed he would not. With an echo of his old self, he cackled derisively when his son suggested the establishment of a suitably worthy charity might be an appropriate solution. 'Bribe my way into the Almighty's good books, you mean? It is a little late for that I think.' Giovanni resigned himself to ignorance. His father was stubborn but not a fool. He had had fourteen years to form an alternative plan for the continuation of his name.

'So, you will return to England?' the count asked as he rose to take his departure.

'I have no fixed plans.'

'I heard that you were much in demand. Do you not have a list of anxious clients awaiting you?'

Giovanni shook his head. 'I have no fixed

plans,' he repeated. He was mid-bow when Count Fancini made the astonishing request. 'You want me to take your likeness?' he repeated in disbelief.

'A parting gift,' the old man said with a toothless smile, 'I do not want to be remembered like this. Do you think you can make of this withered visage a thing of beauty?'

Giovanni laughed. 'Still, you doubt me. I shall prove you wrong.'

'Do not expect to be paid. It is a father's last request of his errant son.'

'Then I shall honour it. And in doing so perhaps I might finally please you.'

But Giovanni never did get the opportunity to find out if he had, for the count died before the portrait was completed, and in any case, it was a painting done to please himself. This canvas had all the truth of the one he had left for Cressie. An old man, once powerful now fallen, admired but bereft.

One gift the count granted him. Not his final words, but his last words to Giovanni. 'It was a lie that those fisher-folk washed their hands of you,' he told his son. 'They wrote many times begging to visit, to see you just once more. I forced them to write, saying that they wanted you to cease communication.'

'*Bastardo!*'

Count Fancini laughed. 'Look at you. When I see you like that, I know you are indeed my son. Unclench those fists, boy, you can do nothing to hurt me now. I am already dead.'

'But my letters? I wrote to them…'

'Every week. And every week, I had them burned.'

'Knowing you, I should have guessed.'

Count Fancini's smile was as vicious as Giovanni remembered it. 'You were always too trusting.' His smile faded, his mouth settling into its usual sneer. 'You never took my name,' he said. 'Di Matteo. The name of those commoners. That is how you are known, not Fancini.'

'I did not think you would wish such a venerable name as yours associated with such a menial trade as mine.'

'I did not think you would make such a success of it.'

Did the count really think him a success? Giovanni had framed the question when he saw the look in his father's eye. His silence denied the count a last opportunity to deride his profession. Whatever were the old man's true thoughts on the subject, he took them to the grave. When next Giovanni returned to the palazzo, his father was unconscious.

He took the unfinished canvas back to his lodgings and completed it there. He attended the funeral, keeping a discreet distance from the other mourners as the count's body was interred in the magnificent family crypt. Taking his customary evening stroll along the banks of the Arno at the end of that momentous day, idly speculating about the path his future might follow, Giovanni realised with a start that for the first time in his life he was truly free. Free of his past. Not exactly washed free of his sins, but cleansed all the same. He had done what he had done. He had been wrong. He had paid a heavy price. Now he was free to choose his future. And he could not contemplate any future which did not involve Cressie.

Cressie, who deserved better than he, but whom, he also realised with a blinding flash as bright as the sun's rays on the stained glass of Brunelleschi's Duomo, he had not actually allowed to choose for herself. He had decided for her by leaving. He had nobly decided he would not inflict himself on her, but what if he was wrong? He had not asked her. *Dio*, what if he was mistaken?

He ran through the narrow streets of Firenze towards his lodgings. He must pack. He must return to England. *Pronto.* He ran as if his very life depended on it. Which in fact it did.

The late afternoon sun cast its golden rays through the dormer windows of the attic, a dimple in one of the glass panes sending shards of light shimmering on to Cressie's dress. In the weeks since Giovanni had left Killellan, summer had arrived, Bella had continued to grow thinner, Cordelia had remained incommunicado save for a brief note to reassure her sister that she was quite well, and Cressie had tried very hard not to pine. Giovanni was gone. At times she was angry at him, but most often she simply felt regret. He loved her. She had only to look at the *Cressie* portrait to see that but loving her and wanting to be with her were two different things. He had been gone months, without a word. Being in love did not necessarily mean being together. It was a tragedy, but she had to accept it for reality. She had her proof in his silence. She was, after all, a mathematician.

Looking up at the wall above her writing desk where the drafts for her soon-to-be-published geometry primer lay waiting to undergo final corrections, for her practical experience had paid its dividends in persuading Mr Freyworth to publish, Cressie studied the framed triptych. She had been tempted to have them hung in the portrait gallery, but not even the anticipated horror on her father's face, if he ever returned from Russia, could persuade her to make them public. If Giovanni had wished them to be seen by anyone other than her, he would have taken them with him, or told her so. This, rather than embarrassment, was why she had decided after much thought not to submit them to the Royal Academy on his behalf. The portraits told their story, hers and Giovanni's. So she had hung them here in the studio where they had been painted, where their story had been played out, and claimed the attic for her study. She had thrown herself into her work, for there was nothing else for it.

The boys' new governess had taken up her position last week. Cressie had insisted that Freddie, George, James and Harry have a say in the selection process, and her brothers had taken to Miss Langton, who had five brothers of her own, immediately. She was teaching them from Cressie's newest primer. The publishing firm, which would print the first, was already clamouring for the second. It seemed that Cressie had hit upon quite a gap in the market for school books. Lord Armstrong knew of none of these developments. He would return expecting a new son, to find instead a new governess, two departed daughters and most likely a newly independent wife. Almost, she wished she could be here to see it. Almost.

Cressie pushed her chair back and roamed restlessly over to the window. The arrangements for her visit to Celia were also in train. Her eldest sister made no promises, but she was encouraging. And touchingly, lovingly eager to be reunited with Cressie.

The crunch of gravel through the open window alerted her to the arrival of a carriage. Most likely Lady Innellan, who had become quite a bosom-bow of Bella's. Looking out, she saw not the Innellan barouche, but a travelling coach. The door of the coach was thrown open and a familiar long, trousered leg appeared. The occupant leapt to the ground without waiting for the step to be lowered. Cressie felt faint. The blood thrummed in her head. It couldn't be, it simply couldn't, could it?

He was tanned. His hair had grown. Abandoning what little decorum she possessed, Cressie leaned precariously out of the dormer window and cried out to him.

'Giovanni!'

He looked around in confusion.

'Gi-o-vann-i!'

He looked up. He smiled, that particular smile he saved for her. And then he ran across the carriageway, up the steps and into the house.

She met him at the door to the attic and threw herself at him. He didn't hesitate, he didn't recoil or make the least show of resistance. He swept her up into his arms, carrying her over the threshold of the attic as if she were a bride. He had not shaved. His chin was blue-black with stubble. He looked tired, but also different somehow. She couldn't put a name to it. She stopped trying when he set her down and pulled her tight against him, and kissed her.

'Cressie.' He kissed her again. 'Cressie, Cressie, Cressie.'

He kissed her again. His stubble grazed her skin. His lips were soft on hers, his mouth warm. She stood on her tiptoes to twine her arms around his neck. He smelt of dust and travel. Of the lemon soap he always used. Of sweat a little and of Giovanni a lot. She closed her eyes and breathed him in, saying his name.

He was kissing her forehead now, her eyelids, her brows, her cheeks. He was kissing her ear, pushing her rebellious hair back to nibble on her lobe. She wanted to climb inside him, wrap him around her, make of them one skin which could never be separated again. 'I missed you,' she said, almost laughing at the inadequacy of the words. 'You never sent word, and I missed you terribly.'

'Cressie, I have so much to tell you, so much I need to say.'

'You came back, that's all that matters.'

Giovanni lifted his head to look deep into her eyes. 'But there is one thing of paramount importance I need to say.'

'You have already said it. You said it there, though I would very much like to hear the words.' She pointed at the triptych. Giovanni gazed at the framed paintings as if he had not seen them before, then he smiled again, a slow, sensual smile that wound its way around her heart.

'I did not realise it was so obvious.'

'I am very glad it was,' Cressie said. 'It is all I had to cling on to.'

'I love you, Cressie.' Giovanni pulled her back into his arms. He touched her forehead. Her cheek. Her throat. She almost cried with the bliss of it. 'I love you more even than that painting can say. I don't deserve you, but…'

'Don't say that, Giovanni.'

'What I was going to say, if you would let me finish, *tesoro*.'

'*Tesoro?* What is that?'

'Darling. My darling Cressie, I know that I don't deserve you, but I am asking anyway. I went to Italy to—to confront my past. I saw my father. No, later I will tell you all. I saw him, I made my peace with him and with myself.' He took her hands and placed them over his heart. 'This is yours if you will take it, Cressie. *Ti amo*.'

She could feel his heart beating beneath her hand. She could see now what was different about him. He no longer carried the long shadow of unhappiness with him. 'I don't care about the past, Giovanni. We have both done things we have regretted. We've both wasted a lot of time trying to be what others wanted from us. I would not wish it undone, for I would not change you, and really, I don't care. All I'm interested in is the future.' Cressie took his hand and placed it over her own heart. Feverishly beating, it fluttered in her breast as if trying to escape. '*Ti amo, tesoro*. I love you so much, Giovanni.'

This time his kiss was crushing, his lips hungry, famished, feasting on hers. Their tongues touched, igniting the fierce flame of passion which had smouldered between them too long unsated. His hands framed her face, his fingers tangling in the wild curls of her hair, tugging it free from its ribbon, spreading it out over her back.

He gathered her close, sinking his face into her hair and breathing deeply. 'Lavender. And Cressie. How I have missed that.' He kissed her mouth again, tenderly this time, then with increasing passion. His hands were feverish, on her back, on her waist, on her bottom, on her breasts. He was trembling. 'I don't know what to do,' he said, with a lopsided smile. 'I feel as if—it is stupid. I feel as if this is the first time. I don't know what to do.'

His words, the way he looked at her, heated, loving, and yet almost bashful, she thought she might actually faint with the depth of her love for him. She felt like laughing hysterically, like crying, like declaiming her love from the attic window. 'Make love to me, Giovanni,' she said, 'that's all I want. That's all you have to do.'

With a confidence she was far from feeling, Cressie locked the door of the attic and led Giovanni over to the Egyptian chair and pushed him down on to it. She glanced over at the image of herself hanging on the wall. *Cressie.* Fingers shaking, she wrestled with the hooks of her gown. It was not the most elegant of undressing, but she had no doubt of how it was being received. Giovanni was riveted as she shrugged herself out of her dress. Standing in her undergarments, she played his words from the whispering gallery over in her mind.

'Corsets,' she said, placing herself before him. His breath was warm on her nape as his fingers struggled with the ties. When she turned around, his pupils were almost black. Colour slashed his cheeks. His breathing was ragged. She slipped out of her petticoats. Turning sideways, she propped one leg on a footstool, and leaned over, feeling her pantalettes stretch tight over her bottom, rewarded by Giovanni's sharp intake of breath. The line of beauty. She slipped off her shoe and rolled down her stocking. She had never seen a face so stark with passion. It made her feverish, damp with anticipation. The knot in her belly was aching. She turned to repeat the process. Bend. Shoe. Stocking.

She had only her chemise and pantalettes now. Quickly, she dispensed with them. A glance at the portrait—not that she needed to be reminded. He caught her looking, and a smile dawned. Cressie lay down on the *chaise-longue*. She stretched her arms over her head.

She arched her back. Her nipples were hard. She turned her head to smile. Cressie's smile. It came to her so easily, looking as she was at the man she loved. Seductive. Provocative. Confident.

Giovanni was on his feet now, casting clothing wildly across the room, yanking so hard at his shirt that the buttons flew. Cressie held out her hand to him. Naked, his chest heaving, his eyes wild, his erection jutting up thick and heavy, he looked at her as if she were…

'Beautiful,' Giovanni said, kneeling before her. '*Tesoro, sei bellissima.* I do not think I have ever seen anyone so beautiful as you. Cressie. My very own Cressie.'

She thought she had never seen anyone so beautiful as he as he leaned over her to kiss her. She thought she had never been so happy as she was now, as his lips touched hers, as she opened her mouth to him. She was so hot and so tense and every bit of her tingled and throbbed, she thought she would climax, just from him kissing her. Then he kissed his way down to her breast and took her nipple in his mouth, sucking slowly, a gentle tugging pull that made her cry out, and Cressie stopped thinking altogether.

An aeon he spent kissing her breasts, stroking them, cupping them, crushing his face between them. She was writhing, struggling to hold herself in, when he kissed his way down her stomach. 'Softest,' he murmured, reverently parting her legs, pulling her over on the *chaise-longue*, tucking his hands under her bottom to lever her towards him. 'Softest,' he said again, his voice husky with passion as he kissed her thighs, licked the yielding flesh.

Heat built inside her. She thought she had experienced passion with him before, but this was quite different. His touch inflamed her, made her want to scream her frustration, to surrender to the fire which he was kissing into an inferno, and yet she didn't want to surrender to it just yet. When his tongue touched the damp folds of her sex, she whimpered. Though he was gentle, a mere whisper of a feather-light touch, she could hardly hear it. She arched her back, dug her heels into the chaise, her hands into his shoulders. 'Giovanni.' His tongue was rougher now. 'Yes. Please. Oh, Giovanni.' And yet more. She came like a tempest, great rolling waves gripping her, squeezing her, shaking her, turning her inside out.

She could hear herself crying out, but it was such a strange sound and she was so far away, riding the crest of her orgasm, that she couldn't associate it with herself. As she shuddered, he licked her again, until she thought she could bear no more. Sliding on to the floor beside him, twining her legs around him, her arms around him, she pulled him on top of her, panting, pleading.

He kissed her hard. He angled himself against her. Then he hesitated. 'I'm afraid,' he said in a strangled voice. 'I have never wanted anything so much. Just watching you, I am so…I'm afraid I won't be able to…I don't want it to be over.'

'Giovanni, it's never going to be over until we die. Please,' Cressie said desperately, 'make love to me.'

'Cressie, in truth I think I may die if I do not.'

He kissed her swiftly and entered her slowly. Delightful. Delectable. Delicious. Luscious. Nothing was sufficient to describe it, the slow penetration as he slid into her, gradually merging his body with hers. Braced above her, his chest glistened with sweat, heaving with the effort of restraint, she thought she had never seen him more beautiful. He kissed her again, holding himself still inside her. She could feel the blood pulsing through his shaft. It made her muscles pulse, an echo, a summons. They were the same. The same.

He withdrew slowly, breath rasping. She gripped him tight. He pushed his way into her again. Stars exploding. They couldn't be, but they were, right behind her lids. She forced her eyes open. His face was starkly beautiful, his eyes focused on her face. She arched up. He swallowed. He thrust. Not so slowly this time. Then he thrust again. Harder. *Frisson*. Friction. She hadn't ever. 'Haven't ever,' she gasped in a vain attempt to tell him what he was doing to her. He thrust again and she shuddered. It was different but the same, this climax. More violent. Not just hers. Claiming. It rolled over her, gripped her, made her grip him, made her clutch at him, cry out his name wildly as he thrust one last time and fell on top of her with a harsh cry just as wild as her own.

'I painted his portrait, before he died,' Giovanni said much later, when they had wrapped themselves in each other and were sprawled on the *chaise-longue*, their bodies dappled with the light of the sinking sun and he had told her of the reunion with the count which was not a reunion. 'I will show you it later. I think it is good.' Giovanni stroked her hair. 'He asked me, but I didn't really paint it for him, I painted it for me.'

'You don't regret it, turning down such a huge inheritance?'

'I could not keep it, Cressie. I know that it is the one thing which would have reconciled your father to our...'

'Liaison?' Cressie said with a chuckle.

Giovanni's hand stilled. 'There is nothing temporary about what I feel for you. I will give you my name, I will give you all that I have if you will take it, but even if you don't, I will never let you go.'

Cressie rolled over to prop herself on his chest. She touched his forehead. His cheek. His throat. He smiled at her in recognition of the gesture. 'I have no intentions of going anywhere far from your side.'

'You don't think I made a mistake, turning down the count's estates?'

'You would have made a serious mistake, let me tell you, Giovanni di Matteo, if you had come here bearing riches with which to bribe my father. Of course you didn't make a mistake.'

'But your father—it is not him so much as what he can do.'

Cressie nodded. 'I know. He could forbid my seeing my brothers, but I doubt very much if Bella would allow it. She knows how fond they are of me, and though she seems to love my father, she loves her sons more. As to my father—to be frank, I think the less I see him the easier it will be for me to love him.'

Giovanni gave a bark of laughter. 'My thoughts exactly.' His hand moved down her spine to stroke the curve of her bottom. 'Do you want to marry me, Cressie?'

'I don't know. I want to be with you always, I know that much.'

'I won't have my children called bastards.'

'They will be our children regardless. But if we are lucky enough to be blessed, then you may most certainly do me the honour of bestowing your name upon me.'

'*Grazie, signorina.* You have a very naughty smile, did you know that?'

'I did not, until you painted it.' Cressie wriggled her bottom, and felt a most satisfactory response from beneath her. She smiled again, quite deliberately, and equally deliberately brushed her breasts across his chest. 'Giovanni, do you still believe we are kindred spirits, you and I?'

'I am certain of it.'

Another wriggle. He was definitely hard. She was definitely ready. 'Does that mean you like what I like?'

'Yes, it does.'

Cressie smiled, her new-found seductive smile. She kissed his mouth. Then she slid down on to the attic floor between his legs. 'Good, then let me show you exactly what I like,' she said.

Historical Note

The inspiration for writing a heroine who was a mathematician was sparked when I read Benjamin Woolley's biography of Lord Byron's only legitimate child, Ada. Estranged from her husband almost immediately after her marriage, Byron's wife, Annabella, was terrified that her daughter might have inherited her father's wild temperament, and introduced a strict regime of formal studies, including philosophies based on reason and logic, in an attempt to counter any such tendencies. My heroine was born thirteen years before Ada, but the two have read many of the same textbooks and share an acquaintance in Charles Babbage, whose counting machine is credited with being the progenitor of the computer.

The idea of having Cressie write a mathematical 'theory' of beauty which mirrored the technique which Giovanni used in his portraits came from two sources. I first came across William Hogarth's 'line of beauty' when I took an arts foundation course with the Open University. Jenny Uglow's excellent biography of the artist, *Hogarth: A Life and a World*, taught me a bit more on the subject, which I filed away, vaguely thinking that it might come in useful some day. Then, on a recent visit to Hampton Court with one of my sisters (sisters do tend to play a vital role in my life and my books), I saw Sir Peter Lely's paintings of the 'Windsor Beauties' and was much struck by the theory that he'd actually painted each of the individual women using a sort of 'template' of beauty in order for the portraits to be more acclaimed. It was here, in Hampton Court, that the idea for Giovanni's side of the story was born.

At the time Giovanni was painting, ready-mixed oils would have been unavailable. He may have made his own pigments, but would most likely have ordered them from a catalogue and mixed them himself. Much of the technical detail of his craft I gleaned from reading about the English artist Turner. Giovanni's travelling box of oils is actually based on the one found in Turner's studio. There are 'models' for the three paintings which Giovanni does of Cressie: *'Lady Cressida'* is based on one by the portraitist Thomas Lawrence, *'Mr Brown'* takes its inspiration from Goya and *'Cressie'* is inspired by Goya's famous painting *'The Naked Maja'*, reputedly the first portrait to depict pubic hair. Though Giovanni precedes the Impressionists by some years, I've tried to show his artistic journey from the glossy, idealised style of portraiture popular during the Regency to the more 'impressionistic' style which took hold towards the end of the nineteenth century. However, I'm no artist, so any mistakes I've made in describing Giovanni's painting technique are most definitely all my own work.

Finally, for those who are interested, a few historical facts and figures and slight historical liberties I have taken. Though it was not exactly common, there is a precedent for Giovanni's father, Count Fancini, making his illegitimate son his heir. Guilio de' Medici was the Earl of Florence's natural son, for example. Lord Armstrong's trip to Russia to discuss the problem of Greek independence was actually made by the Duke of Wellington in 1826 and not 1828. Killellan Manor is based on Pollok

House in Glasgow, which lies within the country park housing the amazing Burrell Collection, and which is very familiar territory for me. There is no whispering gallery in the cellar there—that particular piece of architecture was inspired by New York's Grand Central Terminus. If you wish to know still more about the inspiration behind this book, please do check out my *Pinterest* page.

* * * * *

A sneaky peek at next month...

HISTORICAL

IGNITE YOUR IMAGINATION, STEP INTO THE PAST...

My wish list for next month's titles...

In stores from 7th June 2013:

❏ Reforming the Viscount – Annie Burrows

❏ A Reputation for Notoriety – Diane Gaston

❏ The Substitute Countess – Lyn Stone

❏ The Sword Dancer – Jeannie Lin

❏ His Lady of Castlemora – Joanna Fulford

❏ The Honour-Bound Gambler – Lisa Plumley

Available at WHSmith, Tesco, Asda, Eason, Amazon and Apple

Just can't wait?

The World of Mills & Boon®

There's a Mills & Boon® series that's perfect for you. We publish ten series and, with new titles every month, you never have to wait long for your favourite to come along.

Blaze
Scorching hot, sexy reads
4 new stories every month

By Request
Relive the romance with the best of the best
9 new stories every month

Cherish™
Romance to melt the heart every time
12 new stories every month

Desire™
Passionate and dramatic love stories
8 new stories every month